December and Mae

by

Sharon Shipley

Dedication

To: Skip Shipley,
a most patient and brilliant husband…

Acknowledgments

to Nan Swanson,
a most patient and empathic editor.

Prologue

Snagged on brambles and rusted barb wire destined to saw ankles and trip feet, stumbling over icy dead stalks and victim of the odd prairie dog hole, the girl finally gasped, hands on knees, sobbing for breath that wasn't there, when she could go no further.

They were coming.

She could hear them, their raucous, raging, drunken bawling behind her. They'd kill her this time, if feeling mean, or if liquored up enough. She shuddered, not from cold but from the memory of her oldest brother with that queer look on his face, hovering by her pallet behind the wood stove, these last three nights before she ran away. She'd mumbled about "using the jakes" and scarpered out with just the clothes she slept in, wishing now she ran better prepared.

She looked over her shoulder. *Closer now!* She heard the clods of earth tossed aside by their boots, thumping the ground, and their harsh winter breath and curses and promises of what they would do to her if she did not stop or when they caught up with her. She looked back. By the buttermilk light of the moon, she spied them leaping over ruts and clumps of henbit and boneberry bushes, baying like ravening hounds.

She had to put distance.

She *had* to.

Her breath, ragged now, sobbing, tearing up the dark

with rasping like rusty saws... Her knees felt like custard. She could no longer feel her numb feet, though they bled and left a telling trail for those hounds from hell chasing after.

First of August this far north, hoar frost made the barren-scape glitter, yet the night seemed above freezing pond water. A blessing, as she'd barely enough rags and a squashed hat to clothe her slight body and those rags were all she owned at any state.

She halted to stare at the luminous disc floating in a black sea of sky, seeming to lead her on, lending her a last strength.

She pelted on. A jackrabbit skittered across her path...she sprawled flat, listening to the scurrying of an invisible night world, and her own ragged breathing; at least she couldn't hear them anymore, nor could they spy her. Their cries faded off in another direction, like the mist from her breath. She stiffly rose; with each step on the lumpy uneven terrain, she either felt the jarring jolt clamp her teeth and jaws together or else she was falling off the edge of the earth.

The girl dropped to her knees again and wished she could sleep under that glowing moon washing her with silver. A minute of not telling herself she wasn't sure she could rise again. Her body, prone now on the crackling frosted weeds alternately urged her to wait, rest, *go back*.

She could hear them again. They veered back from the thicket of treeline, which she herself was hoping to reach, as too impenetrable. Most likely, for the first time in their miserable lives, they were right. She gritted her teeth and staggered up. She wouldn't be the doomed hare to their murderous hounds. Now they blundered in circles. She imagined them sniffing frozen clods for her scent. Baying, cursing, yelling in agony as one or another stumbled in the dark.

She heard her name called. A promise of pain. An expletive on their tongues. She detected manic glee. Never a good sign.

Suddenly she was airborne, not as dandelion fluff but as a tossed boulder flung to the earth, sailing right over a deep ditch, though not manmade, landing hard, knocking breath from her lungs, skinning knees and elbows. A rock wedged under her stomach. She began sobbing with hurt and frustration, instantly clamping her mouth tight till her jaws ached.

They, the five of them, raced past, three brothers and two uncles by the sound of them, shambling, leaping, legs stretched wide in pursuit, arms flailing. She timidly raised her aching head. The night swallowed them in a dark cloak. Their baying grew fainter. It did not return.

Stiffly the girl rose. She swayed, bewildered, fighting tears. A few escaped, trickling her cheek, adding to her misery. The cold wet itch irritated worse than a blow. Wasn't certain sure where she was, which way she ran. She turned full circle. Even their ramshackle hut was preferable to this aching cold, but even the hut was a chimera of her longings.

Thanking all the stars… In the distance loomed a square gray ghost. A lean-to of a stagecoach stop, though she did not know it.

The road she approached seemed to her a silver river of dust leading to the town of Laramie. She thought Laramie lay that way. Sanctuary. From there, hitch a train. Maybe. Was there a train? Ignorant of such luxuries, she hugged herself, dancing from cold. Had to find shelter, soon, or it would not matter if they caught her. Her brothers would find a frozen corpse. The lean-to would do for now. However, in the darkness, she tripped on a thick clump of frozen henbit, and when she clambered up, shifted slightly west.

A pinprick of light showed faint, yellow as a cat's eye in the boundless night—*there, again.* As if tree branches were waving across a faraway welcoming window.

Giving a last look at the stagecoach stop, and on her last strength, the girl made for the light.

Chapter One: Luke

Lucian Devereaux Farnsworth.

By his exterior, it was as if a mountain had a rock slide, leaving craggy outcroppings, broken, reshaped by harsh winters, some brawls, the war between the gray and the blue, horse falls, brutal labor and not a few gunfights, mended and forged anew by scorching Wyoming summers, lending him now, at the age of fifty-four, unexpectedly striking features.

Luke's nose bore a hawk-like ridge. A scar sliced a gunmetal brow. His eyes, when he squinted at a fellow, seemed more flint than rain-sky gray—even strong men found diplomatic ways to retreat when those eyes stalked them from under fierce iron brows. Taller than most men around and yet unbent, with arms corded with iron bands, his grip was that of a vise, with scarred fists punishing as anvils.

Liz, his sister, didn't fear him at all, giving good as she got with their rare-as-hen's-teeth squabbles. And, if they would divulge it, he resembled James Corbett, the famous pugilist, according to Liz's twittering female friends, who watched him sideways under lashes and pursed cupid-bow simpers.

"Luke Farnsworth! Why! Mr. Farnsworth! I do declare, you look just like that handsome devil James Corbett!"

Not only would Lucian Farnsworth disavow the

charge, but deny he'd ever heard of the notorious boxer that left the weaker sex swooning, or so his sister's quilting bees never wearied of declaring. He'd perused, in the privacy of his sitting room, a month-old *Laramie Sentinel* with Corbett's picture and dates of his bouts long past.

After one chance overhearing, Lucian tried to avoid the cracked mirror above the towel roller in the kitchen.

True, that Corbet fellow is a well-made handsome devil, with a full head of hair like my own, Luke conceded. He did look like him, though his own hair was admittedly on the iron-metal-rifle side.

The rest, all hogwash.

One woman had tittered, "He had eyes hard as silver bullets."

"Silver bullets. Hunh?"

'Spose I should be flattered.

Maybe he was.

A little.

Luke sucked in the tiny softness above his gun belt. But a man who boxed for money? Foppish. A good bar brawl, wrestling calves to the ground, that's what men did.

Risking a glance for Liz, Luke turned sideways, lifting his rather massive chest and shoulders. Still, his summers approached fall now. Luke grunted, took a slug of Liz's day-old tar, and gazed out the kitchen at nothing in particular.

Luke Farnsworth, broken-nosed but Lord and Master of over forty thousand acres, give or take, of good Wyoming prairie, some acres of pine forest, a few lakes and streams, a foothill onto a mountain range, and an untold thousand head of cattle, part interest in a thriving copper mine, silent partner in a Red Butte ironmongery, and a varying number of roustabouts, escalating from ten to twenty-five during drives or harvest season, when Liz set the long table groaning with hearty fare under the oak… He dashed the dregs in the new zinc sink, crammed on his battered Stetson and headed for work now the sun had decided to creep out from covers of darkness.

****

Besides, something caught his attention.

A scrawny scrap of a thing garbed in rags, or some conglomeration thereof, with an undefinable hat jammed low on the head, lugged a bucket, slopping half the water, from trough to stable, on some mysterious errand.

Luke leaned closer, squinting. Who in hades *was* that?

Wouldn't call Liz.

She'd accuse him of needing specs again. He squinted. Spindly legs, narrow shoulders. He didn't have short roustabouts thin as grasshoppers! Luke stalked to the door where he didn't need to see through the uneven panes, but the mysterious unkenned boy had disappeared.

Luke nibbled his mustache. "Hunh!" *Talk to Liz about hiring help without my say-so.* "'Less it's kitchen house help," he amended. *Speak of the devil.*

Liz strode in, flustered as usual, tying her apron, checking the wood crate with a jaundiced eye, rattling the poker in the fire box like killing snakes, all the while snatching the coffeepot to refill, and gave her brother a distracted look he kenned well—*Do not be a-bothering me whilst work's to be done.*

Hell with that.

"What the Sam Hill you about now, Lizzie?" Luke shot an accusing thumb at the stable. The figure reappeared, single-mindedly heading to the well. "Since when do you hire the hands? That one," he jabbed his thumb again, "looks fit to *die* on me. Couldn't lasso a dead dog."

He chuckled to remove the barb.

Liz threw him a sisterly *what are you pothering about whilst I'm busy fetching you a breakfast?* look, but proceeded to grind more beans and tossed grounds in the battered pot to boil before bending to peer outside.

Liz, seeing no one, resolutely turned from the window, raised a questioning brow, shrugged and went back to stir oatmeal destined to be laced with blackstrap, and dragged down the flour tin. "Hands be gathering like starving coyotes yodeling away if hot biscuits aren't meltin' butter by seven, so don't be pestering me with nonsense." Later, brushing the tops with butter, Liz deftly plopped dough rounds on the bacon-greased sheet, popped open the blackened oven and stuck more kindling in the fire box.

A little smile played across her lips.

"Ah there's that now," she muttered, eyeing with satisfaction the glass dome of fresh churned butter already on the table, ham frying and eggs in the big iron skillet ready to douse with bacon fat for her and Luke, and the huge enamel coffeepot she'd already tossed eggshells into, to make the brew stronger, boiling away and already thick as tar. All was right under Heaven.

****

Luke headed out, clapping on an old battered Stetson after sweeping back a lion's mane of silvery gray. He wore scuffed boots, a threadbare pair of five-button denim jeans skimming his long muscular legs, and a worn gray plaid shirt with patches on the elbows. Laggards straggling from the bunkhouse trailing squabbles, tomfoolery, and braggadocio, bee-lined to the long-benched table outside the kitchen, where Liz plunked down a clatter of tin plates, a cauldron of steaming oats, bacon and blackstrap, along with cream so thick a spoon could stand up.

Steam rose from the barn roof. A rising sun heated the dried wood shakes.

Luke glanced over as Old Tom fetched tin mugs and the coffee urn. He did a double-take. He could swear he spied a pale oval face staring at the scene from the stable doorway. He blinked. No one there now. He had the impression the face—the figure, if there was one lost in the gloom—appeared hungry. He shook his head. Liz might be right. He did need specs. Probably just one of the hands inspecting his horse.

Biskits, the bunkhouse cook and bone mender, looked disdainful at the fare as something the cat sicked up, but as usual tucked in. Luke couldn't recall when the devil's bargain of Biskits not doing breakfast was sealed, but it was dyed in the wool now, at least while the weather was yet temperate.

Bit past it anyway. Biskits mostly mended saddles and dressed his wranglers' cuts, bumps and breaks, and he hadn't the heart either to pension off Corky or Old Tom, still the best smithy in the county, no matter his eighty years on God's green earth…closest to a foreman he had.

Luke, pulling his own belt in a notch, checked his hands' flat stomachs and low-slung gun belts, even now threatening to slide off their narrow hips from the weight.

Squinting under his battered Stetson, Luke listened, resigned, to his roustabouts, fretting between gusty chewing over the new mustang with the rough coat, one they vowed was "the devil's own and couldn't be broke" that awaited them.

Bone idle. Anxious to dabble in the delights of the local sin city, this being Friday. By local, Luke meant twenty miles to Laramie, or maybe even farther to Red Butte.

****

By eight o'clock the sun's hammer beat down on the anvil of hardpan, wild horse and man alike. Luke and the feed salesman, Nate Solomon, the only Jewish fellow for fifty miles around, and his helper, Hurly, along with Old Tom and Biskits, hung elbows over the split rails of one of Luke's multiple corrals whilst judging Gimpy Joe's attempt to saddle the rowdy pestiferous horse bought at the Red Butte auction last week.

So far, its only talents were eating, crapping horse apples, and trying its damnedest to break bones or heads, or bite anyone with the effrontery to approach from the rear, with long yellow teeth like shovels.

Gimpy Joe, the toes of his boots dragging furrows in a whirligig pattern around the paddock, clung to a tangled mane still stuck with burrs while Luke listened with half an ear to another of Nate's tall tales of his latest amorous conquests.

"I tell you, Luke, I had to beat her off. You recall. That Ledbetter gal? The one with freckles and the—" He cupped two rounds over his frayed tweed coat. "Well, I slipped her a box of horehound candy and a pink garter. I said she could have it if she allowed me to put it on her purty little leg, and let me tell you, she—"

Luke chuckled gamely, nodded and tried to cut him off. Heard most of them before, or some like it anyway. Even so, Nathaniel was always good for a jaw or two, better than the telegraph. But then Nate's gossip, as a feed and sundry salesman, turned decidedly morbid, as it had lately. He looked up at Luke, with a pallbearer's gloom. "You hear?" He shook his grizzled head. "Greiner passed on last week. Only fifty-seven. Lemuel Johnston too."

Luke inhaled. *And I'm going on fifty-five.* Luke nodded in empathy, recalling missing acquaintances gone the last year to their heavenly reward—though one of them, he wasn't too sure of the heavenly reward part.

"That a fact. Lem? Was what?"

"Fifty or thereabout, not too young to have a bad ticker, reckon," Nate offered with the expression of an old hound dog, his gray dewlaps wobbling side to side.

Luke rubbed his chest. "No, didn't know. Should have, only lived a mile down the pike."

"Found him. Laid there all day, 'fore the hands thought to check."

"'Taint right when nobody misses you," Hurly, the assistant muttered.

Old Tom, kibbitzing, spat tobacco through any teeth left. "Makes three this month. Hope I go in mah sleep. Jes' wake up seein' the Pearly Gates bangin' shut behind me, and a purty angel sayin', 'Welcome, Tom. We bin awaitin' fer ye.' " He cackled.

"Don't we all," the salesman offered gloomily in his litany of accidents, early deaths, blood poisonings, snake bites, heads caved in by horse hooves, or who had whose infant on *either* side of the sheets. Tales collected like currency on his sales rounds, all the while keeping an eye on Gimpy Joe, still being dragged by the horse from Hades, for further fodder to impart down the road at his next stop.

Luke nodded at his so-called bronco buster, whose skinny rump had just bit the dust. *Hard*. He winced. "Expect a few twinges, 'specially when you hit dirt often as we have."

"Ahh, if it's not the ticker, it's the liver."

"Stop making love to that jug then, Nate," Luke jested.

"No siree. Ain't likker, nor gettin' kicked in the head by a horse. Age gets us in the end." This Hurly offered.

Nate contributed, "'at's right. Spotty fever, Doc said, and you hear tell of Norbert Peters? Lungs filled up. Doc says galloping consumption, and he was in his thirties."

"Can't say I did," Luke offered civilly, wishing mightily they'd change the subject.

Old Tom nodded. "Ayyup. And old man Ledbetter had a lunger. 'Course, he was seventy-five…"

Luke shook his head, resigned. Old Tom too made any obituary column unnecessary with his daily assessment of who died, who had banns read, but curiosity bit finally.

"Who else? Only heard of Jakes down at the feed store," Luke challenged. Harry Jakes had died of lockjaw. Around horses, tetanus was a common thread and a subject of dread.

"Didn't hear? New Methodist parson over in Red Butte! Hardly time to unpack 'is prayer books when over he keeled." Hurly made a diving motion. "Congestion of the humors, Doc said."

Luke snorted, watching the next buster swat the

recalcitrant horse, who wasn't putting up with any horse breaking either. "Congestion of the humors" meant doc was clueless.

Leaning elbows on splintery rails, Luke threw a half vexed and half amused glance at his dour companions. "Why all the gloomy gab? We sound like old hens."

"A good woman will cure *that* for ya," Nate boasted. "A randy filly sure makes *me* feel like a springtime rooster."

Luke sighed inwardly.

"Oh, and you have one, randy er otherwise?" Old Tom cackled. Luke had never noticed before how irritating Old Tom's cackle was. Like a burr in the britches.

"Durn tootin'! Got me a little filly in *every* ranch from here to Buford, *or* Cheyenne City."

Luke, watching the next unlucky roustabout limp off, side-eyed Nate. The feed salesman clapped Luke's shoulder. Hanging on, he whispered in his ear, "Like hammers, Luke boy. Don't use 'em, gets rusty, my friend."

Luke shook him off. "Not certain sure I get the connection."

"No! Luke! By golly. Really! May've been tootin' my own trumpet a tad loud, but…"

Nate leaned closer, gathering his cronies in with a come-hither gesture and lowered his voice. "But some of these rancher's daughters get awful stony lonesome out there with nothin' but the wind whistlin' up their skirts and prairie dogs. Plum glad to see a stranger, *any* stranger." Nate nudged Luke's ribs. "And they need more than seed, gewgaws and cattle feed, let me tell you! Lord help me, but those little gals help *me* out a treat. I vow I can hardly walk straight."

"That so?" Luke said evenly, hearing Old Tom snort, while Biskits just looked on, wistful.

"And they seem to cotton to me." Nate looked smug. "Don't know why. Twice their age…"

Three times, Luke amended.

*"*But, shucks, they seem to find me good-lookin', or maybe just figger I can give them a hard time, if you know what I mean." He thumped Luke's chest. "Word gets around, when you have the knowhow."

Old Tom and Luke shared glances. Luke had to laugh at his old friend. "You are a hellion on wheels, Nate."

Sobering, Luke gazed unseeing at the last attempt to corral the horse from hell. Didn't even want to recall when *he* last had a good romp. Must be months. *The widow. Martha*.

Lately, thoughts of inheritances and gravestones came uninvited. Thoughts that he hadn't been with women *that* way much since his beloved Katie passed on to her reward—and God kenned his lovely Kate deserved a reward. Melancholy swept in like a nor'easter out of nowhere, drenching Luke's spirits. Pastor Huckaby had assured him his sweet Katherine "went to a better place." A childlike woman Luke missed more than he could say. Her passing left him with no particular passion, save keeping his vast empire thriving.

"Hope my daughter and son-in-law appreciate it," Luke muttered, unwitting. He came to Nate's latest episode and slapped his shoulder.

"That's good, Nate. Keep it up. Best be getting to work 'fore noon, though."

Nate winked and leered. "'At's what I'm doing, my

friend, keeping it straight up like a good little wooden soldier."

Luke forced a laugh and after shaking hands on a new order of buckwheat seed, Liz some hair bobs and "Doctor Hartshorn's Number 8 Liniment," he waved Nate Solomon off, with Hurly busy taking notes on a slate.

He turned back toward the house, but halted a hitch. *What the Hades? There's that odd figure again in the stable doorway, sweeping this time.*

He tracked a few of the hands sauntering over, sniggering something. One tugged the boy's short hair. Luke squinted. With the rising sun blazing orange and hot as a fried duck egg now, a black cutout figure was all he could make out. Before he could investigate, one of the hands limped over, whining about something or other. He put on a patient face, but he didn't have truck with complainers. By that time, the slight odd figure, whoever it was, had vanished again.

"Get on back to chores! Almost noon! That means all of you!"

It was barely eight-thirty in the morning.
****

Luke lingered, eyeing Gimpy Joe, Rudy, Matt Diggs, and Rusty and Dusty, the twins with one brain between them. He held his patience for a full five minutes while they each timidly approached the demon horse, then skipped away, falling over their own big boots. Rudy, swinging a lariat, sidled over again, while Dusty nervously held a saddle. He could excuse Matt Diggs with the broke leg.

The horse from hell clamped shovel-like teeth on Rudy's shoulder, released him, then reared, slashing razer-sharp hooves an inch from Dusty's head. Rudy yelped and skittered off, leaping the fence without touching a rail. Luke watched, stone-faced. Wasn't like them.

"Hell's bells, Rudy, I'll do it!"

Luke didn't want to admit it, but he had to show the young bucks he had sand. Truth, he couldn't wait to break a bronco again. He vaulted over the fence, an act he'd regret later, stalking to the wildest horse ever lassoed, most likely a cross between a wild Indian pony and a cavalry horse—one of the big Clydesdales for hauling cannon in the civil war that finally ground to a halt in bloody splendor a few years back.

No doubt I'll have a date with Dr. Hartshorn's liniment come bedtime. The stallion raised thick rubbery lips above coral gums in a sneer. Luke eyed with respect the huge head sawing up and down, and the wicked rolling eye. Teeth like yellowed ivory spades snapped at Luke's ear as he ducked under.

Damn! It unsettled him, still aware, from the corner of his mind and eye, of the grasshopper figure dressed in rags, gripping a hay rake handle, now watching squint-eyed beneath a squashed hat and chopped-off hair like a black brush. But that too he didn't show and soon forgot about as he attempted to master the horse.

****

With hands full of sticky bread dough for the week's rations, Liz looked out. Glancing, frustrated, at the wall clock and down at the dough needing to rise, she almost wiped them on the apron covering her drab brown house dress and rushed out to stop her brother's fool-headedness.

Instead, keeping an eye on the battle between horse

and man, she groused, "Darn fool. As if being thrown like an old rag doll last year wasn't enough. That horse should be black as Satan for all its ill manners and ugly disposition." She grumbled while pummeling the dough, shaking flour on the board, savagely kneading in her concern.

With grudging pride, Liz eyed the calamitous struggle for domination as Luke, boot heels digging, leg muscles taut and straining, back rippling, apparently ragged the boys now hanging over the split-rail corral as he battled the horse's will. The horse was more teaching *him* a lesson, almost dragging him, but Luke, running alongside, was getting the upper hand despite his age, keeping up just like one of the boys.

Liz stretched her lean mouth in a grin. Her brother grabbed the tangled matted mane and, making a running leap, vaulted onto the stallion's hitching back, albeit landing a tad off center.

Luke's strong thighs held a death grip on its barreled ribcage, flexing, unflexing beneath tight, faded earth-stained denims. Back muscles writhed, twisting, bunching, lengthening, threatening to rip his old blue shirt to smithereens, left arm flung out straight, rump a full foot off the saddle as the horse from Hades made figure eights and killer bucks.

Luke, her brother, looked ten years younger.

She pressed her lips and, giving the dough a final wallop, plopped it in the big bowl for a second rising. She dusted her hands and straightened the tight bun on her nape. "'Spose I won't say beans. Lucian sure don't like gettin' *old*, but 'pride goeth before a fall,' " Liz muttered with all the unctuousness of a parson's wife. A giggle, and a murmured, "Proverbs 16:18," escaped

Liz's prim lips. She pummeled a new batch of dough, shook flour on the board and savagely began cutting rounds with the end of a glass.

Liz, with suppressed pride, stopped watching out the window, however, as the wicked mustang from Hades jounced on legs like springs. She'd just got a good gander at the raggedy boy Luke had mentioned, peeking beneath the top rail on the far side of the corral.

Supposed she'd feed it afore she shooed the panhandler on its way. Hobos, renegades, drifters, defectors, and other such occasionally passed the ranch for a handout. "Land o' Goshen. What next?" Liz snorted, as close to cussing as Liz ever went. She thought too she might have some leftover cornbread. A tad dry, but it would do.

****

Luke felt eyes and hidden smirks as his hands, and even Biskits and Old Tom, held up the rail fence whilst he slung the saddle over the rambunctious horse's rump, privately blessing the stallion for allowing it, *after the third try—still respectable*, whilst the horse from hell performed the polka and schottische. Sweating bullets not to show stiff joints, Luke vaulted into the saddle like he broke mustangs every day before breakfast. Which he had, till recently, when that dad-blasted piebald bronco back in June threw him into next Sunday.

The mount took off like a jackrabbit with Saint Vitus dance. After a rowdy session with much silver hair flying, arm waving, knuckle gripping, hat sailing, rump thumping and cussing a blue streak, *somewhere* amidst the churned dust, Luke became aware of two unblinking gray-green eyes scowling below a hank of black hair and squashed hat, from a dirt-grimed face. Hands gripping

18

the rail were small and pale, with short black-rimmed nails.

However, with his inattention, the horse from hell quivered, stopping so sudden Luke was near tossed over its big thrashing head. If he didn't know better, he'd swear it had Satan's sense of humor. Trotting tamely up to the fence, it nosed Biskits, docile as a baby lamb, snorting something rude at Luke. Then it broke wind.

In truth, Rudy had wore the beast out some.

"Okay, listen up, guys," Luke announced from his semi-quelled horse. "Roundin' cattle next week, as you well ken, so get your high-jinks and drinkin' in the next couple days."

"Yeah, boss. You got it, boss. Yes, sirree-bob, boss, don't mind if we go inta town, ag'in then?" chorused his hands.

"You didn't get all of your hootin' and hollerin' done last payday?" he teased, kenning well from the silence from the bunkhouse. Pay packet day, filled with a silver dollar amongst other jingling coin.

"Yes, sir, Mr. Luke, but…" They looked at each other shifty-like. "Got a mind to go to prayer meetin'." Stifled sniggers.

"Does church have anything to do with the Red Dog saloon and what's going on upstairs? Not your keeper, jailer or sermon-spoutin' parson. How-some-ever, be careful you don't pick up somethin' you might regret on the trail."

Luke wagged a scarred finger. "A little Bible-thumpin' down at the church house come Sunday wouldn't hurt any a you scallywags, 'cept the roof might cave in."

They grinned, shifty, digging in the dust with the

pointy-toed boots affected from Mexican *caballeros*. Keeping his face rock hard, Luke had a crawly feeling like a caterpillar down his back.

His cronies' jawing came back to him. "*'At's right and did you hear…*" and grim recounts of the latest fallen soldier to infirmity, old age, or mysterious hair-raising illness.

Luke had listened with half an ear. Least so he told himself.

Like he bit into a rotten apple and the taste lingered.

The mocking striplings before him made the taste all the bitterer. When had he become "a codger"?

When had he stopped going into town?

****

Luke glanced at the horizon. The sun had at last wore itself out, beating the hard pan to brick, and now, laying slantwise, sending batons of purple shadow from the stables across the paddocks to the big house. "Gowan, have a hootenanny, but come sunrise, Monday…"

Luke left the warning unfinished. Puking, splitting head, wobbly-kneed, by God they were still expected to put in a week's ride. "Get gone," he said wearily, and stalked off trying not to limp. "Maybe your last tumble for a while."

"We won't ride 'em too hard, Mr. Luke." More sniggers in the gloaming.

Luke made a mouth. Didn't cotton much to their speaking of women in such a disrespectful manner. Even if they *were* doxies. Especially doxies whom he suspected had a harder time than they made out under their cheerful face paint.

"*Old Lucian young once*," one smirked.

20

Hank Perry hung back with a cheeky grin on his freckled face. "Maybe last time for you too, huh, boss? Why not come on along? Keep us outta trouble." Digging pointy toes in the dirt, with smarmy grins, they looked shifty again. "Lotta purty gals at the Red Dog."

Luke saw they were breaking each other's ribs. Again. *Like to break a few heads.* He swatted their notion aside with one muscular hand.

"Don't need you to pick me out a gal, boys." He nodded heavy. "I can find my own."

I've had my day. Wasn't sure if they believed him, or something else tickled their funny-bones. Nate's jawing came back to him. Couldn't hide a wistful linger, either, as his wranglers hustled off even while slicking hair and buttoning on fresh shirts.

Luke pumped a bucket of well water and slicked his own hair, scrubbed the back of his neck, swabbing his face and large-knuckled, scarred hands of the day's grime. Scanned his worn blue cambric shirt. Checked his boots. Wouldn't do to drag horse-leavings and dirt into Elizabeth's spotless kitchen. However, as he headed for the kitchen, something bothered him like a speck in the eye he couldn't dislodge.

Something unsettling back at the corrals. What was that?

He shook his head. Hunh? Getting old. Like Liz warned.

****

As Luke winged his battered Stetson onto the hook by the door, he eyed the table with equal hunger and distaste, kenning he should be grateful, yet he always sensed Elizabeth put herself out as if he were going to toss her on the midden heap like an egg gone bad if she hadn't. 'Sides, who could eat all this? The Argo-starched cloth, so white it dazzled, groaned with platters, cruets, bowls, and pitchers. Ham, chicken *and* chops?

"Sure looks good, Lizzie, and smells better," he said instead. Beans, bacon, and cornbread would have suited just fine, but Luke stuck a white napkin, so crisp it could cut cold butter, in his shirt neck.

Another waste, all that ironing and such, but he made good work of lumpy mashed potatoes with skins, roasted turnips, black-eyed peas, bread-and-butter pickles, ham, pork steak, fried chicken, cornbread, apple butter, hot fluffy biscuits melting in your mouth without butter, Swiss chard… He was mopping gravy…when he stopped and stared, forlorn, at his near-empty plate…

Was this his life?

Making Liz happy by indulging her in her own brand of dictatorship?

He was getting stout. Need to awl an extra notch in his belt soon. He frowned at Liz's back whilst she puttered about the stove.

Something was off.

The clattery sound of dishes being scrubbed in Liz's new zinc sink.

Yet there was Liz pouring tea at the big black Majestic cook stove.

Luke checked behind him. That *boy* he'd spied at the corral, hellbent over the detritus of Elizabeth's efforts! Narrow rump, too-large hat clapped so far down his ears got bent sideways, scut of shaggy black hair sticking out, and Liz's apron so long it dragged the floor. Sure had his work cut out, Luke mused, eyeing crusted iron skillets, big lidded pots, bake tins, mountains of mixing bowls, wood paddles and whisks.

Liz serenely poured his coffee, plunking down a golden-labeled bottle of Old Overholt instead of the corn likker kept in the cupboard as "good for headaches and toothaches," though "corn was the mother of all headaches," she professed, when Luke's good whiskey added a companionable tot to her own cup of India tea.

"Where'd *he* hale from?"

Luke with an expression of disbelief, jerked his chin at the figure hunched over the sink like he wanted to hide himself, busily wiping a rose pattern off a plate. Liz just smiled in her cup. One of those *vexing* smiles when Liz had one over on him. "Meant to be taking you to task." Luke grinned, taking out the sting. "Since when do *you* hire the hands?"

His sister, twinkling bright as the North Star, glanced over her shoulder. "Just showed up lookin' for work. Didn't have the heart."

Luke poured more whiskey. "Seems too…" He searched for a word, then whispered, "…*feeble* to be much use."

Liz still had that smile, irritating Luke some, like hair down his shirt. Vexed, he dug out tobacco and papers. "So, what hay bale you find him under?" Tunking tobacco along the flimsy parchment, he licked the length, not much caring about the answer but feeling he had to make conversation. Liz didn't get out much. Only hen parties, quilting at the long stretcher taking up the front parlor, The Ladies' Aid, or after Sunday meeting with his daughter, Beth.

"I was busy with the chickens," she said offhand. "One of the Saurbachs," she reflected. "I think. They have a passel. Seemed unchristian to turn a *lad* away who's wantin' work 'stead of a handout."

"Ah, *Saur*bachs." Luke had an inkling the church halfway supported the vast Saurbach brood, from what he'd heard. "Well, see now, you have a heart soft as milk custard."

"Better 'n rock candy."

She nudged a saucer for his ashes, irritating him more. Wasn't about to douse the butt in coffee dregs!

Well, dang it. He wasn't.

"*Saur*bachs, you said." He made a face.

She emptied his saucer in the slops bucket, plunking down the clean one. "Just came to the back door, that big old hat in hand."

Luke patted his stomach, sighing, impatient. A Hawthorne novel and a bottle of Monogram rye awaited him in the parlor. "Right. Don't have to sell me like some flannel-mouth snake-oil salesman. Reckon you did the right thing, Lizzie."

Liz rolled a sardonic look. "Not with this 'un."

Luke didn't bite. He stretched, yawned and couldn't think of anything else. Restless, like the first zephyr of Spring blew winter away with Her erotic scents. Too early, by thunder, to go to bed, and *The Scarlet Letter* suddenly had no appeal.

Wonder what the boys are up to? Not too late to saddle up the skewbald gelding.

Maybe that's what *he* was these days.

A damned *gelding.*

Luke tried brushing away morbid notions. Nevertheless, the morning's dirge of mournful gossip still nettled him. Biting his mustache, he checked the dark. *Ah, what's the use. Twenty miles to town, twenty back and what then?* Luke once more reached for the brown glass bottle of Old Overholt. He could drink here.

Yet, grinning to himself, he couldn't josh fetching barmaids *here*—one with the charming gap between her teeth, or watch the rowdier girls put on a little jig showing their knickers and tight garters on the saloon's tiny stage, allowing thoughts to range to the rooms upstairs, or to fade.

What was wrong with him? Luke shot a wry look at the bottle, with a feeling no *preacher* could put to rights.

He nodded to Elizabeth.

"Don't mind if I do."

She splashed him another large tot. "Think on naming the new stallion Hell-Fire," he half jested. Liz frowned but he couldn't get a rise out of her.

"Sounds about right."

After that, Luke put all thought of heading into town aside.

"Gets lonesome here," she murmured, taking a sip. "Appreciate you bein' here."

"Sometimes it do." They sat and drank, each in their own brown thoughts.

"Day after tomorrow's Sunday."

"Aye, that it is." Stubbing out his second hand-rolled, Luke kenned what was coming.

"Your daughter's expecting you."

"Always is."

"What's the matter, Lukey?"

He tried not to show irritation over the childhood moniker.

"Nothin'. Did I say?" Luke poured another generous shot. He was getting pie-eyed. Dang! Another early night sprawled half-dozing in his worn leather chair, with a danged book he'd read three times on his lap, plus his onery, one-eared cat gnawing on his knuckles.

"Why not a *Saturday*?" Irritation gave his voice a burr. He drank quick to feel the burn. "What we do *every* Sunday. Like they *expect* it."

"Did you get crossed with a bear at birth?"

He threw her a sour look. "Beth'll just have some old widow woman waiting like a chicken hawk ready to swoop down on me."

"What's wrong with that? Maybe wouldn't snap my head off like a broke-back snake if you had a bit of sweetening."

His grin would have melted cold steel.

"I have you, Lizzie."

She snorted, studying the stove as if it had just landed from space. He detected moisture in her eyes and her mouth crumpled. "Is that what you think of me? Spinster on the shelf, drying up like a grape too long on the vine?" Cheeks flaming, she slurred words and mixed her images.

"Lord, no, Liz! Where'd you get that? You are single by choice—a brave headstrong filly, were and still are. Why, any buck would be—"

"Not by choice. Don't you be shinin' me!"

He flinched from her bitterness. Like walnut gall.

"Just happened." Liz made a long face that told him he should cut the evening short. Didn't want to think too much on what she forfeited.

"About Sunday after church, Lizzie. We'll see. Sounds just the ticket. See the baby. Growin' like a wild carrot, I bet."

"Don't butter me, neither. Thought maybe you might wanna stay home rather than go to your daughter's every week. Thought maybe Beth might want to be alone with her husband!"

"Okay, okay, Lizzie, got your point."

Not really.

Elizabeth said the opposite two minutes ago. Luke didn't wonder about Liz's conflicting emotions.

"Never mind, saves me a lot of cooking." She sniffed.

Lucian *had been* married. He kenned enough not to ask. A waste of a good woman, too. Women ran ranches on their stony lonesome, owned businesses. Was it his fault? Like she said, it just *happened* with the slow leak of years.

An icy hand squeezed Luke's heart.

Did not that reflect on him too?

The slow leak of years?

A pleasant face came to mind, like an errant breeze.

A widow woman without kith nor kin, save a young'un. Lovely Martha, or even one of the gals down at the Red Dog, like storm-battered roses but still eminently desirable, or perhaps the unmarried schoolmarm, Miss Lottie, though, in truth, she warded off suiters with a withering scowl. He s'posed a good thing or he might have asked her out for a buggy ride.

He ended, soothing, "Why, you're queen of the house, Lizzie. No one could take your place."

She threw him a look that said *withering dismissal*.

"I was just," she muttered, rising unsteadily, and with the barest slur of her voice, "gonna take this little piece of pie out to the…"

Liz hesitated as if she tripped over the raised brick by the hand pump. "*Boy* out there. Then, off to bed. Long day. I'm all right," she said, as if she hurled stones at her brother.

"I'll take it. Go on, get your proper rest, Lizzie."

She looked with longing to the stairs. "Well. Don't scare the—*lad* none."

She had that strange look again. Pinched, like a drawstring bag keeping something bursting to get out.

Like a laugh?

What did Liz have to find so danged humorous? Liz *was* getting on strange, Luke groused.

"I'll be sweet as this pie." Luke made a googly face.

"Oh, get out there, you no-good. Don't forget to fetch the plate back. That was Grannie's!" she said unnecessarily.

Luke studied her a moment. "May head into town later. Don't wait up." His voice had more snap than he meant. He dragged his attentions back to his sister like they were a reluctant calf resisting the branding iron. "I am apologetic, Liz." He hesitated, then added, "Anything I can bring back, if I ride in?"

"Your good manners." Liz, nose in the air, swept upstairs, carrying her kerosene lamp with the painted irises. "And maybe a bag of horehound, if you stay over and the dry goods is open."

Liz had her way of ferreting out what he was up to.

Luke checked the mirror above the wash basin. A habit rarely indulged.

Scary?

Maybe.

His leonine shock of silverish hair did look kinda wolfish. He flattened it. Otherwise? Luke showed teeth in a practice grin.

Teeth, whole and white.

Running a large muscular palm, rasping whiskers along a square jaw, decided against it. Furrows plowed his forehead. A stern mouth framed by a steel gray mustache. Skin tan as an old used saddle. Silvery eyes rimmed in black, like looking down a rifle barrel, scowled under ferocious brows.

Not *too* scary.

Practiced another smile.

Nothing scary there.

Ah, well. What did it matter? Some runaway. Most like, he'd hightail it off by morning carrying anything not nailed down. Like Liz said.

Toting the pie with a face that would sour milk, all Luke could think on was that flask of Monogram Rye and Nathaniel Hawthorne. Or maybe that trip into town. He wasn't through drinkin'. Luke stopped short at the barn door.

"*Crying? Must have lace on his britches,*" Luke muttered as he called out. "Hey, *boy!*" He lifted the lantern and peered in the dark. Coughed. Scuffled his boots.

Legs scrunched, knees tight, head tucked, the boy hastily wiped his eyes, jumping up ready to scarper, then tripped over some bit of tatter trailing from his rags. Two huge eyes glared back at Luke from a tear-stained, grubby face centered by a small red runny nose under the squashed hat.

Luke halted, disgusted. The evening was wasting. He frowned at the pie. Glanced at the house and, sighing deep, looked back at the boy.

The boy rassled out a broken pen knife from a ragged pouch of some kind deep in his layers of rags, holding it in front. "Don't you come any closer. I'll stick you! I'll stick you good!"

Luke sucked a tooth and strived not to roll his eyes. The voice seemed strained, like the boy was trying, not too successfully, to deepen it. "S'pose you don't care for this pie, then?" Had half a mind to toss it.

The boy's gaze snapped to the plate Luke still held, eyes big with hunger. Instead of contrition, to Luke's consternation the urchin jabbed the knife higher. "That don't work, mister!" The boy backed to the far opening…tall double doors leading away from the house to the fields and trees and road beyond. He stuck the knife somewhere back in his rags and began tugging at the iron handles.

Luke, striding after him, proper vexed now, was caught at the sight of the fragile column of neck between the hacked-off hair and what served as a collar. Swiveling, the boy, back to the door, desperately looked about and snatched a broken axe handle, making a stand, yelling, "You leave me be! I ken your kind! I'll hit you good! I will!" The boy swung the axe handle like a scythe.

My kind? Luke rarely lost his temper, but when tired and set upon, he did. Whiskey waiting, nice little fire laid by… His one or two hours of peace, garnered at end of day like a miser with gold. Dang it! Plus, his unfavorite one-eared cat awaited with its usual tail-lashing so it could lounge over his book.

"Hell's fire! Get over here and quit the blamed foolishment!"

The boy threw a half-empty bottle of horse liniment snatched from the top of a stall door where it had been abandoned. The bottle broke, splashing the smelly stuff on Luke's boots while Luke did a quick sidestep to avoid the damage. The boy, trying to go around Luke, tripped over a hay rake and, rucking up straw, scrabbled back on his rump.

"Dagnabit! Not gonna hurt you none!" Luke roared. "Stop it now!"

"Yah. Heard that afore! Ain't hurtin' enything a yours neither, an' I want nothin' to do with you. Get out of my way, you old cuss. I'll hightail it so fast…"

Luke was aware he blocked the other entrance, and the rear door the boy tried to open was locked and barred for the night.

"Gol dang it! I brung you a slab of pie! Eat it or wear it!"

He stomped closer. Suddenly the boy ran past with his out-slung arm just touching the plate—the pie flew into a pile of none-too-clean straw.

Luke saw red and grabbed sideways and backward. They both went down, with Luke twisting on one knee and an elbow. Nevertheless, he snagged some cloth and a limb, feeling the thinness of bone, hoping he hadn't broke anything, even though he wanted to smack the snarling, raging, bundle of bones upside the head.

The lad landed on his side, wistfully eyeing the smashed pie, but began to scarper once more, leaving behind a piece of dirty rag in Luke's fist. Luke made a flying leap from his prone position and snatched the boy about the waist—*and let go like his hair was on fire. Or the lad's was…*

Or he had lost all reason. *Judas! Bosoms! Breasts.* His hands had grabbed *bosoms.* Soft, warm and smallish, but still.

"Hell's bells!" he hollered.

Luke stared at his offending hands.

Felt his face grow mahogany, exploding, "You're a damned little old *gal!*"

The lad—he couldn't think of any other word yet—

snarled in reply and snatched up a hayfork, thrusting it out like he—*she*—meant business.

Eyes the shade of clear water in the dirty face looked mightily offended. "Don't be gettin' any ideas, neither, you old devil. Leave me be, or I'll stick you, *good*."

She thrust the tines an inch from Luke's midriff. Luke sucked in.

"*All y*ou varmints are *alike*."

Luke jumped back. She pressed forward, still poking sharp tines clotted with barnyard filth perilously close to his stomach.

Luke halted.

A stall door might have had something to do with it. Be damned if he'd show discomfort though, even though his stomach muscles tried to turn to iron bars.

"Liz know you're a gal?" He said, accusatory instead.

"S'pect so. Don't I *look* like one, you old bastard?"

No. Not a whisker. "Bastard, hunh? I'm getting a tad weary of you calling me names."

She shoved back the crumpled hat that had fallen over her eyes.

And Luke beheld a girl who looked like an angry kitten.

Tar-black fringe of hacked hair drooped over one eye and stuck out over each ear. Huge eyes the color of rainwater, or a winter stream, fringed in a thicket of black lashes. He remembered the corral then. Those eyes. Watching between the rails. The small grubby hands he had noted absently, gripping those same rails.

His scrutiny traveled soft pink cheeks under the grime, to a delicate pointed chin—surprised Liz hadn't scrubbed her within an inch of her life—and pale, fresh-as-cream flesh beneath an open shirt front, if one could call the tatters she wore "clothing." The straggly red ribbon tied around the hacked-off hair, unseen till now under the hat, almost undid him.

Tears welled, threatening to spill tracks down those cheeks.

Ducking so he could not see, she swiped her hand under her nose.

He'd rather face a jab to his breadbasket than face those tears. "Dad blast it! There now. Startled me's all. No need to be scared, or stiff jawed. Like I said," Luke spoke softer, "big old slab of peach pie waiting fer ya, if ya want it, or leave it. All the same to me."

Her eyes wandered, reluctant, to the flakey smashed pie, like she hadn't seen pie, or kindness, if ever. Fortunately, Grandmother's plate was intact. The filthy hayfork drooped, to Luke's eternal relief.

"For—*me*? To eat? *By myself?*" She looked slantwise with suspicion. Liz had cut a whole fourth.

A fish bone stuck in Luke's craw. "Wasn't to look at, or grow wings and fly." Luke sighed. "I'll fetch another," he began, when the girl dropped the hayfork and dashed to the pile of straw, snatching up handfuls of pie, mixed with hay, and cramming wads of fruit, juice and crust willy nilly into her mouth till her cheeks bulged like a chipmunk's.

Luke waited till she picked leftover crumbs from the plate, then the straw, then licked the plate, sensing if he stopped her, he would miss a finger or two.

"Didn't Liz feed you none?"

"Your woman? Yeah. *Some.*" Luke could imagine the table scraps Liz set out on the tin plate she used for the odd prairie bums.

She nodded at the empty plate. "Ain't never had enythin' so good as this in all my born days." It was an accusation.

"You are like my daughter Bethy when she was about ten. How old are you, anyway?" Luke blurted.

"Don't rightly know, do I?" Another accusation. She backhanded juice from her lips with belligerence, licking the back of her hand. "What's it to you, mister? Maybe sixteen? Why?"

He doubted it. "Look younger's all." Act it, too.

She shrugged, indifferent. "Tried to figure it up onct." She nodded inwardly, more at ease, or the question took her back. "Sixteen's closest, cause my nearest brother's fifteen, *maybe,* and I come before him. I *think* he was fifteen. He doesn't rightly ken neither, cause Ma don't—doesn't write down nothin' in a Bible or such."

She squirmed. "Called me the runt, but I'm strong," she quickly added, eyeing the hayfork again.

"Mmm." Doubt flavored his grunt. Luke dug out papers and tobacco, rolling a cigarette one-handed, and squatted against a bale. She looked at the butt hungrily. He didn't bite. Shouldn't smoke if you were a woman, least in his circles, but suspicioned some did, including Liz. "How many brothers and sisters?" Really didn't care.

"Fifteen, one's on the way…should be popping out any day now," she said as if mentioning the weather. Even by farming and ranching standards that was a high number.

"Your ma must be busy."

She mulled. "Not 'zactly. With each kid, she doles out more chores, and Pa don't do nuthin'. I figure by the

34

next un, she can stay in bed the whole darn day." She twisted a pained smile.

Judging by her rags—tattered, frayed overalls cut off from an adult's after they were too tired of work and half-falling into the ragbag, one strap stuck with a rusty safety pin, the other drooping from a knotted string, revealing the top mound of a rounded white bosom poking the colorless rag—the parents didn't do much for their offspring either way.

He looked off when her shirt slipped off one side, uncovering a satiny shoulder the shade of one of Elizabeth's cream envelopes and her slender neck, with a ring of grime at the nape. Two different types of footwear, too, Luke noted. Boot on one foot, scruffy Indian moccasin on the other, with not a speck of stocking. Her ankle appeared too thin and white for the cold. "Why'd ya leave home?"

She set her jaw. "That's for me to know, mister. And don't be gittin' any ideas 'cause yer stinkin' drunk er somethin'."

He hadn't had that much. He didn't ken why he uttered the next words. "You start working for me." He said with no inflection. She scowled for his troubles.

"Guess I need to ken your name if yer to keep on. I'm Lucian Farnsworth. Luke."

She frowned, narrowing her eyes. Judging and finding him wanting. "Maybe. Maybe not. Depends." She stuck her small chin out, snapping, "Pearly-Mae. But mostly Mae, or *Hey, you.*"

"Pearly-Mae. That's pretty." Almost said, "Pretty as you, under all that dirt," but kenned she'd throw rocks at him. "Reckon I'll call you *Mae.*" And she was, under the grime and too-thin face like a half-starved cat that needed feeding, well—*pretty*. Those big eyes, maybe too big because of the scrawniness, surrounded by lashes soft as shredded velvet under two black brows like silky commas. Above the small pointed chin, her soft pink upper lip protruded slightly over the lower one.

Yes, a feral scrawny kitten, he decided.

"But it's just a job, mister. Nothing else!"

He sighed. *What would I want truck with a filthy, dirty-mouthed, obnoxious gal tramp*, he yearned to shoot back. Sorry he offered. He could smell trouble off her, as well as a certain perfume. *The scent of youth.* Not objectionable. He smelled worse from his roustabouts.

"So, you up and decided to cut and run," he challenged.

"Warn't like that. They—*made* me." She bit her lip as if to hold more back.

Luke studied his smoke. "Go on."

"Sez I was not eny use and if I wanted vittles, go out and make my own way, but to bring home cash money most every pay. They sent me here." She added innocently, or so he thought, "I warn't going to."

She hesitated slightly, studying the straw-littered dirt and added, "Then, there was my brother, and—and my uncle, and…" She mumbled it almost to herself, without further explanation.

Luke took a drag, nodding darkly, flicked tobacco off his tongue. "Sent you?"

She gave him a look that peeled the skin off. "Said onct, heard you was well-heeled and why not help out a neighbor by takin' on extry mouths." Her mouth crumpled. "Pa stood there at the door with a big old stick. Said I warn't welcome no more." A slow tear tracked a clear line in the smudge. She scowled. "I was ready to light out anyways."

"How'd you ken where we lived?"

"Didn't, did I?" She looked up boldly, watching him.

"It's a big place. Not easy to stumble on."

She shrugged as if the vagaries of the universe didn't apply to her. "Figgered it out, though, didn't I, onct I was here."

Luke wasn't certain he quite believed her. He could arm himself, like that King Arthur fella, against arrows through the gizzard, getting thrown from a horse and a broke head, but the sight of this gal with tears trembling on her lashes unmanned him. *Dang it seven ways to Sunday. Wish't Liz was here.*

He began to pick up the plate, when he heard, "Either that, or get hitched." He turned back.

"Hitched?"

She folded her arms and nodded sulky. "Drover. One got a sheep farm."

Luke took on a faraway look.

He kenned the drover. A mulish slovenly cuss he ran across once, down at the feed store in Red Butte.

Anyone with a lick-spittle of sense kenned sheep were scarce the trouble to drive the smelly contrary things to market. If the feller took one bath a year, it was Christmas. He recalled flabby flesh, hair limp and yellow as grass found under a rock. Had a weak left eye. Never kenned where he was looking, and the way he beat his sheep dog, had a cruel streak like a cancerous knot on a tree.

He smiled grim. The lout never found out *what* happened to his sheep dog, now resting comfortably before Luke's fireplace.

"So, you scarpered?"

She lifted her shoulders.

"Why him?"

*"*He asked. Well, plagued Pa some. Said he'd give him five sheep if he could marry up with me. Only thing, Pa didn't cotton to mutton or lamb, and…"

Grunting like he swallowed gravel instead of a laugh, Luke waved her off. "I'll pay you a bit. Keep some back. Only give them a part. If *any.* You don't have to, you ken? Miss Elizabeth'll be your banker."

She shot a shrewd glance and nodded.

"Feel some better now?"

She dug her toe in and nodded, sulky.

Luke heaved a sigh. "First thing, proper boots." Maybe a dress. Thinking of Liz, he held back. But jeans. He'd see if one of the skinniest hands had castoffs. Even those would be better than the scraps half hanging off her, especially after their tussle.

She smiled.

Luke started. It was like the sun broke out on a bubbling brook. Mischief, fun, sweetness, all hidden till now, rippled across her face. A high clear laugh tinkled like a chandelier in the wind.

"Settled then," he gruffed.

"Yes, sir," she whispered. "I'll do anything you ask, sir."

Luke looked down.

She had ahold of his hand.

A slim cool small-fingered thing with tiny callouses, lost in his large scarred tanned paw. He wasn't sure what to make of it. He felt a stir from some unkenned regions lost in the past, drawing his hand back as if hers was made of flames from the burning pits of Hell, and gave it a quick pat.

"Enough of that now." He flushed, stern.

She cocked her head, studying him with a wisdom that unsettled him like a burr under the saddle.

He should leave, but of a sudden, with a sensation with which he was unfamiliar—it felt comfortable with nowhere particular to go, despite Elizabeth's habit to go to bed with the chickens, when the sky was alive with stars. He settled back against a hay bale.

Mae began to ramble, which made it easier, letting her stories wash over him in a soothing tide. He got to chuckling, captivated by recollections of her many siblings and their wicked stunts against feckless parents.

****

"So, my oldest brother and me, his name's Sammy, we got back at Pa for the beatin' he gave Sammy, over *nothin'* this time." She giggled.

"Pa stole a pig. Says he's gonna butcher it, though he never did, and it made a big old mud wallow after that bad storm…"

Luke nodded. He recollected the one. A real humdinger, when the sky turned the color and weight of anvils and lightning forked the ground with vicious eye-blinding stabs. He nodded—*Go on.*

"Anyhow, we put straw and grass and I don't know what all over that big old wallow."

Mae was laughing so hard now she could hardly speak. "And then, Sammy yelled…"

Luke laughed along. It felt freeing. "So, what then?"

"S-Sammy yelled, 'Hey, Pa! You stink worse'n rotten eggs and look like a pile of horse apples,' and Pa came barreling out, hit that mud puddle like he was dancin', belly-flopped, rolled over and sat the seat of his britches smack in the mud clean to his waist. And when he stood, he slipped and fell face f-first. Like a tar b-baby."

"*Hahahah!*" Luke's basso voice rang out.

Good thing the hands weren't about. Or, he amended, checking Elizabeth's window for the glow of kerosene—*Lizzie*. But why shouldn't he be out here? His ranch. Still, probably should go in. But then, Luke found they both chuckled to beat the band over another tale concerning a wasp nest and her sister and a stick. When the dust settled, Luke asked quiet-like, "Your dad hard on you too?"

She rolled her eyes. "Likkered up, or just wanted to feel better and beat on somebody." Luke kenned the type. Angry at the world. Only way to blow off steam was pummel with hurtful words, brutal fists, or worse.

"Ma's no better. Tried at first. Easier to go 'long." Mae shrugged. Luke now noted the scar bisecting one brow, the crooked little finger, and the bruise he had thought a shadow on her slender neck.

Getting late now. S'posed she could kip in the kitchen, but what if he wanted to wander in his altogether? Some nights when Liz was tucked in and he restless, he did just that. More and more lately. He'd search out windows or saunter to the porch and check the moon in his birthday suit, relishing the chill on his lean flanks and bare chest, then haul clear cold well water in for a drink.

He chuckled. Now that *would* scare the bejeebers out of any young thing. Nope, wouldn't do. Still, plate in hand, studying the stoic figure, he hesitated. "Getting on late. Tonight, sleep in the kitchen. Only got two bedrooms." Guess he'd curtail nightly wanderings for a time.

Mae scowled and kicking at straw, looked away.

"Your woman said I could sleep in the stable."

"Darn decent of her," he muttered.

"Yup. Said red up the dishes and you can sleep in the barn, 'cause it's dark, like you said, but then I got to go."

"So...." Luke was aware he'd been out here a long time and Liz could teach General Sherman a thing or two about interrogation. "Let's go."

"Yeah, mister. But...already made me a bed. Here. Ain't sleepin' in no house with you."

Luke sighed again, startled when she took his hand in her impossibly small one. Guessed she finally decided he wasn't that Jack the Ripper fella he'd read about, in London, over in Europe. Leading a mystified, edgy Luke deeper in the stable, Mae showed him like any house-proud female...an empty horse stall Luke surveyed with no little interest.

Horse blanket neatly folded across a hay mound with an old saddle for a pillow. Ragged jacket on a hook. Rusty tin can from the dump holding drooping Shasta daisies. She'd removed a lantern and it too hung on the same rusty nail fastening a horseshoe. The small space seemed warm and inviting with the lantern light melting the red plaid horse blanket in a buttery glow.

Luke felt a lump big as a turnip. He spied a piece of ham meat in a crust of bread wrapped in a faded red bandana peeking out of the hay.

"Looks right nice. Did right proud. But mayhap we can do better. Maybe a *piller*? I'll ask Miss Elizabeth."

Mae held out her hand for a formal shake. "I'll work like the devil for you, Mister Luke. Haven't never been afraid of it. Just you tell me anything you want. I'm sorry 'bout the pie…"

"Ummm. Good night then. Ah…" He looked out at the darkness. "You aren't scared?" Luke nodded at the night.

"Ain't scared a nothin'. Nicest room I done ever had." Mae wrapped arms about herself in a hug of contentment.

Luke studied his boots. "Fine, then. Help Miss Lizzie out in the kitchen and such at first. Not getting any younger, I reckon, and could use a hand. Whatever she asks. Won't be over much." Without another word and oddly reluctant, Luke strode away.

Looking back, Mae appeared lost, framed in the vast doorway, with the dark interior behind her. It was all Luke could do to keep from running back and dragging her to the house, Liz be damned about "help sleeping or eating in her home."

****

Lucian Farnsworth strode into the kitchen with a scowl that would turn a grape to sour wine. To his consternation, Liz was still up in her nighty and raising her teacup with the roses to her lips, eyes shining over the rim. "You need your sight tested, old man, for spectacles."

Luke sailed his hat on the hook. "Why'd ya not tell me!"

"Not often I get one over on you." Liz didn't try to hide her smirk.

"Don't have to look so all-fired pleased. Sure as shootin' *looked* like a boy!"

Suddenly their faces crumpled, Luke sputtering not to laugh and Liz, gasping from the same affliction, grabbed the corn likker this time, from the shelf. "Might help us sleep, finally."

"Sure are somethin', Liz." Luke splashed a shot in his old cup and added to hers. "So, she's to stay?"

Liz eyed him. "You were out there a spell?" She always could read him like a hymnal. "We don't ken anything about her other than she's a Sauerbeck." It was a warning.

"That shouldn't damn her."

They sat and sipped in uneasy silence, each in their own dark alley of thoughts.

"Long day tomorrow," Luke said, abrupt, drank the dregs and kissed his sis on the forehead. She didn't seem to notice. He steered away from her sad face, shaking his head, and watched Liz slowly make her way upstairs. Women were an unknown planet sometimes.

Too early for bed, too late to read. Luke rocked on the porch, smoking Sweet Caporals and watching the indigo midnight sky. A dim light glowed in the stable. Another in the bunkhouse. Was this all there was? He pondered, as if a dark masked stranger had tapped him on the shoulder, asking for the time. The slow slide into old age?

He stubbed the butt on the heel of his boot without answers.

Dawn would come too soon.

****

Next dawn, Luke, in his usual blue cambric work shirt so scrubbed it resembled gray silk, a worn black leather vest, taut faded denims, loose in the waist but skimming his long leg muscles like paint, plus scuffed wedge-heeled boots, took his first wincing sip of scalding tar as he gazed idly out the window at the closest corral to see if any of his hands were out and about.

The sun already threatened a cook-oven of a fall day. Be good to work in relative cool. He drew a tin cup of cold well water piped in to the new zinc sink Lizzie had wanted as the latest thing. Glancing out again, he dashed the rest.

Damn.

Trouble already brewing like a nor'easter.

Roustabouts surrounded Mae as she tried to toss a bridle up over a horse's head—Betsy, his old brood mare—missing by a mile. Least she reckoned which horse was tamest. He watched her hopping about, trying to wedge one small moccasin in a stirrup. One of the hands, grinning foolishly, cupped her bottom to *help* her up.

She scowled and swatted him off. Luke had been on the rifle end of her scowls. Even so, as she desperately tried to grab the pommel, the mild mare dragged her about some. Luke swore out a breath when she almost slipped under Betsy's nervous prancing hooves. Mae hopped aside.

Arms folded, she leaned against the splintered rail, glowering at the wranglers. Luke had to chuckle. She still resembled an angry feral cat. Ignoring the entertained hands, Mae grabbed Betsy's reins. Hanging onto them with her teeth, she climbed the split rail and gingerly lifted a leg over the saddle.

Betsy sat docilely as if that was her intention all along.

Hearing Liz arrive, still pinning up her hair, Luke spoke over his shoulder.

"What's a gal like that doin' in the stable?" He said

it before he thought.

"Can you see her in the bunkhouse with the *hands*?" She hooted, startling him some. "They'd think it was Christmas, New Year's *and* their birthdays all rolled into one." She glanced mockingly at him. "Can't have a gal stirrin' 'em up. Like kerosene to a match." Liz smirked, nodding toward the window. "'sides, for what they're thinkin', they can go in to The Red Dog. 'Course, she looks like she's *been* in a few bunkhouses to me."

Luke didn't comment. Start another fire. "Wasn't thinking, Liz. Right. Ain't fittin'."

The stable was three steps away from the bunkhouse. "I'll have a palaver with them too."

Liz scoffed. "Be gone 'fore the week's out anyway. Probably with my best silver," she repeated, like a mantra. "I've dealt with these tramps before. Not worth the effort. Keep an eye on her."

Luke could not tell if that was a threat or a prediction. He looked out again. When Mae couldn't get Betsy to budge, Luke watched her try to dismount, to the accompaniment of his bronco-busters' ribald comments, and finally slide down Betsy's broad side, showing them her little rounded rear end.

Luke scowled. Time to get to work himself. He strode out. When Mae looked over, he thumbed toward the kitchen. He shook his head, watching her drag over to the kitchen door as if going to the hangman. He didn't see Mae again for the next few days; Liz had her on a cleaning tear and almost forgot about her, what with one hundred twenty head of cattle found lost in a fold of hills and a trek into town to talk with his lawyer about fence lines in contention.

Chapter Two: Widow Alcie

The sleek Sunday-go-meeting surrey with Old Tom at the reins was hitched and ready when Liz stepped out in her best cranberry bombazine straight from Chicago, courtesy of Sears Roebuck catalogue and the Wells Fargo Stage Coach Company, plus her usual cameo brooch that had belonged to their ma.

Luke, fiddling a gold watch looped about his gray velvet vest, was spiffed up too. New black suit, high-collared shirt, black bolo, and Stetson freshly brushed, the gold watch and chain, and his boots, lick-spittle shining. His choice would be clean jeans and his best shirt. But Liz liked to put on the ritz.

As she raised a boot to the iron step, Liz smirked over at the barn. Luke followed the arrow of her discontent. There Mae crouched, forlorn, in the barn doorway, arms about her knees, wistfully watching. She ducked at their attention, scratching dirt with a stick and appearing interested in a rock.

"See here," Luke muttered, "why can't she go?"

Liz, prissily straightening her skirts and clutching her Bible, looked at him as if he'd just grown another head. "That gal hasn't set foot inside a church since the day she was put on this earth," she hooted. "Land a Goshen, Luke. Church roof would fall in if any of the Saurbachs warmed their fannies in one of the new pews. 'Sides, she can't go dressed like a tramp."

"What might you be telling me, Lizzie? That you deny this poor little scrap a bit of pleasure in life? Maybe riding into town or going to a shindig come harvest time or a church social? That would cost you nothing."

"Pshaw! What would she want to go to a harvest dance for? She'd be like a pig with a ribbon tied round the ear! She's hardly house broke, or worn shoes! Folks would laugh and make us out as prize fools." She huffed and fussed with her hat.

"She doesn't have to look like she just crawled out of the dustbin. You've made sure she stayed that way."

Rarely did brother and sister lock horns, but when they did, the hands either made themselves scarce or lined up for the rounds. Old Tom glanced about, disapproving.

"*I've* made her that way? I burnt those pestiferous shreds! I scrubbed her raw. She now wears shoes, in case you had not noted. And the bits and pieces I've given her, which weren't exactly rags!"

"Liz, do you not recall you aren't that old? And what it's like to be young? She can learn. You could teach her. Even a simple dance. How to talk to other females her age."

"Hmmmph! Leave that up to you! You seem to have a fascination for her."

****

Liz watched her brother, vexed. She rarely experienced freight trains of clouds as if brewing on the western horizon, black as a coal train thundering toward her. That was her brother's expression. But when they did appear, even Liz felt thunderstruck. But she wasn't sure where or how to avoid Luke's wrath when his mood came storming in, carrying a whiff of brimstone.

Luke. Always so easygoing, so kind, so thoughtful, she forgot this dark obstinate side of him, and now he was going on the warpath over this ragamuffin, against his own blood kin, *his own sister.* She was going to say something tart, but her brother's head was lowered like a bull ready to charge, nailing her from under thick black brows.

Liz tapped Old Tom, who affected not to be listening, to hurry up.

Luke shook his head, clicked his tongue and vaulted up, itching to take the reins, but Liz for some unfathomed reason said it warn't proper on Sundays.

Hell's bells, Old Tom wasn't their servant, and he'd have another talk with Liz about getting Mae proper duds, church or no church.

Old Tom clucked to the sleek black yearling, twitched the reins, and the surrey jolted off leaving Mae to watch wistfully till out of sight.

****

Sunday after church, Beth thrust the baby, a boy, at her father.

Grinning down at the little bundle of chubby cuteness, Luke strolled her vast kitchen, cradling the boy, tickling his waving hands with his mustache and cooing in a way that would have gob-smacked his wranglers. Luke smiled into the child's wide blue-turning-to-brown eyes. Someday, his spread would belong to this little scrap… His thoughts were interrupted by Beth's cry.

He swiveled with the baby to see a short female at the door stoop, greeted by his daughter calling out as if seeing the Second Coming, "Heavens to Betsy, look who's come to visit, Pa. What a nice surprise!"

Somehow the last didn't ring quite true. And there was Beth ushering in a short, pleasingly plump, dark-haired female, fortyish, sporting a purple hat with stuffed blackbirds quivering on its brim and youthful curls fringing her forehead. The newcomer, crammed into lavender velvet, glanced eagerly about, resting on Luke a tad long as if she were a starving wolf and he a fat juicy rabbit.

Placing the baby over his shoulder, Luke groaned inwardly but, bowing slightly, put on his company face. "Madam."

"I begged her to come visit any old time. Wasn't that right, Alcie?" Beth enthused.

Shuck of his Sunday jacket for more comfort, Luke was still gussied up a tad for dinner with his daughter and son-in-law. He looked like a swell in the gray shirt with a bolo tie studded with a striking piece of turquoise, his Sunday-go-meeting black whipcord trousers with thin stripes and best black leather vest. He didn't recognize it of himself, but Luke cut a striking masculine figure—shoulders like a barn door, square jaw, rangy legs, neat hips, six-three, hair like quicksilver and steel gray eyes.

Both his daughter Beth and his sister Liz, chattering like sparrows, hugged the woman, and, divesting her of her sealskin jacket, shot a smug glance behind Luke's back. They reckoned he couldn't see, but didn't reckon on Luke catching the exchange in the hall-tree mirror.

"Lucian, this is Mrs. Alcie Hastings…" Judging by her mourning attire, no matter how rich, Beth needn't inform him, "…recently widowed."

"Why, sure," Luke said politely, handing back the child to Beth and shaking the newcomer's limp, moist, plump, outstretched hand. Luke quelled the urge to wipe his on his pants afterward.

"Lucian! My, what an attractive name. So noble!"

"Um. Thank you, Miz Alcie. I think I might have known your husband, Ed…"

"My, yes, dear Edward. Married thirty years. One gets lonely. Do you find that? Sometimes I sit there at night and don't know what to do…" She tittered but never took a breath before she continued, "Do you ever talk to your dear wife? I find it so comforting. My, you do have a lovely, well-run ranch. Your dear daughter told me. My Ed used to keep our place spick and span, in apple-pie order, 'everything in its place and a place for everything,' he always said, and ah, then I always said…" She took a breath. "But dear, you can never find anything without my help…"

Luke, lost in a tidal wave of comments, opened his mouth to speak, while his daughter looked on as if Alcie was giving Lincoln's Gettysburg Address.

Luke tempered his thoughts as Alcie rambled on. The woman was edgy, as was he.

"…just not the same without a man about the house. I was acquainted with your dear wife. You might not know, but we were good friends, though never invited to your place, but we did meet at the Ladies' Aid Society and quilting bees. I vow, she was lovely, too, and I did have her over at our home for tea one afternoon, but as I said I never had the pleasure of seeing *your* lovely ranch…"

Luke nodded and smiled till his jaws ached. He'd rather face a grizzly in his underwear.

Alcie eventually wound down when Beth herded them to the big clawfoot table and placed the baby in his cradle, only to resume the chatter after they were all seated. Luke shot a glance at Beth that said, *We will speak later.* He plastered on a smile and took the time to draw the chair out for Alcie the widow—*the hungry widow,* it turned out, but that did not halt the flow of words.

He looked with despair over Beth's usual Sunday spread, as no one wanted to eat whiles Alcie was full steam ahead. All getting cold. Chicken and dumplings, ham, beef ribs, sugared yams, cornbread and biscuits, big slabs of butter, scorched-just-right runner beans crumbled with bacon, black-eyed peas, and squash pie cooling on the sideboard, alongside Beth's famous chocolate spice cake.

Luke loved Beth's hot fluffy biscuits, so short they melted without the butter, but politely returned Alcie's conversational parlays while they cooled. "He hailed from Illinois, your Ed, didn't he?" Luke interrupted, as Beth passed along the melting butter, watermelon conserve, gravy and smashed potatoes. Luke made full use of the opportunity. "I recollect his folks were from there…"

His daughter made significant looks to pass the biscuits, now grown cold, while Luke made his comments to Alcie and managed to add, "You fattening me up for the round-up?" as he winked at Beth, nodding at the cake, hoping to head the widow off at the pass.

Beth laughed, with Alcie nonplussed at being shunted aside, but not for long. "Oh, my, yes! Chocolate cake! My Ed always said my cake was so light it nearly floated off the plate."

Even Beth seemed annoyed at that.

But the widow Alcie could not be deterred. "I often thought of returning to the Midwest, but…" she airily waved a hand while gnawing on a chicken leg. "There's no one left there, you see," and gazed fondly at Beth, who was now looking a bit desperate herself, Luke was gratified to note.

"Your sweet daughter here—oh, might I have the teeniest bit more of that sugared ham? It is nice to have someone worry about you, and some of that redeye gravy too, 'fore you put it away. Why, I feel she is almost like my *own* daughter," Alcie vowed between bites. This announcement was followed by silence as heavy as a coal scuttle.

Beth's husband, Matthew, gamely eating, ignored the whole conversation.

Lucky stiff.

Alcie was okay, a fine woman, yet he didn't cotton to women with dumpling faces, even if she did have rather fine eyes, if a tad set close. His Katherine had been lean, fit, and majestic as an Arabian horse all her short life. This woman you could say was *comfortable.*

A nice woman, even if she did keep up a wave of conversation he was drowning in—something about how dear his daughter was, and "nice to have a companion, though one misses the companionship *of a man…*" and she knew how close they were, and that he should come over sometime for supper, "even if I do say it myself, I set a table almost as fine as this…"

Might as well hit him over the head with an anvil.

"Besides…" She tittered. "…I could do with some manly thoughts on insurance issues. Ed took out some, you know, *quite a bit*," she added meaningfully. "He certainly did not leave me high and dry. I have a tidy sum, but I don't understand words like 'fiduciary' and 'annuitized,' and then there is the farm equipment—my, my, I don't ken a backhoe from a cream separator," and she tittered again. God help him.

"Sounds as if it might be understandably over your head, a fine lady like you, perhaps," he suggested politely. "Your proper place may be back east with familiar folks, *like you'd have there.*"

Then Alcie looked at him with eyes like two Smith-and-Wesson gun barrels. "I don't know what you mean! I *have* no one left there." Her voice rose almost to a screech. "Without a man I am *nothing*!" She snapped down her fork. "How could you even *think…*?"

Even Beth's husband glanced up from snitching another slice of Beth's cake.

Alcie heaved to a calm. "I have always been rather—sheltered, I know, and my dear husband's death was…" She tucked a lacy kerchief to her smallish dry eyes. Luke was aware of Liz's and Beth's punitive looks nailing him to the wall, and he felt the burn.

"No, no. Not at all, not at all, be happy to go read your books and set you up straight, so's that you can do it on your own. Maybe Beth would like to go with me and visit."

He eyed his daughter in a manner which left no doubt what he expected. Alcie sputtered, "Why—why! That is entirely unnecessary!" She looked at their stricken faces. Matthew had halted eating.

Alcie changed like a weathervane in a windstorm, her smile now as sweet as honey oozing from the comb. "Oh, *could* you! That would be so gal-*lant*, Mr. Farnsworth. May I call you Lucas? I feel as if I know you now. You may call on me at any time."

"It's Lucian or Luke. Don't stand on ceremony here." He looked desperately at his daughter. His son-in-law was again industriously chewing, nose practically in his plate. Where did he put it all?

"I sure do love that dress you have on," Beth cut in. "I know you do all your own sewing. There's not a dressmaker in the county could come up with that. Isn't it right pretty, Pa?"

"Yes, very fine, I'm right fond of purple…" *The color of an old bruise.*

"Well as you may *recall,* I'm still in mourning, but I shall soon be out of—"

The silence lengthened. Luke stuck a finger between his neck and collar. "Umm. Not here. Doesn't mean much. Back east you have to stand on formality, I suppose…black for a few days, then gray, then purple, or lavender…hell, I don't know."

"Pa, there's no need to get huffy…"

"Or use profanity," Alcie sniffed.

Liz added to the mix, rolling her eyes at Alcie. "I've tried, Lord help me, Alcie, but he *will* take the Lord's name in vain."

"My deportment does not need your *help*, Elizabeth."

Matthew, his son-in-law, nervous as a hound dog in a room full of rocking chairs, stifled a grin behind his coffee cup.

Oh, to be back at the ranch. Mae's perfect little face swam before Luke's eyes. Time with her seemed a sweet flowing stream in comparison to this. Belatedly, he became aware they watched him oddly as he stared into space with a smile on his mug.

"What's funny, Pa? Share it with us." It was a command.

Luke decided to keep his big mouth shut, the safest

route through this minefield, so he smiled, nodded and made a bland comment, to his daughter's annoyance and the widow Alcie's consternation. Liz just watched her brother like a cat ready to pounce on a mouse emerging from its hole.

After they sipped coffee and nibbled a last piece of cake while listening to a gramophone record of a man called Caruso, who sounded as if he could call hogs across three counties, his daughter still didn't get the message that her matchmaking was dying along with the tenor's last bellow.

Beth gave it one more shot to bring down her quarry. "Pa. Maybe you'd like to be taking Miz Alcie home. Getting on late. You could hitch your horse up to her carriage, to get home on."

"Why, *yes*," urged his helpful sister Liz. "I was planning to stay over. Gives me a chance to visit my little nephew."

Luke thought desperate thoughts. If he took the widow home, she might invite him in, presaging a spider's web of entanglement. "Much as that would be my privilege, ma'am, I need to head on back. You too, Liz."

Why are womenfolk such pitfalls?

"You can't stir up a mess of oatmeal?" Liz exploded while Alcie glared.

Luke, as the target of those Smith-and-Wesson eyes, had visions of her holding him prisoner. "Nothing I'd like better, Miz Alcie. However, I have to get up early for, well, you know, the…the, umm, round-up. Best be hightailing it home. Past my bedtime anyway." *Dang. Explaining too much.*

Alcie looked sadly at him for a moment and then,

swatting him with a small lacy fan, simpered, "Oh, I understand. You *men!* I have my boy with me."

The woman had more moods than a peddler had pots and pans. She meant the boy waiting throughout dinner by the stove with his own plate, stowing its contents away as fast as he could in a way that showed what sort of mingy household the widow Alcie managed, despite her affluence.

His big-hearted son-in-law interrupted, "Why don't I take you on home, Miz Alcie?"

The widow shot him a look that would fry an egg. "I don't want to put you out…"

"No trouble a-tall. I could use the fresh air…been working all day on the manure spreader, all bolloxed up…" Matthew trailed off at the look his wife gave him, then mulishly crammed on his hat and yanked his coat from the hook, leaving the widow little choice but to hastily wrap her fur and summon her boy.

Luke could read his mind. Lord knew Matthew needed a break, if taking a widow home was a holiday. Beth never wanted him far from sight, unless Luke himself was around.

"All right, then, guess that does it. Thanks, Bethy, for your usual glorious grub."

Luke gave the widow a stiff bow and offered, "Nice making your acquaintance, Alcie."

"Yes, indeed. I hope we may kindle that friendship." *She did not give up easy.* She winced, a stiff little smile tightening like a purse string, and held out her plump hand—expecting it to be kissed, Luke guessed too late, bumping her forehead and knocking her bonnet askew as he bent. Alcie turned on her heel and swept out, twitching her finger at her boy. "Come, Jeb. Make haste.

56

These people have important *things* to do," she said pointedly.

After she left Luke rounded on his daughter. "*Whew!* I know you have my best interests at heart, Beth, *But...*" He shook his finger in her face. "Little missy! Let's stop the matchmaking! I'm fine. I have my work. I have the ranch. I have my boys to look after, and Liz to keep me—company."

"But, Pa!"

"Enough! My back is up about this. No more!"

"But Pa, I only..."

He cupped Beth's cheek and said kindly, "You mean well. I have my memories, kitten."

Beth folded her arms. "Sure, Pa, but memories don't keep you warm at night."

Liz gasped.

Beth rounded on her, snapping, "Liz. Maybe you'd like to see to the kids, if this conversation is too adult for you."

"Well, really, Beth! Such manners. What has gotten into you, I'd like to know? Katherine did not raise you this way, and you needn't be crude." Liz walked slowly to the stairs, huffing, "I don't know what the big *secret* is anyway."

Luke watched her leave with mixed feelings. Since when was he scared of Beth?

Beth waited till her aunt was upstairs. "You need, like a, well, a...*fast* woman," Beth hissed once Liz was out of hearing. "When's the last time you had a good— ?" She made a vague gesture.

He chopped his hand to stopper her words. "Beth!" Luke shook his leonine head, swiping back a lock of gunmetal hair. "Always been a right caution, Beth, but this is the limit." He began to cram on his hat.

"I mean it, Pa! We are *adults*. I'm a married *woman*. I ken what it's all about. I'm not a blushing *girl*! We've always talked things over. We have no secrets. How—how *is* your, well—*love* life? You are still a young, vigorous man—you are fine-looking—*any* woman…"

He threw an ironic look at Beth that said, *I give up.*

"Really, Pa! Look in the mirror when you shave, for a change. You *are* a nice-looking man! Why, any woman would be proud to be on your arm."

Luke made a negative noise. He placed his hat back on the table.

Beth watched with an impish smile, like when she was twelve. "Pa? Do you have a lady friend?"

"Disrespectful daughter of mine, she'd be *no* lady if she cavorted in the way *you* mean."

"Pa! I only want you happy."

Luke knuckled the table hard. "No more, Beth Anne."

Beth slowly took her seat. Luke hesitated, brushing the cloth of imaginary crumbs. "And yes, I was stepping out with a—a *woman* who will remain known to me alone, Miss Snoopy-Drawers. I don't wish to offend the lady."

"Pa. I wouldn't gossip."

"Not until you told your best friend, and she?" He snorted. "Only way to keep a secret amongst three females is if two of them are dead." Laughing, Luke clapped back on his Stetson. "And I am *very* fond of you, little darlin'. Tell Liz I've gone on and to take her time. I'll survive fryin' my own eggs."

"Don't go yet, Pa."

He turned back sighing.

"'Sides, been a while since we've had a good father-daughter talk."

Luke fiddled his Stetson. "Thought that's what we *been* doin'. I am kinda done in, sweetheart." They both looked to the door when Matthew stomped in. "Back so soon?" Beth rolled her eyes at Luke. "He can't stay away from me."

Matthew shucked his boots, flushing. "Been tryin' to get Bethy to go with me to the big feed and livestock show in Chicago. We could have a hog-killin' time for a change. Eat out. Fancy grub..." He glanced blushingly at Beth. "Soft sheets."

"I'd rather spend time with my father!"

Matthew tossed his wife a wounded look.

But Beth had turned to her dad. "He knows we can't leave. There's the hog slaughtering and..."

"You should go, Bethy. Time gets away and all you have to show for it is, well—blood pudding, sausage and ham."

"He's right, Bethy."

"Matthew, you stay out of this. It's between my Pa and me. You have nothing to do with this." They watched Matthew trudge upstairs mumbling something about "tired."

Beth poured Luke a glass of something vaguely prune-colored and one for herself. "Does Elizabeth take care of you, Pa? She's getting up there. Maybe you should move here. Sell the ranch."

Luke threw her a look. "You don't mean that." Hurt. The spread would be little Matthew Junior's someday. "Elizabeth's fine. And neither one of us is the undertaker's friend." He took a sip of the hootch his daughter made from raisins—he preferred rye, but this jack had quite a kick—sputtering it out at his daughter's next words.

"You are right, Pa." She raised an airy hand. "But Liz probably keeps you tied down. Cowhands all go into town and…" Now she did look away for a second. "Well, you know?" She gave an elaborate shrug. "I know what goes on upstairs at the Red Dog. Maybe that's why a good woman like Alcie…"

Luke stared at her. "You are something. You just don't give up, do you? And Alcie is about as exciting as a plate of cold beans."

"Even cold beans taste good if you're hungry enough."

He began to protest, but Beth had a mischievous smile.

Luke shook his head. Still, he felt uneasy. What she said was true, in a way. He *didn't* like Liz to feel lonely and unappreciated, so he'd stayed close to the hearth until it became an expected habit. Luke twirled the empty cake plate.

"I been to town. Saw the widow Tharp for a time or two. *He wouldn't tell her about Martha…*

"What happened?"

"She gave me calf-foot jelly."

"Oh, how terrible! What calumny! She gave you a gift."

"It was for an old man."

"Pa! You are not old!' Beth rapped the table. "Why you are hardly over fifty!"

"Well aware of that fact, sweetheart. I am. And *happy.* Don't fret."

His son-in-law had come back down, poured a cup of joe, and hung about, pretending not to listen. Finally, he plunked down across from them.

"Beth, I don't see why we can't go."

"My father *needs* me right now, Matthew."

"Bethy, I can look after myself just fine. An old broom kens all the corners, and that's me." Luke clapped on his hat. "An old broom! Sweep out your own house, missy."

With a grin, his son-in-law walked Luke to the door, slapping him on the shoulder. Luke winked and murmured, "*Chicago…*" in his ear.

****

Outside, moon glow turned the night's ice-coated weeds, Hell-Fire's plumes of breath, and the dusty road to Laramie, all sparkling with hoar frost, into a silvery magic.

Luke vaulted onto his horse and sat dazzled by the night's brilliance. "I should raise more hell," he informed Hell-Fire. "Go in with the boys and, if nothing else, have a few drinks. Maybe next time, by God." Hell-Fire nodded his great head and snorted as if to say, "*Rubbish.*"

Yet even Luke surmised he'd never intrude on their opportunity to proclaim grievances about their boss in the saltiest of terms.

****

Beth, sitting before her dresser vanity, gave a final brush to her long wheat-colored hair and plaited a thick braid. Matthew, buttoning his nightshirt, rounded on his wife. "Beth, what in tarnation was that all about?"

Beth watched him in the mirror. "Look. Obviously, my father needs help finding female companionship. To turn down a wealthy, nice-looking widow like Alcie shows he—he just needs a little push."

"And you want to be stirring every pot."

Brandishing the brush, Beth rounded on him. "Don't want to hear another word. My father is going through a *very* hard time right now. You can tell. *Something* is eating at him. Partly age, I suppose." She said it with complaisance while finger-scooping from a tin of Pompeian Night Crème and smearing the fluffy shine onto her cheeks.

Matthew squinted at her in the mirror. He set his jaw and had a look in his eye Beth had never seen before. Manly. Determined. "Seemed fine to me, till you women started peckin' him to death. And Beth, *we* need a getaway. Let's forget about your pa for one dad-blamed minute and think about *us*! We ain't been nowhere special since our danged honeymoon, and that was just a dang weekend in Red Butte to buy those heifers!"

Beth threw the brush. It bounced off the wall behind Matthew. "I am not going *anywhere*. I told you—Pa is vulnerable right now. I can't just *abandon* him."

"But me, you can," Matthew muttered. He looked at his wife, reflected in the mirror, with a bleak defeated expression. "I'm going to sit up for a while."

Beth didn't seem to notice when he left.

****

Despite its dreamlike beauty, the moon, shining huge as a wheel of cheese in the black plate of sky, made the prairie with the far mountains etched in silver as remote as Luke felt.

Five more miles back to the ranch.

Wisht he was tucked in bed with a tot of rye.

Wisht he was back with the widow.

Spirited Martha!

The thought brought a stirring in his loins that his saddle did not assuage. Memories and temptations denied far too long crowded unbidden.

Too long since he'd enjoyed the special sweetness of a woman.

He liked Martha. Enjoyed her spirited clever company last spring when all was rampant and blossoming. However, then the cattle drive, then harvest, and then *winter* made travel treacherous, and then? How had it gotten so long since he'd had company outside of the wranglers and his family? Wasn't just physical, either. But that too, for Luke was a hot-blooded man, truth be told. Luke yearned for a woman's touch, her voice, like a drink of spring water on a scorching day.

Memories blossomed like a newly opened rose. The way Martha undressed unashamedly. His dear Katie, till the Lord took her, still disrobed behind a Japan screen; he never once saw her naked except by accident, and it haunted him for days...not the secrecy but his ardor for her.

Martha was eager to gallop, canter, pace, or enjoy a slow gentle ride, consuming a nighttime of playful action ofttimes whenever his mood or hers coincided. And the way she teasingly unhooked her corset and drew down her shimmy revealing one bosom at a time, the way she grabbed him by the john henry, she could have led him anywhere.

Growing warmer by the second, and feeling his denims tighten uncomfortably, Luke grinned at his overheated notions.

The thing was, he kenned Elizabeth got lonely and even spooked, out on the ranch, alone with the hands, though they wouldn't touch a hair on her head or he'd thrash them to next Sunday and hold their heads in the horse trough. Yet it somehow never seemed the right time to go *courting* Martha, in bed or out. Besides, Liz didn't cotton to her, or for truth, Martha to Liz.

He flushed, feeling his face heat in the chill breeze. Half a mind to go there now. He was near the fork, with cold wind whispering in his ear. Lizzie was safe at Beth's. Another hour…be midnight.

"Hell-Fire, am I a doddering old fool?"

His horse whickered a wicked comment he could not translate. Luke laughed, gusting out a plume of smoke, flicked the reins and dug his spurs toward town.

He'd show Martha he was still fit enough even though his thatch was more silver than black nowadays. Luke figured women loved surprises, indicated by their romance novels. Luke would rather set fire to his own hair than admit he once delved into one of Beth's after warning her not to read such rubbish.

What was the name of that book? Oh, yeah, *Jane Eyre.* He rather admired the male character. A tough old varmint. Laughing out loud again, Luke tugged Hell-Fire toward Laramie, urging the horse to a wild gallop they both relished.

Chapter Three: Martha

Luke tromped up on Martha's porch steps in partial warning and brashly tapped the brass lion's head knocker. Must be nigh on to eleven o'clock by his big watch.

"I'm coming. I'm coming. Hold your horses!"

Martha's brown eyes peered beyond the curtain. The door soon whammed open. "Lucian! Evermore! What in God's name are you doing here this time of night?"

Not exactly a welcome. 'Sides, her voice had not her usual flirtatious lilt.

After checking both ways, Martha clutched her wrapper tighter, then, stepping outside, blocked his way, Luke noted, briefly irritated. Unexpectedly strong, too. He looked quizzically at her slender hand pressing his chest. Might as well be an iron bar.

"Well, Martha? May I come in?" He touched his hat. "I ken it is beyond any polite lady's hour for entertaining." He tried on a roguish smile, which for some reason fell flat as a hoecake.

"Luke? Is everything all right? I was asleep. You'll wake Carrie…" came the torrent of words spilling from his former beloved's mouth. Her face, in the light from the half-sized kerosene night-lamp—the tiny globe printed with roses he well recalled sitting on her bedside table, guttered rosier than he recalled on her cheek…but Luke felt he was already sinking into her warm soft feather bed, feeling her silky body comforting him and he, hers…as before.

"Well, better come on in out of the cold."

He detected a sigh. Luke stepped into the parlor. Gazing at Martha lovingly, he lowered his voice. "Don't know what got over me," he chuckled, bashful, grinning from beneath the hat brim. "All a sudden, my horse just turned up here like it knew better than this old cuss." He smiled down at her and cupped her cheek.

She set the tiny lamp hastily on a side table. Luke, removing his Stetson, tried to take her in his arms. He held off twiddling his hat. "Maybe we should have supper some night, Martha…take the buggy and ride into Cheyenne." 'Bout time he made his intentions known. No more sneaking…

"Luke!" She half-laughed, pushing him again. "Why *are* you here?" Suddenly his will and another part of his anatomy wilted.

"Why, Martha, I just had to see you," he added lamely.

"Oh, really!" With a bemused smile, she folded arms over her ample bosom. "After all this time? I can well imagine."

"No, not that way. Yes, that way too, dammit, but Martha, I've made, well, a terrible mistake." Why had he not told her he loved her? Not like Katie. Why had he not seen it till now? "I let work and responsibilities get in the way of our…"

She laughed in the full-throated way he aways prized. "Our *what*?" A twinkle, not all lantern glow, formed in her eyes. "Lucian, *dear*." She placed a cool palm on his jaw. "We had many a lovely tumble."

On her comfy featherbed, Martha was a racy

strumpet who talked like a miner. Nevertheless, she was always proper out of it, no matter how rambunctious. Luke was vaguely shocked at her admission but warmed to the idea. "Is Carrie asleep? *Are* you lonesome?" Carrie was her young daughter she was left with when Hank passed on.

Martha plopped on a velvet settee, when it appeared Luke was about to embrace her again, and gazed up at him earnestly. "You helped me when I needed it most, Lucian dear. When I thought my life—*that* part of my life—was forever over, and I missed it. I missed a man's body. Your strong arms," she continued wistfully, shaking her head. "A good man in my life and for my daughter, so she wouldn't get spoiled by her mama."

"Well, I...*Damn* it! Come here, then."

"No, Luke dearest. You see..."

No, he didn't gosh-darn see. She looked down shyly, grinning like a lovelorn schoolgirl. "You see... we—Joe and me..."

"Joe?" Luke felt a frown form between his eyes, his brows pinched.

"That's right. Joe, the sheriff. Joe Garner. We are getting married. Banns read last Sunday-go-meeting."

He didn't hear. She was Lutheran.

Luke stepped back a bit, not liking the feeling he'd been punched in the midriff but managing a pleased smile. Barely. "Well, well, that's—that's *swell,* Martha. Joe's a fine, *fine*, upright man, and a bit older than..."

"Oh, Luke, he's younger than you." She grinned reproving.

"Might be, at that. You find him..." He made a vague gesture.

"I find him strong and reliable and kind. Carrie is

my main rival in his affections. He adores her."

"Banns already read, hunh? Well, well. I'm right happy for you, Martha. Joe's a solid character. Couldn't be better for you. When is the—the blessed day?"

"Three weeks, Sunday, Luke. You are invited."

"You bet. You bet. I will be there with bells on."

Like hell I will.

"Congratulations, Martha. Joe is a fine, fine man and a very lucky one. I hope you two will both be very happy and…" He plucked his hat from the side table before he could make more of a fool of himself. "I'm right happy for you." How many times had he said that?

She nodded sweetly and was closing the door on him. "See you soon, then, Luke. And Luke?"

He looked down at her pretty upturned face.

"It was all good." She stood on tiptoes and kissed his cheek.

What am I, her grandfather? He kissed her fingers, saluted her with his hat and, walking backward off the step, clapped it back on. "See you, Martha. Best of luck. It's a fine, fine match."

****

It was a long ride back to The L Devereux Ranch.

He and Martha had a thing in bed. Out of it, Martha, bless her, was a good woman. But not for him. Somehow, even if she owned Katie's sweet disposition, there was always a patronizing air, if Luke could put feelings into words.

More troublesome, he could not see Liz tolerating another female as strong-willed as Martha. His sister would be polite enough, but with a frosty edge that would chill any new life partner for him. She had adored Katherine.

He patted Hell-Fire's mane. "We'll grow old side by side, old friend. Two old bachelors. Or 'bachelorette' in Liz's case." He chuckled. "The gingham dog and the calico cat…" The old nursery rhyme floated though his memory. "Side by side on the table sat…"

****

The spirted clip-clop of a stallion eager for his stall, a good rubdown, and a bucket of oats entered Mae's dream as she awakened to Betsy's whinny of welcome, a *huff*ing and a gentle, "Whoa, boy." She detected the creak of stirrups, followed by the brisk scratching of a curry brush, the sounds of affixing the oat bag, and a final, "Goodnight, you old son-of-a-gun. Have to find you a filly pretty soon." Hell-Fire whickered assent.

Mae giggled quietly. *He talked to Hell-Fire,* filing the fact away like violets in a scrapbook.

It gave Mae, perched in the hay loft just out of the way of the window, pleasure she could not define—of pride, anticipation, a feeling of safety and wonder—to watch Luke, unaware as he went about his business of the day—or across the corrals wrangling a horse, or ordering the hands about with such command and authority.

The striding way he walked like a powerful animal, graceful and attentive. The way his wranglers were instantly alert and did his bidding without question.

She had never crossed path with a man like that. Certainly not within her family of weak ne'er-do-wells and grifters, her shifty uncles and sly, untrustworthy pa. You had to count your fingers if you shook hands with *him*.

She felt giddy when she saw how Luke's broad shoulders strained the bleached blue fabric of his shirt.

How muscles, hard as iron, still flexed and rippled beneath. Feeling her fingers tingle as if they longed to touch him. Or the stern way he eyed his ranch hands when doling chores of the day under the dark shadow of his hat. The deep cleft, flashing on one side of his jaw when he laughed or quirked his mouth when commanding a horse. Someone who would always be there, like the mountains, like the water, the very air she breathed...

Mae shrank, folding arms about her knees as Luke walked away and the sound of his boot heels faded. Mae ran to the loading window to watch her boss's square-shouldered, rangy figure stride to the ranch house. The moon gleamed on twin revolvers riding lean hips and lit his hair like strands of silver.

Then the night enveloped Luke, the kitchen door ratcheted open and closed, a lantern came alive, steadied, and dimmed.

Mae observed his shadow against the curtains.

Then, that too faded.

Chapter Four: Hell-Fire and Mae

Next dawn, Luke drained the last of Liz's black tar and stepped out into morning chill. He checked the buttermilk sky. Winter just around fall's corner. But not yet. In Wyoming, snow one day, 89 degrees and sun like a sunny-side-up fried egg the next. By noon, lacy frost in nameless streams running through his spread would be a gurgling memory, with heat scorching the flannel on his back.

Settling the black Stetson, he inhaled the crisp air deeply, comfortable in old boots and denims covering long loose-limbed legs and his warm faded red flannel shirt and fleece-lined vest, striding toward the corrals where some commotion was going on.

Luke roared a warning.

Curly was boosting Mae onto a saddle—only the saddle wasn't on Betsy but the stallion from Hell. *His* damned horse…and even *he* couldn't always judge…

Luke dashed his mug, breaking it on the stone stoop, and raced, waving his hat, calling out the hand. In place of his action halting what was happening, Hell-Fire's rolling wicked eye caught the waving Stetson, and the stallion reared. Mae hung on, grasping the mane for all she was worth, but still sliding down Hell Fire's rump, slick as melted butter.

Contrary, Hell-Fire bucked rear legs and Mae's slight body near sailed over the rusty mane to be dashed to the ground, if she hadn't clutched it in a death grip and wrapped her thighs tight. Her eyes were big with fear—and, he detected distractedly—*delight*. Hell-Fire once more kicked front hooves out, near taking Curly's head off—and tossing Mae like a rag doll back in the saddle with a resounding *whump*, then sailed over the fence in one graceful, powerful leap, thudding wildly off in a harebrained pattern, and within a flash in the pan, Hell-Fire was a careening dot with Mae's tiny figure hunched on top, bouncing and clutching his mane for all she was worth. Luke dashed for the nearest mount—slow-plodding Betsy, as it turned out. He growled, glaring at Curly, "Consarn it!"

"She ast me to!" Curly quailed under the onslaught of Luke's scowl.

No time. Rein-lashing startled Betsy, Luke tore after Mae.

He prodded poor old Betsy hard. Mae in the far distance barely hung on even though Hell-Fire gave her a fine gallop. Luke caught up after a few bone-rattling miles in time to see Mae thrown over the half-wild horse's head and landing hard, splayed, tumbling beneath Hell-Fire, where she narrowly missed being trampled by tons of horseflesh as Hell-Fire, kenning a despised green rider on his back, stamped and reared high. Iron-hard hooves with razor-sharp edges thudded inches from Mae's face, after which the mount from Hades thundered off, hell-bent for freedom.

With a fierce tug of reins, Luke leapt off Betsy before she skidded to a stop, and ran to what seemed a crumpled heap of rags sprawled across prickle grass and rocks. Mae's chest was still as a grave. A bloody gash marred her forehead near the hairline. Pale as a sleeping angel, she appeared dead.

Luke studied her quiet form, dreading to move or touch her for fear of what he'd find—an inert body cooling as he touched, yet he felt urged to do it, to crush her slight form to his chest, enfold her, keep her safe. Kiss her hair.

"Mae…*Mae!" Dammit. Wake up! You fool girl!*

He patted her hand—her face. Angry and scared, and angry with himself for being so. She sucked deep in a long shuddering pain-filled sigh.

"Don't move," he growled. Gingerly running his hand down her back, Luke checked her slight bones. He probed her foot. Her neck. He once had a wrangler frozen in place from a broke neck in a fall too similar. The man wasted away with withered limbs till he passed on two years later, a shrunken wreck. "You feel this?" He barked at her without meaning to.

She nodded as if waking from a dream. "Wanted to learn…ride proper…for when we all go out cattle drivin'," she slurred. "Wanted…t' help…be with…"

"Damnation! Why'd ya let Curly put you on that devil?"

He felt a rib. Mae sucked in, wincing. "Just wanted—" She gasped. "…surprise you."

"Dammit, girl! I'll teach you to ride! Let's see the damage."

Too gruff, Luke turned her over and pulled up her shirt, gently probing her ribcage with strong, knowledgeable fingers. Already her left side turned the shade of a beet. Forehead and hip and upper arms bore ugly scrapes where Hell-Fire had dragged her across the rocky scree with her foot caught in the stirrups. Her skin and clothes were stuck with cockle burrs like cloves in a ham. One by one Luke plucked them out.

He couldn't help but notice, he told himself, when her body was relieved of layers of cloth, her figure was anything but childish. Under all that, her waist was a handspan, his handspan, elegantly swelling into trim but womanly hips. With a rush of feeling, he noted dimples above her buttocks close to the spine. Hastily Luke lowered and neatened her clothes. No wonder Liz wanted to keep her covered.

Breathing too hard, Luke eased her up.

Mae remained stoic and chastened, even though her face was knitted in pain.

"You'll need alcohol on those. Sting like a bear," he threatened. A black eye, too, Luke surmised. Lord alone kenned what the rest of her resembled, inside and out. Yet the land was thick with scrub; that helped some, he figured. When she took a step, the wince was visible, along with the bit lip and a hitch.

Scooping her up, he cradled her under his chin. She had the weight of a lofting feather, her tiny body nestled against his huge burly chest like a sprite to a bear. He draped her gently across Betsy's saddle, then stirruped his boot and swung a leg over before settling Mae, moaning while striving not to, behind the pommel with her back to his chest.

Let Hell-Fire wander home on his own, or go to the devil.

Shortly after arriving back at the ranch, Luke strode out with a bottle of Doctor Hartshorn's Number 8 Liniment. His hands already anticipated silky warm skin and smoothing down that ethereal slope of waist to hip, the small cup of her back…when he looked down at his hands. He looked off. Suddenly Luke strode back, wordlessly thrusting the bottle to Liz, jerked his head to the stable.

"Gal needs attention."

Liz raised a brow but nodded, grabbed up a cloth and headed out.

Mae relaxed all day, restless, and on the second morning was pitching hay, joshing with the hands, and striving not to limp in his presence. Curly was sent to muck out the privy.

Hell-Fire ambled back of his own accord but did not appear chastened.

****

Mae was at the far end of the stable attaching a feed bucket to the roan mare ready to foal. Luke fumbled a length of rope and straightened a bridle on the wall.

Mae glanced at him shyly. She dropped a bucket of oats and swiped her forehead. "Mr. Luke? I'm thankin' you for yesterday."

Luke nodded and nudged the bridle where it hung, an inch to the left and fiddled with a halter. Be damned if he could think of a thing to say. She waited.

"It's been brought to my attention…" he began, stiff as cold leather—actually Liz had argued, "The gal hasn't been to church on Sundays!" And in her contrary way, snorted and s'posed again that the girl hadn't ever set foot inside a church, and that the whole building would cave in if any Saurbachs sat in one of the new pews.

"That you haven't been off the place," Luke ended lamely, shuffling one boot in the straw. "Reckon it isn't proper for you to head in with the hands when they go a-roistering."

"No, sir. I'm right happy, Mr. Farnsworth. I mean Luke." She cast her gaze down. "I play with the kittens and I'm sewing me a dress. Miss Liz gave it to me." Hands behind her, twisting her upper body back and forth, Mae seemed pleased as a June bug.

Luke looked on bemused. "Oh, ah, well. I look forward to the grand entrance." Maybe Liz had done the right thing. "Bet it'll be the prettiest dress in all Laramie."

That iced the cake a bit thick.

"Hope so, Mr. Luke."

"Oh. Sure as shootin'," he lied.

"Never had me a dress." Mae wiggled with pleasure. "Guess I'd best be gettin' on with it then." She twisted her hands together and blushed like a wild rose.

Luke swallowed hard. "Maybe you can wear it into, um, a church meeting, or pot luck, or there's a big harvest do coming up soon… Most everybody above earth around here kicks up their heels." The harvest hoedown *was* the social event of the season, attracting bigwigs from both Laramie and Red Butte, all and sundry to the furthest out and the poorest clodhoppers.

Luke hid his hands in his back pockets. For some reason they trembled. He was aware his speech tumbled out like rocks down a waterfall, or maybe like a runaway freight train on broken tracks. He felt sweat down his back.

"Is that something you might like?"

He bent to pick up a nail so she couldn't see his face.

Mae looked suddenly grave. "I—I reckon I would be liking that mighty fine, Mr. Luke. But I ain't…never learned to dance none."

Luke looked down at her small graceful figure, feeling his rough hands about her waist and her pressed to him, circling her around a dance floor. "I can take care of that. Could dance up a storm, in my day, long as I don't step on toes," he demurred. "We—we'll have to, ah, do that then."

Her face lightened. A ray of sun hit Mae's head. Sparkles of dust circled like a halo, her shirt open to the third button, with one hanging off, revealed the gentle slope of her long pale column of neck and gentle round of a paper-white bosom.

Luke, framed in the stable doorway, looked away. Couldn't think of anything else to say. He was breathing hard. What the Sam Hill was wrong with him! He walked off, unsettled, then turned back, striding purposefully now.

Pitching a forkful of dirty straw into a barrow, Mae looked up anxiously at his stony expression. Shading her eyes, she stepped out of the light. "Yes, Mr. Luke? Somethin' wrong?"

"I was wondering too…" Luke looked up to the lofty rafters for help and back at Mae. "Maybe time we went riding. I mentioned I could maybe teach you. Proper-like."

"Yes, sir?"

"Been a long time since I inspected my spread. Fences and such," he ended, for want of a reason. "Good time to acquaint yourself with the workings of a big ranch like this, good time to learn, if you're, ah, going to stay on."

Lord, lame as a hobbled horse.

Her questioning eyes were on him. A stray beam through the rafter lit her face. She really was fetching, so young, he mused. Even more. Pretty inside. Her lips, the same color as the polished coral pin Liz prized, satiny moist as she ran her tongue along them. Cheeks smooth as fresh cream. Large eyes of undefinable color, like rain water on window glass, irises ringed in black, as were her eyes, with thick inky featherings of lashes fanning cheeks, as blushed as tea roses and filled out some since she had proper vittles, he noted.

Luke realized the face looking back had bloomed from a grubby child-like female to a youngish...*woman*? No. Not quite. Somewhere in between.

Lost in Mae's face, still upturned with a look of consternation and wonder, Luke didn't hear her response, if she made one. He suddenly, with unquenchable yearning, wanted to kiss that soft mouth. Feel the silky cool smoothness against his own. Tickle her with his mustache. Hold her slim waist tightly against him. Feel her small bosoms pressing his chest.

He suddenly felt sick of himself.

Luke's ardor faded like ashes in the wind. Lord, no better than those randy roustabouts, or that old reprobate Nate Solomon. He should be horse-whipped in front of the whole Baptist congregation. Mae still studied him disconcertedly, head cocked, her hair grown out some like a black waterfall, hanging sideways past her shoulders.

She broke the spell as she looked down, scruffing a toe and twisting one hand in the other, saying softly. "Iffen you think so, I'd purely be happy to go on a ride and learn quick as I can."

"Settled then." Luke backed awkwardly. She called when he was at the wide doors. "When, Mr. Luke?"

Damnation, he had a mare to foal any day now. Couldn't leave it all to Joe or Old Tom. His voice suddenly stern and boss-like, growled, "Soon. I'll have Liz fetch us some grub. We'll make a day of it. Be ready."

As he stalked off, he heard her address the scruffy one-eared mouser. "That's my *boss,* cat! That's Mr. Luke! He runs this whole great big ranch all by hisself! He owns everything, from here to Kingdom Come!"

More than that. More than a boss.

He smiled gloomily, shaking his head. Swacked his old work Stetson against his thigh. Straightened it reasonably well and clapped it back on. Wasn't conscious he wore his best workaday shirt of gray cambric, the one Liz said matched his eyes. Wasn't aware his long legs moved easily in well-worn jeans the shade of a winter sky, fit tight across his butt, or that his shirt was strapping tight across work-broadened shoulders, or wondered if Mae watched as he strode off. Wasn't in his nature. But she was.

Mae sat with her nimble knees below her chin, hands clasped, gazing out of her barn loft window, watching him go. The setting sun cast a bronze glow to her usually pale face making her eyes the shade of gold, They stood out startling and clear. She felt warm, an unusual situation for her—to feel safe. Welcomed. Noticed.

"Luke," she whispered.

She hugged herself.

Below, the roustabouts argued, joshing, ribbing. She didn't envy their companionship. Didn't know men that well. Only brothers and odd uncles, and her pa of course, but they were "cut from a different cloth" she overheard Liz say once about one of them.

These young wranglers were healthy in a raw sunburnt way, some even good-looking, with lean, whip-thin bodies, work-broadened shoulders and narrow hips, thighs bulging with muscle from all the riding, obvious in the bow-legged way they swaggered in their boots, and then her eye rested on the one odd figure, not odd in a bad way, but different.

Luke. Her boss.

She watched his figure as he strode to the house, long taut muscles, flexing, unflexing, neck thickened with cords and muscle, thick hair glinting silver like moonlight. His outline, bulkier, more solid, work-hardened hands swinging easily at his sides, recalling the deep squint lines between his nose and mouth. In place of age, he seemed carved from granite, bronzed and broken-nosed, a jaw made of iron.

Mae grinned, fiddling with her toes. He looked as if he could rope a bull, or kill snakes and things that lurked under a bed. Luke's was the form that favorably filled her thoughts, pleasured her mind, and lifted her wide smile, without her kenning. She would never dream of it, as not fitting.

****

Before heading in for his usual evening with Liz, Luke leaned on a split rail corral fence, gazing out over his spread, clear to the far setting sun, making the whole shebang look like from another planet. That red one called Mars, past heaven's gates. Prairie grass and shrubs, the juniper trees rimmed in sulphureous fire, cast black shadows all pointing toward him. Twenty acres or so of scrub was all he inherited from his mule-skinner pa, plus half a lean-to, the one he and his sister were raised in by a feckless dad, and a ma long gone to her reward.

The lean-to was still extant, humbled beneath showy, expensive yet gracious add-ons of stone and timber and slate roofs. All the rest he'd done himself, beginning with the starter-dough of his lucky gamble— going in on the copper mine.

Luke grunted, quelling a joyful laugh as not seemly. Nevertheless, he now owned a spread of over forty *thousand* acres, all his, and a house grand as anything he saw in that one trip back east to far-off Chicago, on a street called Lakeshore Drive, with proper windows, gables and dormers, rich rugs, polished floors. Good glass panes, and one of stained glass sporting a proud stallion, the Farnsworth name, and his branding symbol. He would defend all of it to his last breath.

A pity and a shame he had none to pass it on to except his son-in-law—who was, truth be told, not the savviest rancher this side of Cheyenne, or their boy, who might not take to ranching at all.

Mae's face floated across his mind for some vexatious reason. Luke shook his leonine head as if to swat a gnat and stomped up on the porch as the sun painted his back scarlet.

Chapter Five: The Dress

Mae fumbled with the needle, her pink tongue stuck out the side of her mouth in fierce concentration as she stabbed at muddy brown cloth. Wisht she had a big old mirror. She peered in the horse trough when she brushed her hair, but maybe she could buy a little one with her first pay, next time Nate drove by. Mae's face lit up, imagining. Never earned cash money before or bought anything in her whole entire life.

She mentally inventoried his stock, small items set out in lidded bins along his wagon sides or stuffed in trunks, and the dull aprons and house dresses or men's denim jackets and long johns hauled out of boxes and hung from a rail whenever he halted. Mayhap ribbons and stick candy, lemon drops, or horehound.

She shook her head. "That's for little 'uns. Best get me some lavender toilet water."

More grown up.

Working at night by lantern light, the dress took most of the month whilst Mr. Luke was off with his cattle run to Cheyenne depot and other business in Laramie. She'd overheard one of the roustabouts jaw over the trip.

Mae spread the material over her lap. Miz Liz was nice to give her a whole dress to make over. Didn't cotton much for the color, and the thread Liz gave her was bright yellow, but it was the first honest-to-gosh grownup rig she ever owned. Didn't think to ask Liz to help, nor did Miss Elizabeth offer.

Mae ripped it out several times when she couldn't get the waist to fit right, and hemmed it up some. Now, at last, she stood with the sweep of a lopsided skirt pooling at her toes.

A bit long, but with shoes? Wisht she had proper shoes. The waist was nice and snug, though the top ballooned over her small breasts some, but that was okay; she looked like a lady.

Newly hemmed gown on, Mae twirled in the lamplight.

"*Oohh!*" She cried in fright when she nearly knocked over the lantern. Nevertheless, the skirts whipped about pleasurably, and she succeeded in *not* burning down the stable.

Mae laughed aloud. She considered her image bit by bit in the small piece of cracked mirror scavenged yesterday in the ranch's dump, in a little gully beyond the stable. She cocked her head. Maybe a little old bit of lace, if she had some, or embroider flowers or somethin' to take away the mud brown.

She eyed the yellow thread. Sure would like to learn fancy stitching like she saw Miss Elizabeth do. Maybe around the neck and wrist bands…

****

The month was hectic for Luke.

He and the hands had bushwacked three suspected cattle rustlers and hustled them into Laramie's newly elected sheriff's office—the same Jimson boys caught harrying off a pregnant heifer and three yearlings last year. Plus he'd stalked his spread with the part-Arapaho water diviner for a new well closer to northern pastures. Then met again with the sheriff to talk him out of jailing his best hand, Roscoe, over a saloon fight that hadn't killed anyone or done much damage outside of a dented spittoon that somehow found itself wedged on Roscoe's opponent's head. That was, of course, *after* the Cheyenne run. And then haggling over some new rich bottom land…

Luke was content and eager for home.

****

Liz looked up, startled, as a hail of fall leaves swirled into the kitchen.

"Well, speak of the devil. Didn't 'spect you till next week."

Luke shucked off his sheepskin jacket, unwound the bandana from his lower face, and dragged off thick cowhide gloves. His nose and cheeks glowed redder than the firebox.

Liz hustled over, relieving him of the heavy outdoor clothing. "Get yourself warm. I'll heat up some coffee."

Luke winked. "Hit's the spot. I'm colder than a witch's—" He trailed off at Liz's expression. "Sale went better than I s'posed, and the old so-and-so was more eager to get rid of that bottom land and hightail it to California than even *he* knew."

"You always could hornswoggle harder than Nate." She smiled, approving, and plunked down the scalding coffee.

"I only mentioned the gold rush a few times." He winked, taking a searching sip. Luke eyed the table set for one while Liz was busy rectifying that. He looked around the empty kitchen. "Where's Mae? Should be fetching her dinner. Thought by now she'd be eating with us, supper time." He frowned at Liz. "Don't know why in tarnation she can't eat in here."

Liz looked vexed at her brother. Her face said—*just get back and already fussing.* In her other house dress, grim gray this one, Liz knuckled both hips. "Then *all* the hands would raise a ruckus 'cause we showed partiality. 'Sides, Mae's still—" she rolled her eyes, as if *she* had to sew it, "makin' her a dress anyways. Been at it near a year!"

"Ay, heard that." He thought of how cold it must be up in an uninsulated stable. Reading his mind, Liz grunted. "I give her extra blankets and keep the stable doors shut. Livestock warm it up some and it's right cozy."

Luke cast a glance at her obstinate face and poured more day-old coffee from the pot from the back stove plate, then flinched at bitterness near matching his thoughts. He made quick work of thick ham sandwiches with thunder-and-lightning pickles, a slab of raisin pie and homebrewed beer fetched by Liz from the spring house. He wouldn't start a dust-up now, saying through a mouthful, "Great grub as usual, Liz."

Liz, perched with her own beer, smiled archly, saying cryptically, "The devil's hands."

Luke raised a questioning brow.

"Told you. I gave her an old dress of mine to rip up, do whatever she can with it."

"That was mighty *Christian*." The way Luke looked at his sister should have told her he meant no such thing, but she took it to heart.

"Of course, we must help the less fortunate and do our duty. Not that I could not have used…"

Her brother slammed down the empty glass and stalked up the stairs before she could finish.

Liz, a crease between her brows, looked after him

thoughtfully, murmuring, "That Mae. Always causing trouble."

Two nights later, before supper, Mae, with eyes glowing, stood diffidently in the kitchen doorway waiting to be noticed, wearing a bedraggled brown dress, the shade of dried mud embellished with knotty masses of crude bright yellow cross-stitches surrounding the neck and wrists, trailing the floor on one side, hiked on the other.

Luke and Liz looked on speechless until Luke muttered from the side of his mouth, *"You had to give her your old ragbag dress?"* He sourly eyed the brown linsey-woolsey gown he recollected Liz wore when she was in one of her tears—cleaning like a madwoman, scouring nail holes. It now drooped across Mae's small bosom, one sleeve loose, the other shorter by a mile, the waist nipped in tight with extra pleats bunched at one side.

Only Liz saw the tightening of his jaw and lightning flashes of his eyes. However, Mae's own eyes shone as she pirouetted, until Liz stiffened, slamming down a fork. "Great land of living, girl! What *have* you *done* with my good *dress?*"

Mae tripped on the longer drape, falling to her knees, then rose with flaming cheeks and stood frozen as a statue, looking anxiously from Luke to Liz.

"Did you give it to the gal, or not?" Luke's tone would make a stone angel quiver.

Mae looked confused, then down at herself, bursting into tears like the skies had opened a gully washer. Dropping to the floor again in a muddy puddle of skirts, she howled, "Ain't never sewed me a dress before! Didn't know how. Just kept lookin' at yours, Miss Liz.

Sorry I messed it up."

"You didn't, Mae," Luke said dangerously soft. "It was, *already*."

He shot a look at Liz that would split a rock.

Mae stood defiantly, hiccupping, and swiped her face fiercely dry. "I'll do it over!"

"*Hmmmmph!*" Liz scowled, not giving in. "Don't know why I gave it to you in the *first* place! Ruined now."

"Said I'll give it back."

"No, you won't," Luke growled. "Liz will give you proper material, or better yet, maybe *buy* you a dress. You work hard enough." He shot a look at Liz.

But before he could finish, Mae savagely tore at the sleeves, ripping one off with little effort, then dragged at the bosom. Before either of the pair watching her could ken her intention, Mae stripped to grim undies by any other name, with the brown skirt half falling from slender rounded hips in a puddle resembling dried mud around her bare feet.

"Mae!" Liz. Outraged. "Put some clothes on! Cover yourself!"

"Here, here now, it's all right." Luke's chair crashed to the floor. He yanked a shawl from the hook. *Did he touch the girl or not?*

Before he could reach her, Mae kicked the dress aside, and there was nothing between her feet and a flimsy shift just skimming the rounded swell of her little bottom. Luke suspected that was *all*.

Lord! How to persuade her *not* to remove anything else?

"No, it isn't all right! This little hoyden should *know* better. No tellin' how *sinful* she acts around the hands!"

Before Luke could do more, Liz grasped the tablecloth, heedless of empty plates and cruets sliding off, and strode over and wrapped it roughly around Mae.

"You'd best march straight back, you little tramp, and put something decent on."

"Liz!" Luke still held the shawl.

"Stay out of this, Luke!"

****

Mae ran out in nothing but her rags, leaving the tablecloth caught in the door. Luke rounded on Liz. "What in tarnation! Brown doesn't even do her *justice*. And I never saw her be anything *but*…maybe not *maidenly,* but *modest* around the hands, no matter how much they pester that poor little mite."

Hands knotted in fists; Liz hunched like a banty hen ready to do battle. "Oh! Oh! So now you ken a female's proper color! What kinda cloth would suit her best, do we think? Justice? *Justice!* I ask you. Well! Since when does a cheap little scheming barn tramp need justice?" Luke felt his hand itch to slap her.

She plopped on a chair, shaking her head in disbelief. "Out of the goodness of my…"

Luke stopped her with a look that would blast a tunnel.

"Liz, if your heart had any goodness, you couldn't pick it up with an eye dropper. Why not *teach* her to sew?" Luke roared. "Get some proper dress material! *Buy* her a damned dress! What's she ever done to you?"

Outside of being young and pretty.

Liz looked poleaxed. Piteously, she wiped her eyes where tears freely sprang. "Never saw in all my born days," she wailed, "you would take a runaway tramp's side over mine. Your own sister, who's done nothing but

88

clean and sew and cook—"

"Mae's not a tramp…" Cutting her off, Luke saw Elizabeth could go on like a tightly wound clock. Even now still muttering, she spread a fresh tablecloth and set crockery out for breakfast. "And I know, Liz You are a saint," he added. "I'm tired. I'm to bed. Make sure she has a plate."

He halted.

Bed did not find favor with him at the moment. "Never mind. I'll take it." Luke began savagely spearing leftover meat and potatoes from the skillet, dipping from a pot of succotash.

Fretting, Liz watched her brother. Liz looked like the ceiling had fallen in on her. She fumbled with her collar. "I suppose I could…" she grunted with a frog in her throat, "find some dress goods over in Laramie. Give me more housekeep money, then, Luke, and I'll go *buy* her some dress goods."

"Yeah, brown!" He threw a pie wedge of cornbread on the plate. "*Why not let her pick it out?*" Luke slammed the table, making crockery bounce.

Liz slapped the table on her own, making more plates jump, and a cup crashed on the floor. "Hmmmph! Leave that up to you! You seem to have a fascination for her."

Luke's head lowered like a bull ready to charge. He nailed her from under his thick black brows. "What might you be telling me, Lizzie? That you deny this poor little scrap a bit of pleasure in life? Something that would cost you nothing? Maybe a shindig at the barn, or—" He bit his tongue from saying more. No profit getting Liz more riled than she was. Also, he was a tad troubled by their quarrel.

Liz held her ground, arms crossed, chin up. Rarely did brother and sister lock horns, but when they did, the hands either made themselves scarce or lined up for the rounds. Before she could continue, they both turned toward the window at a noise or a cry…

Luke balefully scanned a ruckus through the kitchen window, changing his focus toward twin glows in the dusk, where roustabouts smoked on turned-up stumps.

The new hires, suspected runaways from the military, had dropped their cigarette butts, whooping like liver-colored hounds after a rabbit, and handily caught Mae as she stumbled to the stable as if she couldn't see properly, trailing tatters, with her little almost-bare bottom revealed with each blind gait. They tugged at her hair, and one yanked her to the far corral, ripping what was left of her coverings, attempting to kiss her, while the other urged his compadre to drag her to the stable.

A red haze like smoke from a volcano dropped over Luke's eyes.

Knocking the heavy table aside, Luke tore through the screen, forgetting he had the plate. Liz stared at more broken crockery and glared into the dark, eyes blazing so hot they could light the wood stove. She watched Luke stride to the bunkhouse as if stomping out wildfires, while gravy still dripped and spread on the kitchen floor boards that had been fresh scrubbed that afternoon.

****

Luke kenned if a bee was attracted to a flower, Mae was a whole prairie of wildflowers, but his ranch hands didn't need to act like trail bums. They tweaked her hair. He kenned they told barnyard jokes that would make a jaded doxie blush, just to see her reaction, or in passing nudge her into one another. Luke feared they stood below the loading bay just to catch a glimpse, too. Long ago Mae had learned it would be prudent to haul up the ladder when she was in the loft, and she did, when she remembered.

Luke shook his head like an enraged lion. He raced past corrals with hellfire-and-damnation in his eyes. Dang! Still, he was between the devil and the deep blue sea, responsible as any sheriff to see all was in order under his authority. He needed the wranglers, vile and pestiferous as they were. Needed roustabouts strong and loyal, not grudging.

They stood their ground until he gave them a stare that felt like looking down a double-barreled shotgun from the wrong end; his eyes, turned to flint, carved big swathes from their egos. Luke vowed they'd be gone by daybreak if they lasted that long.

More of his wranglers, even Old Tom, usually asleep by now, moseyed from the bunkhouse to see what the hullabaloo was all about, thinking maybe they could scare up more promising entertainment than a worn checkerboard, grimy cards missing the three of diamonds, or girly pictures from Sweet Caporal cigarette wrappers.

"Inside, Mae!" he roared. Clutching her remnants about her, she scampered into the darkened stable.

Before long, Luke, spying her crouched in a dark corner behind a hay bale, came and squatted beside her. "Hush now. Nothing to be 'shamed of."

"It ain't—*isn't* that, Mr. Luke. Nobody never done, *did* that for me *ever*. T-took my side."

Any time.

They stayed in the warm cave of silence surrounded by the musky sweet hay, Luke uncomfortably aware of her white pearl knobs of shoulders like smooth satiny stones where the sun didn't reach. Her long neck pulsed. She gazed up once, her face cameo pale in filtered moonlight. Mae's pale bare legs, jutting from the shimmy-like rag, were elegantly formed, from her doll-like feet to slender ankles to gently molded calves and an ivory pale thigh, with a hint of bottom swell peeking below the rags.

Mae didn't seem concerned. However, Luke was painfully aware, in the back room of his mind, that she wasn't a child.

He constrained his hand from running down that smooth bare length, feeling satiny coolness of her skin, even as a phantom touch. The knowledge was a splash of icy water. He had to stop this. "You're cold," he said throatily. "Now, where's your duds?" He asked, aware his voice was the husky rasp of a corn shucker while he rummaged her garments hanging from hooks. What he opined went together he laid at her feet and turned while Mae quickly shimmied into her things.

"Just a bunch of yahoos with no horse sense."

"Yes, sir," Mae said. Her hair hung down like curtains to hide her face.

Luke tried desperately to think of *something* to say. "No more baby tears." He chuckled to remove the barb. "You're gonna go to that barn dance. Life isn't all work and boys playin' pranks."

"I heared about it." A frown made her eyebrows a straight line of silk.

"'Bout three times a year—a harvest hoedown, and now Wyoming's a state, on the Fourth of July the church has a big potluck, and right before Christmas there's a cake auction where the fellas bid on the ladies' baking."

Mae owned a wistful, faraway smile. "That sounds mighty fine, I reckon. Do they—do they got to wear a dress?"

Luke tried to look as if he pondered it. "Yes. I do believe most young ladies of your, uh—caliber, do wear a dress to kick up their heels."

Mae looked about, worried, as if another gown might suddenly appear.

"Okay, reckon since you are hell-bent a-going..." He swallowed a rock. "We just might have to do something about that."

Mae blushed a shy pleased smile and ducked her head. "That's what I'm thinking, too, Mr. Luke. Don't ken how to dance, either."

"I wouldn't worry." They sat companionably while the moon turned the cornstalks to silvery spears.

"Guess it's past time to get some shuteye. Good night, little Mae."

She stood, gazing solemnly as if they had just made a pact, or a vow. Luke swiped a tear from her cheek with one knuckle, calloused from too many fights and riding the range, before he thought. Never felt anything so silky. He saw clearly his large workworn hand and her youthful cheek, pure, unblemished as a cameo. That rock came back to his throat. Still they stared at each other a long time.

Luke was the first to break away for fear he would drown in her earnestness.

Dammit.

The stable was chillier at night even from last month. Liz was going to get this girl proper coverings or, by God, he would brave the damn dressmaker's shop in Laramie, just opened, so he heard from—*who else—*

Nate Solomon, who professed to have already seduced the proprietor's daughter behind the counter—not the seduction but the daughter—where she reigned over frothy underthings. Again, according to Nate.

A wonder his cowhands weren't suddenly interested in female knickers, not that they weren't already, he mused, when Mae brushed fingers across his hand.

He nodded, saying gruffly, "I'll fix this." He didn't say what. He didn't quite ken, himself.

"I'm thankin' you, Mr. Luke."

Luke looked off into the dark, hearing the horse's sleepy hoof-shuffling and whiffling, keenly aware of Mae's small feet scampering away, feeling a loss, deep as a crevasse.

At last, he turned to an empty stable.

Liz's gaze followed the blob of orange lantern glow. The barn looked cozy and secretive. Liz wrapped arms about herself and rocked. Silent tears rolled down her cheeks.

Chapter Six: The Warning

The sun made Luke's eyes turn molten gold. He raked the roustabouts so hard they could almost feel the skin peel off their noses. "Never had a young lady on this spread since my daughter, Beth. Tolerate a lot from you saddle bums, but one thing I won't. There's a little gal out in the world to work—same as you. I see any o' you pestering her or hanging around the stable unless the barn's on fire, there'll be hell to pay. Any doubts on that score, find yourself on the road with a burr in your britches and *no pay*. In fact, you two!" He pointed at last night's malefactors. "Grab your saddles, hit the road. And you can leave those two army Colts behind. Now, git!" Luke kicked one's rear end for emphasis.

The two miscreants shot a bitter glance at each other. "Ain't givin' up our pistols!" one objected.

"Yeah…" the other groused. "Hell's bells! Jest havin' a li'l fun. She's jest a no-count gal…"

After a hard rock of a fist hit his jaw with a smack like hitting a side of beef with a tree limb, he never got to finish that remark. The new hire kissed dirt with a lopsided jaw and a spray of teeth. On hands and knees, he tried to gargle a bloody oath. "Fuyew! *Basherd.*" Which earned him another hard kick in the rump by the toe of Luke's pointed boot that sent him eating more Wyoming dirt and making a furrow deep enough to plant corn.

His mate leapt on Luke's back, plunging thumbs in Luke's eyes. Luke shook him off like a flea on a dog, at the same time rounding a hard elbow into his breadbasket, followed by a back-elbowed uppercut to the chin just short of taking his head off, and while the culprit was wide open, smashed a scarred fist into his jaw, sailing him across packed dirt to skid another five feet on his rump till hard up against the stone well, where he thumped his head, in the bargain. Luke kenned in his primitive brain he was overdoing it, but pent-up feeling raged against reason.

The first miscreant began to slide away, but Dusty stuck out his boot. Luke dragged him up by his scruff, relieved him of his Colt, and shoved him off, all at the same time, and then did the same for the other unfortunate, holding his bloody crown and cursing. Hefting the two revolvers, Luke growled and stuck them into his belt. "Believe these belong to the U S Army and *real* men. Skedaddle, before I use them."

At their protest, he thundered, "No horses. I'll keep those too. Walk!" Grinning evilly, Luke kenned the fracas was a little over the top, but didn't care. It *felt* good. And he hadn't felt that alive in years and was now rid of two rabblerousers in the bargain.

****

Mae watched it all. Hawking sobs smote the air like broken crockery. She could take care of herself, since knee high to a grasshopper. Still, her chest felt fit to bust. The man she saw, lean, supple as a blacksnake rolling in the dirt, was years younger than Mr. Luke.

****

Lockjawed, his iron-black hair spilling in a silvery waterfall over his eyes, Luke stalked back to the house.

Liz. Right as rain as always. What was that *hoorah* with his hands all about but pride? Yet Mae's innocent face and tinkling laugh invaded his thoughts like marauding pirates without mercy.

Apparently, she'd looked after herself in the past. Dammit. Nothing *childlike* about her. A woman in miniature, with a disturbingly indelicate or even carnal look, when those half-closed luminous eyes regarded him slanchways through lashes black and soft as sooty feathers fanning cheeks as pale as Liz's best porcelain.

Luke, in splinters of fancy, saw her in fancy duds, slender arm linked in his despite her usual stable grime, straw in her hair and smelling of horses. No. Wasn't real. Could never be. What the hell was he thinking? He had to stop this punch drunkenness, this young man's game, before sparks flared like a runaway wildfire scorching his soul, or a poison barb deep in his heart. Yet, he mused wistfully, Mae was a sweet poison, like the peyote the natives smoked, or even the laudanum Liz was fond of when fearsome headaches struck, fooling the partaker into impossible dreams.

Yet if it was sweet poison, he would gladly die for a taste, he was so sick with longing for this fool scrap of a girl.

Abruptly, Luke strode to the woodpile, chopping kindling until his veins bulged and arms felt like hot andirons, sensing Liz's gaze like a blister through the window as the sound of his ax grew frenetic, kindling flew, and the stacked pile was near toppling. Finally, she called with a hint of worry, laughing nervous-like, "Lucian! You split 'nough wood to stoke a locomotive clear to San Francisco!"

Luke halted with a sudden vision of himself. Faces

even peered from the bunkhouse. He slung the ax and headed to the house. Had to stop this madness before he terrorized the entire ranch. Damned fool!

****

But Liz wasn't done when he stepped into the kitchen.

"Lucian Devereaux Farnsworth! You are pushin' sixty! What do you mean, *brawling* like a common field hand!"

Luke winced as Liz dabbed whiskey on his forehead, and she advised, "Only what you deserve!"

"Don't shove me under the grass staring up at daisy roots yet, Liz. I'm—" What in tarnation *was* his last natal day? Didn't give a tinker's dam, even though Liz always made a great fuss-and-feathers, shooing him from her domain until the grand candle-lighting, unveiling her usual apple cake drenched in whiskey.

Be a wonder if it didn't set the house afire after this year.

"Fifty-five!" Liz crowed, "and if that's not pushing sixty, I don't ken what…"

"Still young, Lizzie. Lot of livin' crammed in those five years till sixty, by God. And what the Sam Hill has my *age* got to do with the cost of tea in China?"

She swept him with a look that would scale a fish.

"Don't blaspheme in my kitchen." Still, Liz had an inward look telling him she too was thinking strong on birthdays. She herself was galloping toward thirty-seven.

"What next, Liz? Okay. Fifty-five, fifty-six. Who gives a healthy God damn?"

She let the oath slide for more pithy comments. "That *child* can't be more'n fifteen."

Luke, wiping the sweat from his brow, stiffened. "I

am kind. I don't cotton to my hands bullying a young'un. Why the hullabaloo?" He looked mockingly at her. "You been readin' too many of those mealy-mouthed books filled with fainting couches and such?"

But that would not cut the mustard with Liz. Arms folded, she squinted with the eyes of a hawk spying a mouse rustling through grass a hundred feet below. "Get shuck of her, Lucian, before she makes a laughingstock of you and me to the whole territory. That girl is catnip to the hands and—"

Liz didn't say *you*, yet the word hovered like the smell of scorched toast.

"The day I care, Lizzie girl, you can call Old Tyrus the undertaker. And get the gal some decent clothes." Luke stalked out before Liz could get another word in.

Chapter Seven: Fels Naptha

A vexatious outbreak of some kind ailed the herd. He tracked it down to a few head, then mulled it over with Old Tom, who'd forgot more than Luke ever kenned about cattle. It kept Luke occupied for the next week as he rode the vast range and talked it over with a few more far-flung cattlemen.

Being home again was good, but something on the back of his mind needed tending to.

He slammed through to the kitchen and flung his hat to its roost, spying Mae in place of Liz. Bemused, he watched Mae intensely mouthing the letters on Liz's store-bought newfangled soap, called *Fels Naphtha* for some reason.

She looked up, not acknowledging his sudden arrival but with a look of utter offense. "But this don't— *doesn't* mean noth—anything. It don't spell out a proper word." A look of disgust made Mae's kittenish face comically ferocious.

Luke cut back a snort of laughter and divested himself from his sheepskin jacket. "'Cause it doesn't. Just a made-up name for soap."

Mae eyed the yellowish slab, unconvinced. Then broke out into a merry grin.

"Guess I'm lucky an' didn't take a big old bite out of this, then."

Luke sniffed it, grinning. "Reckon not. Miss Lizbeth

around?"

"Think she's out feeding the chickens and rabbits."

Luke poured a tin mug from the kettle on the back stove lid over the firebox, wincing at its heat, and studied Mae quizzically over the tin rim before checking in with his sister.

"Mae, can you read some and do your calculations?"

Mae abandoned the bar of soap. "Don't know about the calculations part, but I went to the fourth grade somewhat. We kept on the run. So, yes, I learnt my letters. Just can't put them all together, sometimes. I spell out the feed bags, and the bottles of horse liniment, and—"

"I reckon we can do better'n that."

"Ma had a Bible once, but Pa used it some to light the stove with, and warn't much left. Books are dear. My family had no truck with 'em."

Luke watched her, keeping his face impartial. "Think I could scrape up a McGuffey's Reader, somewhere."

"Don't like them—*those* school books. They *are* silly," she declared, scrunching up her nose.

"They are that. I'll see what Liz has for loaning out," and he wondered what sort of wrong-headed romantic ideas he might be putting forth in the way of Mae's education.

Luke shuffled his boots. He was putting it off. "Right now, I got something you might, ah—like." He hoped Biskits and Old Tom, with a little help from Nate, had done his bidding while he was gone.

They would see it together.

He beckoned her. "Come."

Luke stalked past Mae's stall to the ladder. "You

first." Mae clambered up, mystified. She poked her head up through the trap. To her left was a hay-loading bay, twin of the one facing the house, this one with an aspect of mountains draped in misty purple curtains and a lowering sun the shade of a pumpkin.

"There. A door. Lock on the inside. A bar. Drop it down if you want." *Or have to.*

Mae studied the crude door with its leather pull. Rough-cut pine formed a box carved out of a space usually allotted for bins of alfalfa, corn, rye, and wheat seed.

Mae pulled the leather strap, peering in.

Whitewashed walls. Framed print of a basket over-spilling with cabbage roses.

Luke pondered where the boys got that from. Probably Nate. Have to reimburse them. A cot and a crazy-patch quilt to brighten the mote-filled gloom, a feather pillow and heap of wooly blankets. A small chamber pot printed with kittens. *That* must be Nate's contribution, too. A chair, a mirror. Even something serving as a dresser, holding a china basin—true, cracked, but beside it a pitcher and a slab of soap, with linen towels and a sea sponge—filched from Liz, no doubt.

Luke was amused and amazed at his cohorts' obvious enthusiasm and decorating skills. He had supposed they would come up with a crude duplicate of their bunkhouse, raw but homey with an accumulation of twenty years or so of detritus. He'd buy them some good whiskey and a fresh deck of cards and maybe a shirt or two to make all this worth their while.

"Mightn't do in the harsh winter, but we'll figger something." Luke swallowed hard, his face made younger by her shining pleasure as she went about reverently touching objects. "Right," he said, gruff.

He climbed down without looking back, but as he headed toward the day's horses to be broke before the next sale, a grin broke out that near cracked his face.

"Old fool," Liz would scorn. She'd be right. God! Fifty-five, an old codger next birthdate. Make a deal with the devil. What was she? Sixteen? Seventeen? She didn't ken either. So, what difference did it make? *Damned fool.*

Yet Luke found himself crossing Mae's path when he spied her heading to the barn...the kitchen garden...the smokehouse or corrals. He'd nod as a boss to a hand. Her shy smile was payment. Sometimes he would stop, as if he'd just thought of something. "Mae?"

'Yes, sir, Mr. Luke?"

And darn fool that he was, he'd think of something. His devil smirked. Had to get his mind elsewhere.

****

Luke yanked the bridle off the wall, fetched his well-oiled saddle and nearly threw it on Hell-Fire, savagely tightening the bellyband as the horse stamped, as impatient to be out of its confines as Luke was in haste to be away from himself, or the ranch, Mae, or the whole damned lot of them.

Twenty miles into town and it felt like forty after he leaped onto the saddle and galloped off with night wind whistling past his ears. Forgot his hat or it had blown off by the time he got to Laramie, aware he was freezing his bones without even his shearling jacket, not quite sure why he'd left that too. But some obstinate urge made him go on without it. Liz would have his guts for garters if he got under the weather. That was for old duffers roasting dirty socks before the fire, hunched in a rocking chair.

The horse was in the same desperate spirit to put miles between them and the workaday ranch.

****

The saloon's orange glow proclaimed the blessed warmth of spirits and camaraderie. Luke lunged thankfully through thick buffalo hide flaps and into its boozy tobacco-ridden embrace and reek of sweat, beer, spirits, spittoons, leather, and the gals' toilet water.

Luke took stairs two at a time to find Beatrice, better known as Beatie. Whenever he got the hankering or an urge came on him like a maelstrom…there she was, inviting, warm and gap-toothed friendly as usual, with her shift, half off her shoulders, showing a freckled bosom in full bloom.

Fortunately, she was alone, he thought belatedly.

He grinned over at the corner where Beatie kept her little pet mouse in a cage—ofttimes he couldn't tell if it was the squeaking wheel the mouse was racing to the moon on or Beatie's rope bed springs; sometimes they seemed to match in rhythm—just one of her endearing quirks, although at times a tad disconcerting. Beatie even built a little dollhouse for the wretched thing.

At any rate, by the time he got up there, poking his finger through the cage for the little creature to nibble on, his desire was quenched, as if a bucket of rainwater was tossed on his head.

He plunked into the easy chair, gazing fondly at her, not kenning quite what to say. A comfortable silence reigned as he poured a tot of the unnamed firewater she kept at hand, handed it to her and poured one for himself. What in blazes was keeping him from enjoying the delicious warmth of her body and featherbed? Truly, he was growing crazy as a box of frogs.

They kenned each other well. Beatie patted the bed and, in her lazy half-mocking way, purred, "Come on, don't be shy. It's all right, darlin'. You look prickly as a cactus, dearie."

Damn, did it show?

"Always trouble on my mind till I clap eyes on you, Beatrice."

She raised a brow, settling herself comfortably on one hip and stuffing more pillows behind her head. "Lonesome tonight anyways, and really not in the mood either, darlin'."

Luke smiled. Beatie, always so accommodating no matter his disposition.

"We'll be brother and sister tonight," she teased.

Luke laughed wickedly. "That would be a first. Ah, Beatie, I been thinkin'. Brooding, truth be told." He didn't see Beatie's look of alarm or her quick glance at her little ormolu clock with the cupids, the wee innocuous timepiece keeping her customers honest.

Still, she cast a compassionate glance.

"Been feeling sinful lately, not sure what to make of it."

"But honey…" Beatrice pouted. "You," she drawled, for Beatie was from Georgia, for reasons never asked, "are only supposed to be sinful with me."

Luke grinned an ironic grin. "Beatie, I'm muddled as a box of frogs."

"Aye, that ye aire." She cocked her head, giving him a silent, *Go on…*

"Can't get this gal out from under my skin. She's burrowed straight to my heart, not bypassing other portions of this scarred, beaten and broken-down old carcass."

Beatie sighed, impatient. "Stop beggin' for sweet talk, Lucian Farnsworth, and 'beaten' you ain't. I can testify to that." She smirked a saucy leer.

He smiled, appreciative.

"Who is she?" Beatie looked alarmed but only in play. "Another—?" She indicted the saloon with a jerk of saucy red curls that Luke knew by experience were truly her own.

He shook his head. "A young, scared, feisty, skinny, half-starved, filthy little barn cat come scratched at our door. Turns out she's the delight of my miserable existence."

Beatie raised both brows at that and didn't look too happy.

"So, you *burn*." She indicated her body. "But for only one…" She cast a sad glance at a corner.

"Yes, that too, for my sins, but more than that. I see her in fine clothing, sitting beside me at the dinner table, and…" His face turned grim.

"How old is this *ideal*? This childish seducer of older men?"

Beatrice mocked adeptly, shrugging her shoulder until one rosy breast was exposed, then demurely covered herself to her neck. He didn't respond.

"Oh, Luke! Luke," she leaned earnestly forward. "You would not be the first to go all goony for a pretty young face."

"Don't belittle me. I never felt this way before. Mae's—she's so vulnerable. So needy. Even if she doesn't admit it. I could give her so much in return, if only…"

"So how does this barn cat feel about you, you old

buffalo? Or should I say 'rake-hell'?" Beatie quirked a mouth in humor.

Shyness flooded his craggy face. "She likes me a bit."

Beatrice kenned from experience Luke had what it took to satisfy a whole pasha's *hareem* of nubile virgins, if he had a will. She'd miss that. "But you have not told me how old *is* this innocent little virgin?"

Luke grinned like he ate a lemon. "Don't rightly ken. Nor does she."

Beatie airily waved her hand. "Then *give* her a birthday…"

Luke slapped his thigh, preparing to leave. "Always kenned I could count on you, Beatrice. Might do."

"You also ken where to find me, too, if *all* does not go *entirely* to your wishes."

After gazing sadly into his eyes, Beatrice turned her face to the wall.

"Until then, I don't want to see you, Lucian Farnsworth."

****

Luke could no more deny he wanted more of Mae than he could cease breathing. She was spring in the midst of a blizzard, sweetness in a harsh work world. He hadn't felt so light and, yes, joyful since his sweet Katie passed on. He wanted to spy her across the yard as he drank morning coffee. Or again like that one night from below in the dark, as he smoked a hand-rolled while leaning on a corral fence and gazing up at the hayloft window, the one facing the house. Too soon to turn around, he saw her unclothed for a split second as she slipped a nightshift over her head…as if given a rare gift. Then she stood posing before the loading window, looking out at the dark, or the moon, or listening to crickets, or, he fancied, *she kenned his presence.*

Luke swallowed, feeling some emotion he could not contain, a wild beast in a too-small cage, raging to be free.

****

"You've already tried Betsy, here. Gentle as her name. We'll take her out some on the prairie and teach you a few ropes."

Mae showed small white teeth. "Never rid a horse before. Not proper like. Hell-Fire was more how *not* to ride." She smiled, digging a toe of her moccasin into the dirt, and stared at the horse a foot above her. "Like I said, Mister. Only Daisy, our mule."

"'Bout time then. Maybe later, out with the boys herding cattle to the railway station, roundin' strays or checking fences…"

He studied her slight figure. "In time," he amended.

Like hell she'd ride with the boys…more tomfoolery than work from them, and beleaguering for her, but he'd tell Lizzie that anyway, in case she asked why Mae was on the back of a good horse, or remaining *at all,* as she kept not too silently hinting, though Mae was industrious as an ant storing up for the winter.

Lizzie could be withering at times if she thought things weren't right under heaven. And maybe they weren't.

Two things Luke heard early in life: "'Never slap a man who's chewing tobacco," and "Don't get led astray by a pretty woman." That's what his Pa of the stern biblical judgment and the gnarled hands of a tin miner told him. But Mae wasn't a woman.

Chapter Eight: Not Right under Heaven

"I tell you, Beth. It is not right!" Liz stabbed the taut linen round caught in her large embroidery hoop. "Making a right laughingstock of himself before all the hands, *and God*."

Beth stoked the parlor fire to a brighter blaze before resuming the cutting of a gaudy, rough- woven square of cloth, with rapid jerky motions, from a pattern cut from *The Laramie Daily Boomerang*. The "cloth" was so coarse it cut her fingers.

"Oh, Liz!" she scoffed. "I s'pose God has more important matters than spying on Pa. He's just feeling older. He's getting up there, you know, and maybe softening in his dotage."

Beth laughed to show she didn't mean it. Quite.

She examined the stack of coarse-woven feed sacks, crudely printed with roses, pansies, plaids, paisleys, or even red-and-white-checkered squares. Most farmers' and ranchers' wives zealously hoarded them until accruing enough matching bags to stitch a dress, or at least an apron, or children's clothes, or even a husband's shirt. Given the frugal fare on most ranches, if some husbands wore rose-printed shirts, they dared not mind.

"You sure Pa didn't offer a dollar for something from the dry goods store?" Beth held one bag close to her nose, sneezing. "These still smell of chaff and feed."

Liz, sallow cheeks turning a becoming pink, was

suddenly caught up in the underside of her embroidery. "Don't vex me now, Beth. I have to redo this whole mess of French knots. Listening to you babble on, I used the wrong floss!" She'd rather eat a mealworm than tell Beth that Luke had forked over a generous stipend, which she had slipped into the Baptist poor box on her own authority.

"'Sides, beggars can't be choosers." She sniffed.

Beth raised brows. "That from the Good Book?"

Trouble was, studying the pile of feed sacks, there weren't enough to make a dress that *matched* anyway. No beggar worth her salt was likely to choose this conglomeration of prints.

She frowned at the bags, then the paper pattern. "Might as well make a ruffle around the hem and puffed sleeves from the purple and green ones," she muttered, souring her mouth. The skirt and bodice of yellow and red roses would scream against purple-and-green-plaid ruffles. But what could she do?

The clash made her eyes water.

But then, Liz lowered her voice as if she spoke something she would not say in polite society. "He wants her to go to *church,"* she hissed. "Everybody knows the Saurbachs. We'd be talk of the town if we marched down the aisle with that little tramp." She sniffed at Beth's expression. "I overheard them. Oh, I wasn't *snooping*. I do venture in the stable, sometimes."

Beth sighed inwardly. *It was Liz who'd suggested church-going,* but she bit her lip. "I s'pose this is what it's for, then." Beth stroked the rough material with distaste; her brow cocked in disbelief. "Church meetings and such?"

"Hmmmph!" Liz gutturaled. "Just couldn't *make*

myself after she butchered the dress I gave her."

You mean that scratchy old mud-brown one?

He wants to—to—" Liz searched for words. "Dress her like a little play doll!"

"While I am dragooned into stitching this wretched thing, not you."

Liz threw down the embroidery hoop. "Luke thinks he's a young rooster. Cock of the walk! Hear him crow! *I* think that cheap baggage has eyes on him." Liz slapped the table in emphasis. "You mark my words."

"Oh, Liz! Nothing wrong with that. My father, I will have you know, is still a *very* handsome man. Healthy, and certainly well off. Why, there isn't a widow or a spinster in a hundred square miles wouldn't set her cap for Pa. Moreover, if my father wouldn't accept Alcie Hastings, he'd hardly have truck with a scrap like *Mae*!"

She pinned on the newspaper pattern and scissored out a sleeve from the rough sacking. "I wager Pa will spy some pretty widow woman at a barn dance or church social someday."

Looking down to hide her stricken face, Liz made a small noise. "Oh! Look what I've done." Blood sprang from her thumb, soaking the stretched linen.

"'Sides, even if that Mae *is* making eyes, my Pa and I are *very* close. He'd confide if—if anything was on his mind in *that* direction. Or if this Mae got too forward. Why, I'd be the *first* person Pa'd come running to if he wanted advice, which I must say has *always* been *very* well received. Why the idea!" Beth smirked. "You said she was a scrawny little plucked chicken of a thing. You've been reading too much of that Jane Eyre book, something tells me.".

"Something tells me you protest overmuch," Liz

answered, with an archness unlike her.

Beth simmered and miscut the other sleeve. "Drat!"

"Not too old to have a second *family* either, I s'pose." Casting a sharp eye at Beth, Liz murmured as if nothing could be more offhand. "But might offset a tad of inheritance, I would wager, too."

Beth paled and dropped the feed sacks unheeded. "In any case, *that's* not going to happen. Liz, I said, *you* suppose too much. 'Sides, my father always said raising kids was like having chickens peck you to death. *I'd* wager that's the last thing he'd want."

"It's not you'd be set out of house and home, if he got hitched again." Liz's face twisted in anguish.

"Pa would *never*…"

Beth stopped uncertain, adding feebly, "Why—you could live with us… Oh! This whole subject is crazy as a loon! How we do go on!"

"Where's the buttermilk, Bethy?" The women both looked up as if waylaid by bandits.

"In the spring house like always, Matthew! Shouldn't be sneaking up and listening to folks."

Matthew, looking uncomfortably determined, stepped closer. "What do you mean, live here? Liz, you movin' in?"

"Of course not," Beth snapped.

"No need to fight over me! I just get so all-fired *unhappy* about the notion." Liz tossed the embroidery hoop on the floor.

"See here now, I—"

"Matthew, why not you look in on the kids. Think I heard the baby."

"But Lizbeth, I'd be more'n happy for you—"

"Never mind, Matt. It's not happening. Just talk."

"All righty, Beth."

The women watched him plod off muttering under his breath.

Beth turned back. "Why, If I didn't know better, I'd think you are jealous of that Mae creature, Auntie Liz. What's she look like anyway? You said she was kinda small. I declare I'm just going to have to come over and see for myself what barnyard creature has apparently bewitched my pa!"

"You find it all humorous, I see. She's a skinny little ragbag. Hunh! Day I'm jealous of a hoyden like *that*..." Liz lowered her voice. "Next thing to a soiled dove, you ask me. The next step for the likes of one like that. A sin-sick harlot workin' out of a saloon. You mark my words. That's where she belongs!"

Beth glanced askance at her aunt. "Keep an eye on Pa."

She watched Matthew, shaking his head, disappear upstairs, yet suddenly she and Liz seemed talked out.

Chapter Nine: Ride the Wind

Before church service next Sunday, Luke thudded downstairs, jammed on his Stetson, and announced—with "no argument wanted" in his expression—"Out all day…checkin' fences."

Liz looked on, sour-faced, perplexed at Luke's work clothes. "Why tell *me*! Never let *me* in on anything you do, and you shouldn't be laboring on Sunday, the Lord's day of rest."

Luke grunted. "That's what I damn well *am* gonna do, Liz. Rest for a change and not allow Preacher Grimshaw to belabor my ears."

"Great land of living, Luke! Don't need to bite my head off. And you know what I feel about cursing."

Luke grunted and headed out.

He stuck his head back through the doorway with a look of grudging apology. "Might want to take some grub. Might be gone all day."

"You said that!" Liz thrust the long hatpin in her black straw bonnet with the red silk poppies. She just had time to throw some vittles together before it would be time to leave for church.

"Just do it."

"*I swan!*" Liz muttered under her breath. "What will good folks say about my heathenish brother?" Kenning well she relished time alone, and well able to handle the two-person surrey with or without Luke, if she wished to visit some, and besides, she could gossip about her backsliding brother to her heart's content. With those happy thoughts, she slammed together bread, cheese, a thick slice of ham, ginger snaps hard as poker chips, and an apple, wrapping the sandwich makings in oilcloth to stuff in Luke's saddle bags, along with a canteen of hard cider.

Nothing harder on the Sabbath.

Liz looked after him as he charged in, snatched up the bundle, and dashed out again. "Well, I never!" But just then the surrey rolled up with Old Tom at the reins, which told her he meant to visit his ma after services.

It never occurred to Liz to check the stable.

****

Mae, accompanied by the lazy drone of bees, scent of horse flesh and sweet musk of hay, rested her head happily on a saddle, her nose close to a book mouthing words of a tattered *Anne of Green Gables* Luke smuggled out from under Liz's nose. The pictures were pretty, too.

Luke waited till Liz's surrey was a puff of dust down the road, then pointed to Betsy and lifted the bar for the hellion. "Come."

Mae scrambled up, smoothing her hair, grabbing her squashed hat, and ran over to help tighten girths, while Hell-Fire stamped an impatient hoof.

Neither spoke. To be together with the sun on their faces seemed sufficient company on a perfect Indian Summer day. Not for Luke. The sky seemed filled with cotton balls on a dark blue quilt. Luke pointed out late wildflowers, purple creeping Charlie, white bindweed, yellow seed buds of Black Medic, and the russet underwings of a golden eagle soaring effortlessly as they trotted, then cantered along…for to Luke's pleasure, Mae seemed a natural horsewoman. Straight back, chin up, head high, black hair flowing from beneath the squashed hat. He loved just looking at her.

This was a mistake, whispered his angel, vexing his shoulder blades.

Until next time, his devil hissed.

When the sun was like the yolk of a goose egg high overhead, and the horses were sweating, they sat under a juniper tree fronting a lazy stream and shared the lunch Liz packed. Meanwhile their mounts foraged and drank.

"You did well," Luke grunted huskily. Mae threw him an enchanting smile that near outdid him.

****

Next day, Luke strode from the brick smokehouse after checking rows of maroon sausage loops, a fine patina of mold on their shriveled casings, and rows of ham hocks, all hanging against the coming winter and varmints, not to mention black snakes lurking in the cool dusk. He kicked some fallen brick he'd have the wranglers fix before long, and only then headed on to the barn, after he could tarry no longer.

On the way, he shouted over at Curly and Dusty to get on to fixing the shed roof, and for Old Tom to see about liniment for the lame horse. By the time he reached the stable, he'd sorted out three more chores for the boys, and only then ducked into the warm dark.

Mae had stopped filling nose bags, apparently watching him give out orders.

"Hi, Mr. Luke." Her voice came shy, welcoming.

He nodded stern, almost ignoring her.

Mae's expression sobered.

Luke stroked Hell-Fire's nose, exceedingly

conscious of Mae standing way too close. Checked withers and hocks and let him nip a turnip off his palm, all the while sensing the tiny prickle of warmth along his thigh where her hip rested, the delicate hand with dirty fingernails stroking Hell-Fire's neck, within a hairsbreadth of touching his. It seemed a tiny electric shock fritzed between the two as he helplessly gazed at the tiny fingered hand next to his large brown paw.

Feeling unstable as a bag of bobcats, it was all Luke could muster not to cover that small grimy-fingered hand, if even for a second.

He breathed deep. His own hand shook.

A dam broke inside him with memories of suppressed desire from yesterday, sluicing away all but the primitive need of a man and a woman. His devil chortled.

With no deliberation, only desire old and powerful as humankind, Luke fumbled for Mae's arm, dragging her close in awkward embrace, his head and body in a fever he could not cool even as he tried.

He saw Mae's startled face. It seemed an eternity as their limbs tangled in gracelessness, one arm circling her slender pliable waist, with Mae's arm trapped by her side, the other caught between them. Luke's other arm lifted her bottom until they were chest to chest and her wondering eyes met his. Luke dropped his lion-maned head, searching for her lips.

She wriggled to free the arm trapped between, pressed her hand against his chest, but then slid the hand up to drape it tentatively about his neck. "Mr. Luke," she breathed, then turned her face the other way, whether seeking his mouth or avoiding it, he didn't know.

Whispering, groaning, *"Mae. Mae,"* Luke felt her

warm cinnamon-scented breath through his open shirt—
"*Dear little Mae.*" Luke buried his face in her flossy curls, one brawny hand clasping her tighter to him, his other broad scarred hand gently circling the nape of her neck.

She stopped her slight struggles and spoke breathily in a shy whisper… "*Mr. Luke…?*" Was it a rebuke? An invitation? Luke was past caring.

In a fever of passion, he kissed her ear, the top of her head, her cheeks, her throat, feeling her heart thumping away against his chest, and then, lifting her face, Mae tentatively offered her lips to him. Luke took full possession of her mouth, kissing her thoroughly and well, while golden motes, dancing around them in a stray beam, seemed like a blessing.

Burying his face in her neck, Luke held her close a long time, kenning hopelessly he had to let her go, until finally, shuddering, Luke, using all his willpower, settled her down with both hands spanning her waist and released her.

You should leave. Now.

"Mae!" He barked not looking at her. "I'll tend my own damned horse. Get on out of here!" It was a strangled cry.

"Mr. Luke," she began…

"Go now, dammit!"

While you can.

Mae hesitated, took a step, halted and looked back only once, then ran from the stable. Luke braced hands on his knees, berating himself nine ways from Sunday, breathing like he raced Hell-Fire. How could a spit of a gal hogtie him worse than any calf? He had to make this right.

The Lord kenned how.

****

Beth sighed. Liz's monthly visits had turned into *weekly* visits, as she vented her spleen over past offenses against her, or her brother's transgressions, but mostly about that hired girl. Beth almost dreaded the sound of her surrey rattling up.

"Oh, Beth dear! It's worse than I thought!" Liz greeted her niece even before she hopped down from the trap. "Oh, my!" Liz fanned her face and patted her flattish chest. "I have to catch my breath."

Once in the kitchen hanging up her bonnet, Beth tried to head her off. "Auntie Liz? Did I show you the new marble cake recipe in *The Ladies Home Journal*?"

Liz ignored the proffered magazine and took a slurp from the teacup Beth shoved over. Beth picked up her usual chore when Liz came calling, that of hem-stitching the feed sack dress with rapid jerky motions, sighing in a way that said, *Almost done.*

"He made her a room!" Liz snorted as if he'd fashioned a den of iniquity.

Beth looked up with more interest, grinning. "Probably not all that safe otherwise, with randy hot-blooded ranch hands in the bunkhouse feeling their oats with her so close by."

"No need to be crude, Beth Anne! Yet now you mention it, she probably wouldn't mind it if one of those buckos climbed her ladder—*or Luke!*"

Liz's flush would do a beet justice.

Beth looked reproving. "Oh, Auntie Liz! Can you see my pa doing something like that? I'm all grown. Probably sees me in her, when I was young. We are not exactly nearby. Wouldn't surprise me if in the next few years he'll be sitting right here on the porch in the rocker with a cat on his lap. Not a young gal." She hooted. "Really, Auntie Liz! You *do* go on."

Liz scoffed. "And I *think* they've gone out riding. Alone! Heaven knows where."

Beth picked up the gaudy dress again, sighing, looking askance at the travesty she labored over. The rough sacking scraped her fingers, and with the weave so loose, the hem was well on its way to unraveling. Beth twisted her mouth as she held out the garish gown still redolent of grain. Tomato red, pink and yellow roses, with a green-and-purple-plaid ruffled hem and puffed sleeves…

"While I am dragooned into *trying* to put together this gosh-darn dress, not *you*."

She checked it again. "Done all I can, I reckon. Wonder where he wants her to go to in this thing? Wouldn't wish it on the devil's handmaiden." She began wrapping it in old newsprint. "Guess you'll be taking it with you." Her actions indicated she would need to scrub the house down, after Liz left with it.

Liz eyed Beth's industriously tied bundle as if it was a dead possum alongside the road, again fervently wishing she had not donated all that money to the Baptist church and had gone into the dry goods store for a bolt of calico, or maybe ordered from the Sears, Roebuck catalogue instead.

Beth eyed her, bemused, when Liz didn't accept it and decided to needle.

"Matthew heard at the blacksmith's that you have a new hand?"

Liz blushed from the neck up and plopped down again, welcoming the delay of paying the piper, taking instead the chance of gossip. "I must say he has *a foreign* look to him." Not relaying the fact that she found him immensely pleasing...

Chapter Ten: Enter the Serpent

The demon horse had a hoof tucked precariously between Luke's muscled, denim-covered thighs as he inspected Hell-Fire's fetlock. The day was unseasonably hot, with bottle-green horseflies fat as ticks buzzing Hell-Fire, finding delight in Luke's honest sweat too, and making Hell-Fire restive and out of sorts, as was Luke. "Lift it, you damned outlaw, you!" Luke propped the hoof on a stump, suspecting a loose nail caused the limp. Hoped it was. "And not a shin splint…" he muttered.

A silky, melodious voice interrupted his aggravations.

How a voice smooth as whipped cream could be as irritating as the horseflies, Luke didn't ken but felt atavistic distaste for the unknown male behind him just because of the mellow tenor of his voice. Probably south of Texas, across the border, from the sing-song accent, he guessed.

"*Señor* Boss? *Jefe?* May I be of help? I am *muy bueno con los caballos.*"

Luke twisted his head, viewing the man upside down. First, shapely legs in tight black leather gauchos called batwing chaps, weightily adorned with fringe and silver medallions. His gaze traveled up to a vest similarly tarted up, to a bronzed face with ruby lips framed by a glistening pencil mustache. Licorice-black hair under a gaudy sombrero fell over one dark liquid eye. Luke dropped Hell-Fire's hoof. Straightening, sucking in, Luke stood towering over the slight newcomer, looking him over.

The thin mustache curling down at the corners didn't look silly but rather enhanced the expressive bow of the fellow's mouth, Luke thought sourly. Eyes, liquid black as a moon-wink at the bottom of a well, gazed placidly back, sizing *him* up.

The stripling dropped a saddle roll made of a Mexican blanket and pressed one hand across his medallion-spangled chest, announcing, "You have the honor of seeing Raoul Santa-Maria Rodriguez Delgado. Have I that right?"

Luke, feeling for callouses in the proffered brown hand, suspected he had, hating that he gripped a palm hard and scratchy as dried mesquite. *Danged favorable-looking, too,* Luke assessed, *if you cared for the type.* He suspicioned the ladies might, and he surmised a tinge of Indian in there too, somewhere. Still young, by the looks of him. In time, his body would become hardened with healed-over breaks, knees thickened with bone, back bent or even cracked at one point, and legs bowed from riding…

Luke didn't like the punitive slant his mind was taking.

"Allow me, *Señor Jefe?*"

Luke watched, amused, as the newcomer sauntered cat-like to Hell-Fire. He couldn't wait to see Hell-Fire set this obnoxious fella back on his heels…but the man squatted and, effortlessly lifting the hoof, wedged out a jagged rock from under the iron shoe, tossing it while Luke's usually intractable mount waited, docile as a fluffy yellow chick.

Luke made a mouth.

"Forgive me *Jefe*. I know not my place." His smile nearly blinded Luke.

"Yeah, Mr. Delgado. Much obliged. Now—"

"Raoul! *Por favor*, *Señor*."

"Yeah, as I said." Luke pulled himself to his full six-three and sucked in again. He glanced at the road passing the house at a distance. "Where d'you hail from?" Indicating wherever it was he could return to it pronto.

Raoul was impervious. "Oh, Boss, have I the pleasure of seeing *Señor* Farnsworth?"

"You have." It irritated him the way Hell-Fire kept *nosing* the fancy pants and that he kenned his name.

Raoul stroked Hell-Fire's mane. "I am seeking work. I heard you were the *Jefe* around here much to be admired."

Luke thought rapidly. Didn't like the looks of the fellow or his buttering him up like a biscuit. Danged peacock. Nonetheless, Matt was still hobbling about on a crutch Old Tom had whittled. To be fair, the fancy fellow did seem to have a way with horses. Some did. He sighed inwardly. Why not? Couldn't hurt, for a short time. Then give him the boot.

"Right. No contract. Bunkhouse over there." Luke nodded curtly. A few hands wandered out of the long building, scratching their behinds and looking on with unshielded interest. "Twenty a month, damned good grub. Sundays off and a half day of your choosing, less yer needed, plus Friday and Saturday nights."

Raoul gave a two-finger salute. "*Si, Señor Jefe!*" That blinding grin again.

"Make yourself at home, any empty bunk. I'll assign work after breakfast."

"*Hasta luego*, then, *Señor* Boss-Man."

Just then Mae wandered out. Perhaps she'd heard the palaver. Raoul didn't need to say anything—his eyes did the talking. Devouring Mae in a smug glance, he kissed his fingers before shouldering his gaudy roll and sauntering to the bunkhouse.

Luke swore and headed to the kitchen, doing a double-take.

There was Liz on the porch, smoothing her hair, hands fluttering about her apron like blind birds, her eyes fixed on Raoul like he was Angel Gabriel come to fetch her to heaven. Damn!

Raoul rewarded his sister too with a dazzling smile and a wide sweep of his sombrero. "*Señorita*! I was unaware *bonita doncellas* also lived *aqui*." Liz frowned her misunderstanding.

"A lovely, unmarried fine lady," Raoul informed her with another blinding grin.

"Now, how did you figure I was an unmarried lady?" Liz cooed.

"Miss Farnsworth will do." Luke broke in heavily. "Liz! Breakfast near ready?" His bark startled her out of her enchantment. She looked down demurely, scowled at her brother and, twitching her bustle, threw Raoul a simpering "come hither" over her shoulder before entering the kitchen.

Damnation. A fox in the henhouse.

Raoul turned back, winking. "*Si*, Mr. Luke. Boss Man. You have many very beautiful *mujeres*."

Luke clenched his jaw, making a muscle pop. Insolence if he ever heard it.

He gave Raoul the filthiest chores he could think of. Dredging the stable. Repairing pig houses. Scrubbing the bunkhouse floor. Raoul grinned through it all.

At night the bunkhouse mellowed with sonorous guitar strums and melodic singing, interspersed with the chortling of the ranch hands at Raoul's heavily accented tales of female conquest.

Chapter Eleven: Invaders

Mae stretched, gazing contentedly about her cozy aerie. For the first time, she could see her breath. Mourning, she knew she must soon go to the big house, and she wondered if that was a good thing, but no matter, since she recollected the harsh winters, drifts up to the eaves and blustery winds suffered in each ramshackle lean-to her family gravitated to by whimsy or brute choice. Winters were real bone-shakers here in Wyoming.

She froze, not from cold but at a noise below.

The crunch-whisper of trod-on straw.

A whuffle of a horse, most likely Hell-Fire, who never seemed to sleep.

Mae stiffened under the crazy-patch quilt, then sat up.

By careful, spaced footfalls and the crisp crush of straw, something or *someone* rustled below. Not horses. It was the stealth bothered her.

Then. *Whispering.* A grunt. A being hitting something hard, followed by an oath and outcry cut off quick-like. Now Betsy nickered, inquisitive.

"*Shush, goldarn you!*"

Creeping to the ladder, Mae wisht she had a gun like Luke wanted; she'd show those bunkhouse varmints. Most of them only liked to tease her, but… Sure enough, moving shadows below. A lantern light bobbed erratically over barrels and hanging ropes. Mae clapped her hand over her mouth. The bobbing light struck the side of a gaunt cheek. A caved-in mouth, a thin nose broken several times…

Ma!

Her first instinct was to duck. Nevertheless, they heard her scooting back from the square trap, their notice evident from the drawling, mocking voices filtering through the dusty boards.

"You up thar, sugar plum? Seed yer *light.*" A throaty giggle. The second person. Who? "This whar he comes to you like a thief in the night? That old ma-an?" Her sister. One of them. Ruby June?

Mae felt the ladder thrum and shake under her hands. Ma's face with its goblin grin poked through the opening. Mae felt more trapped than if a wrangler had crept up.

"Thar you air, honey lamb. Hope we ain't a dis-*turbin*' nuthin'." She looked hungrily about Mae's cozy retreat. "Gotcha self real nice up here. Easy pickin's."

Mae had a sudden urge to push Ma down the ladder, taking Ruby June, her next oldest sister close behind, with her. They looked nothing alike as sisters, and kenning Ma, perhaps they weren't full sisters. June, big-boned, reddish skin like sandpaper, close-set eyes, hair like straw, always sullen. Still, she was the only one she could confide in, when Ruby June was in a good mood. They'd both talked of running away.

"Ma! Ruby! What do you want here?" Mae blurted. *And how did you find me?*

"You ken what we want, sugar plum. That old feed salesman I run into was nice enough ta tell me where you all was holed up. Want yew home where you belong.

Warn't right, yer pa runnin' you off like that and not tellin' us nothin', till now."

"On my own now, Ma. Makin' my own way." Mae strived to keep her voice from trembling—either from fear or anger, like they would snatch her up and drag her back to wherever they were holed up. "Pa didn't run me off. I left!"

Ruby June joined Ma. They poked about, ignoring her. Ruby had envy painted on her face like the side of a barn.

Her ma bunched her hands on her scrawny hips. "Not bad, though Mr. High-on-the-Horse could do better. Like why aincha in the big house? Didn't yer pa order you to siphon some cash money or somethin', from what I heered?"

She looked about, disgusted. "This don't look like money."

"I like it here. Alone."

"Hunh!" Ma leered knowingly, plunking herself on the small wood chest holding the ewer, and swinging her legs. Mae noted they were bound in rags. Her family had come down in the world, if possible. She felt a pang of guilt for one whole split second.

"Don't s'pose yew got enything to drank, 'sides this here water?" She raised a wispy brow.

Mae shook her head.

Ma sighed. "Look, Mae. I ain't been much of a ma…" Mae and Ruby both rolled their eyes. "Reckon I'm a-tryin' to make up fer it. I was wed young…"

Mae looked away from her furtive face.

"Never had a chanct, like you. Started poppin' out brats like peas in a pod when nigh on fourteen. Worked hard all my life for my kids. Might as well not have a

129

man." She spat on Mae's scrubbed boards. "Hunh! Be easier iffen he died. Meaner than a rabid dog…"

She threatened to go on.

"Yes, Ma, I 'member."

Ma rolled on. "'Tweren't a easy life, as ye well ken. Did best I could." Ma stuck her chin out. "Scrubbed and slaved my fingers to the bone, for you gals, specially."

Mae twerked her mouth. If she ever spied Ma with a broom, she would have been struck deaf and dumb.

"Don't git mixed up with that fambly. He will do you dirt and leave you with a biscuit in the oven. You can't think he wants trash like us."

"Yeh," Ruby popped in. "Git yerself a young boy, like me and Marvin."

"Marvin?"

"Wellsome, he kinda hooked up with us, running from somebody, but in the end…"

Ma broke in. "That's what counts, end of days, what she's sayin'. Marvin is a steady boy, not like yer pa. But a man, some kids, and the Good Book is all you need in life."

Mae watched her, disbelieving. "The *Bible*? When did you ever…?"

"Never mind that, Miss Sassy Mouth! Come on home with us. Yer kin. You don't got to marry up with that old sheepherder feller. Dumb *cuss*." She spat again.

Mae looked at the brown spittle on her clean floor. Her head reeled. Last thing in the world she would wish was her conniving family invading her *home*. A menace even now, as if they could snatch her away at any time without a trace, leaving Luke wondering at her perfidy.

Mae clutched her blankets like a raft in a turbulent stream.

"Ma. Ruby. I ain't—I'm not coming back. Might as well go."

Contrarily, Ruby availed herself of the only chair, looking appreciatively about, her eyes devouring the colorful crazy-patch quilt and the china with the roses and kittens and pictures on the wall, as if she didn't hear.

"Got it real spruced up. I could stay here with you. Maybe, old man'd like two of us better'n one, or maybe..." She gave a sly wink and lifted her flat bosom. "Maybe the old cuss'll take a hankering to a full-growed woman, not some scrawny little barn cat. Whatcha think, Ma?"

Ma grew speculative behind dark calculating eyes. She'd miss Ruby, even if her daughter could inveigle her way in and share the riches, mulling possibilities and jealousy against common sense. "I don't like my daughter livin' alone like this. Ain't fittin'. Think m'be I should look after Pearly Mae myself. Room enough fer two. Though in time, s'pect we should move into the big house. What chew think, sugar plum?"

Mae stood and drew to her full five feet, four inches. "Mr. Luke made me this room. It's mine!" Mae bit her cheek to keep from blurting further.

Ma slapped her skinny thigh. "Oho! Cat outta the bag. You *do* got yer gunsights set on the big boss a this yere spread."

"Nothing like that! He's my boss. Now go!" *Before someone finds you.*

For the first time, Ma looking instinctively over her shoulder and appeared uneasy. "Yah, best git on back. Yer pappy be wonderin' where we got up to, even if he *is* deep in the jug. An you ken how *he* is. We keepin' this little visit a secret. Fer now. Might spoil things here, till

I do some figgurin'. Ain't that right, Ruby June?"

Ruby June grinned. "Why sure, Ma." She winked at her sister.

Mae kenned that look. Ma meant no such thing. But maybe this time she did.

It would benefit them to keep this a secret somehow. Wouldn't it?

And in time, maybe Pa'd just move on, as he was wont to do on a whim, or a perceived hurt.

"Jus 'member!" Ma jabbed a bony, dirt-encrusted finger at Mae's chest. "Iffen you get tired a being nursemaid to a *old* man, and Nate said he was no oil painting—"

Ma looked forlornly about the cozy set-up one last time, and moreover, left the thought unfinished. "Least ways, *I* won't haveta." Was her odd parting shot.

Mae held her breath until she heard feet race across straw and the raucous complaint from their old mule, when ma and her sister both scrambled onto its back. When she turned, she saw her precious brush and comb were missing. She sighed. And she had forgotten to draw water. She peered out. Still early. Mae shinnied down the ladder in her shift. Water and back…then dress for the day.

Mae saw Raoul's unearthly angelic image rippling in the rain barrel alongside her as she dipped water to splash her face. Her dripping hair, hanging in strings, made her shiver as wet dribbled down her shimmy. She looked down, following his eyes. Her damp clothes exposed more than she would wish, especially in front of him.

Mae scowled from beneath a wet hank of hair and lashed out at him grinning at her. "Don't you be comin' up on me like that!"

Raoul flashed blinding white teeth from burnt-sugar skin.

Raoul grabbed her arm. "Don't run away, *chiquita*. Not gonna hurt you. When an hombre sees a *chica bonita* pretty as you, he just wants to be with her. Even just a look. *Comprendo?*"

He rolled R's like a cat's purr.

Mae drew her brows together. Despite his pretty words, she saw a glitter, not meanness but mockery. Like a cat stretching.

"I would be glad to walk you back to the—" He motioned to the stable. "You have never shown me your place." Mae flushed pink. That she should stand there, wet as a drowned cat and let this *cowhand*—no matter how handsome—sweet-talk her! White teeth flashed, obsidian eyes held hers in a practiced way. Mae looked off before she could be dazzled. "I have work," Mae mumbled.

"*Si*, don't we all? Old *cabron!*"

"He's not old."

Raoul smirked.

"Leave go!" Mae tried to wrench away. But Raoul half-closed his eyes, melting her with a lazy smile...*he thought.* Mae boiled. He watched her carefully, black eyes turning to anthracite. "Is that what you wish? You like *viejos?*"

Mae scowled.

Raoul ran his tongue across his lower lip. Laughing, he released her.

Mae crossed her arms and scurried back to the stable.

Chapter Twelve: The Prairie Kiss

Mae's perfect rounded bottom in tight denims outgrown by one of the hands—no lady would ever approve, Luke thought with amusement—lifted rhythmically off the saddle as if she were born on a horse. She bounced with each thud of a hoof, her head high and proud, back straight as if parading troops, hair braided in a long plait hanging from the crushed faded hat she could not be parted with, for a reason Luke never delved into.

Luke wore a new Stetson, which did not escape Liz's scrutiny, and because of the mildness of the day, an open-necked shirt of blue cambric, showing off his broad tanned scarred chest with the faintest hint of iron gray silk peeking out and a silver bracelet cuff with a hunk of rough turquoise, plus his best jeans.

Galloping along in silence, this was their fifth such ride thudding across the prairie to nowhere in particular or wherever wind, whimsy or the horses took them. Though now attuned to her every mood, Luke hazarded a glance as he tore his eyes away from her bottom and rode up beside her. Never once had he taken liberties, as back at the stable. Nevertheless, it occurred to him Mae was unusually silent and kept casting covert, even troubled glances his way.

He placed a hand on her arm, startling her from some reverie. "Are you—*happy*, Mae?" he began, not trusting himself to go further. *Not bored being out here with an old coot?*

Luke sighed inwardly. He sounded lame as a bull on crutches.

She flashed a glance like a flick of heat lightning. Luke's heart thudded. *Tiring of him. Why wouldn't she be?* Rather be playing with the barn cat's kittens, or spending time with someone her own age. Whatever that was.

He studied an eagle winging the sky to the southwest to its nest somewhere in Medicine Bow Mountains, to keep from thinking.

"Somewhat bothers you." He spoke flatly.

Mae closely studied the pommel. "Just wonderin' if this is the right thing? I mean most every week…?" She faltered. "I mean ridin' out here, *alone.*" Mae looked over her shoulder as if even now they were followed. "I mean, not that I'm not a-*liking* it." She shot another anxious look, sending a chill up Luke's spine. "But we been doin' it for a right long time now and…I mean, *out* like this *alone.*"

"Why?" Luke's brows met in a ferocious scowl. "Some fool spoutin' nonsense?" He grabbed Mae's reins, drawing both mounts to a halt. The eagle still circled on the hot thermals ruffling their hair and the horses' manes.

"Out with it."

Mae bit her lip. Small teeth indented the coral silkiness. Luke wished, with a yearning so strong, he could kiss that sweet mouth, but he reined it in as he would a wild stallion. Shaking his head as if stung by a horsefly, Luke closed his eyes.

Was this it? An end to his nonsense and schoolboy

dreams? An old fool, as Liz would vow.

Mae nodded just as fierce. "Just don't ken, Mr. Luke. I done learnt, I *learned* how to ride a long while ago, and folks think—and Miss Lizbeth already said a few words in that direction—and the hands been joshin' me and sayin' things about what-all we bin *doing* out here."

She mocked, imitating a deep voice, "And 'if I'll go a ridin' with them, *too*, and—" She looked off. "They'll be givin' me as…*hard* a ride or as *good* a time as any old—"

Luke's face turned granite as the hills. "I get the idee. Don't need to go on," he said sharper than he meant. "Never mind them. This's about you." *Us.*

"But, Mr. Luke. It ain't—isn't right. Shouldn't be sayin' things about you and—" She twisted the reins around her small hand. "And they—I see the way you *look* at me. I mean, you're a good man. A *kind* man." Mae spoke in a cross between a wail and whisper. "I don't know why you want to be out here with me. I don't know what you *want* of me, or why you even *want* to *be* with me *at all*," she cried in a rush of words. "I can't ride like the boys. I don't know nothin'. I'm so stupid. My pa said so. Can't read or write proper. Maybe we shouldn't—" Mae halted for breath.

She studied the pommel again, half whispering. "I don't want to *hurt* you, Mr. Luke."

Luke couldn't speak, fearful of her next words.

"Too late for that." His voice was choked with grit. Luke soberly watched her with grave silver eyes. "I'll say this only once, Mae, and I won't bother you again. I *care* for you."

He breathed deep, looking to the far hills. "More

than you will ever know. Not like my kin. I feel—such *affection* for you, Mae." He rushed on. "I wake up each morning filled with joy—pleasure that I will set eyes on you again." Luke looked quickly at her. He couldn't see her eyes. "Does that bother you? I ken you can't feel the same. I—understand, an old cowboy like me. So forget I said it."

"No. No, it don't—doesn't." A flush crept her neck. "I—I just don't want them sayin' bad things. You are such a great man, Mr. Luke. I—I like you too. I just don't want you…hurt."

I already am.

Luke gazed at the purple Laramie Ranges wreathed in mist, not seeing them. The horses grew restive and started to amble along. "Let me worry about that. I want to be with you, Mae. I like your company as often as I can have it." *No matter how you feel about me.*

Silence grew thick as the dust their horses stirred in clouds behind them. Mae seemed to be in a study.

He finally had to break the spell. Words came out all tangled. "You don't cotton being out here with me?" Words tumbled from his mouth like rusty nails from a pail. "Have I bothered you in any other way?" Luke rassled bobcats bare-handed, suffered broken bones, and had fought briefly in the war between the states, ending with a musket ball in his shoulder, but nothing set fire to his soul as much as waiting for her reply now.

She shook her head till her hair, blown loose, flew across her face in a waving black curtain. "You don't bother me, Mr. Luke. Not in a bad way."

Luke was a dog with bone. He couldn't stop. "Would you rather be with Jasper? Or Rusty?" *Or that snake Raoul?*

"No, no! Not them." Her pale nose reddened. "I—I like being out with you, Mr. Luke. It makes me feel *special*."

You are.

*"*You are such a great man. Everyone looks up to you."

Mae misread his silence. She laughed, shaky, touching his arm. "Reckon I'm fixin' a whole pot of stew outta one little old turnip." Darting a shy glance through wind-whipped hair, Mae continued. "Reckon if you want to keep ridin' with me, it would be well with me, Mr. Luke. Where—where are we gonna ride to next?"

Looking down, he felt her impossibly small hand on his bicep. He covered it, kissing her fingertips.

"Just Luke. Call me…Luke." He looked at her as if for the last time. "Reckon we should go back. I—I have work to do." He couldn't breathe. Muscular scarred hands equal to calf-roping, well-digging, and not a few fist fights, *shook.*

Without sentient thought, and being more than overpowered by a need going back to the beginning of time, Luke reached one strapping arm around Mae's slim waist, dragging her off Betsy's saddle and onto his thighs, with her left side pressed against his chest. He buried his face in her blow- away hair, breathing in her clean sweet scent, while her hat went off doing cartwheels in the wind.

Go ahead, kiss her. Who would know? his devil urged with diabolical lies.

Bending, he searched for her mouth, her warm, sweet-scented breath on his cheek. Between Mae being half off her saddle, with one arm trapped between them, and the horses' contrary warring strides, the embrace was clumsy.

Mae awkwardly grasped Luke about the midriff to keep from falling. Luke dragged her the rest of the way, twisting her around until she sat facing him. She clasped Luke's neck, burying her face in his shirt, pressing her cheek against sun-warmed skin, fingers touching his face like butterfly wings, breathing Luke's scent of leather, Bay Rum and tobacco, feeling the thudding of his heart, while his hard hands molded her body as if memorizing it. She lifted her face and stroked his bristly jaw.

Two fifteen-year-olds couldn't be any more awkward, Luke kenned. The horses recognized the moment, though, clip-clopping to a halt, snorting their approval and cropping in a leisurely manner whatever greenery the prairie offered.

Her soft mouth was so close he could taste it, delaying the reward until he shook with desire. His hands and arms had a life of their own. He gripped Mae, burying his face in her soft black hair. Luke, his rugged face in shadow, iron-gray locks falling over his bronze forehead, Stetson sailing in the wind along with hers, crushed her body with increasing ardor, feeling himself swell with desire. Her lips were pink, moist, her breath like candy mints and violets, soft—warm. He brushed her mouth, probing, kissing, grinding his lips on hers.

Mae made a little gasp, whispering, *"Luke, Luke,"* when he finally raised his head. He felt her quivering beneath his hands. Mae pressed her head fiercely into his neck. With desperate effort Luke pulled her away, grating with a voice not his own, "We should go back," hearing Liz's words in his ear. *What are you doing, Luke!* And the Baptist circuit preacher thundering from the crude pulpit about the *sins of the flesh*. And Nate snorting—*You too, Luke, old friend?*

Hell-Fire moseyed farther, seeking greener pastures, with Betsy docilely following. Luke's breathing gentled from steam engine back to normal.

"What am I to do with you?" Luke groaned almost to himself.

"Care for me, Mr. Luke."

"More than you ken," Luke whispered.

"I— I liked what you did."

Almost he believed her. He wanted to believe her.

They rode in silence until a chill breeze picked up toward late afternoon. If he had his way, he'd gallop like fury, carrying Mae off to Canada, or the far north town of Deadwood where no one kenned him, leaving cares behind…build a new world, a new life. Again, Liz's words came written on the cold, unforgiving wind: "*What do you think you are doing, Lucian Farnsworth! She's young enough to be your granddaughter.*"

"I wish we didn't have to go back."

Luke felt a flush of wonder. "How can you know what you want?" Bitterness coated his voice with gall. "Never even had a fella, have you? Even for hand-holding."

"Maybe not," Mae whispered. "They tried, but I waited till it felt right. It feels right, Mr. Luke." Then he felt her slim arm curl around his neck again. She lifted her face, her hand on the back of his head, and as if a gully washer broke through a dam of guilt, Luke's last resolve gushed with it and he clutched Mae's slight body as a woman's, not that of a fragile girl, kissed her deeply, running his tongue across her full mouth. The cool tip of hers explored his lips, his tongue, brushing his mustache.

Another earthquake of desire shuddered Luke.

Where could they go?

Something unspeakable will happen, Mae, little Mae, darling little Mae… You have to let go. Pushing her roughly away, Luke felt as if he were pulling a cart filled with rocks. The last time he would own that control. He kenned it. "This can't—*won't* happen again."

Of course not, his devil chortled.

She nodded after a long while, when he supposed she would not. "I'd—I'd like to go a-riding with you again." Her voice was a whisper, a breath of a breeze. He had to strain to hear it.

Luke grated harshly, "You want that?"

Mae nodded again earnestly.

Luke sighed with bitter bleakness.

Mae looked him full in the face. "You told me about a waterfall."

Chapter Thirteen: Liz Complains

Liz plunked down on a kitchen chair by Beth's big round table.

"I declare, I don't like it, Beth. I don't like it one little whit."

Sighing inwardly, Beth paused from pouring tea into her best china from Sears Roebuck catalogue, then finished before setting out a platter of oatmeal cookies made from bacon fat, studded with raisins and still warm and soft. This was the second time in scarce a week. "Care for what, Auntie Liz?"

"Luke! My brother, your precious *father*, is acting all peculiar. *Secretive*!" She bit into a cookie. "Hmmmph! You don't believe me."

"*Really*, Liz. My Pa is the most straightforward open person I know. Nothin' sly about him." Beth's guise was smug to the point of insult, had Liz, after selecting a third cookie, not been picking flecks of crumbs from her tea.

"Hunh! Didn't think I *saw* him straggling back with that girl on Betsy. Lord knows what they were up to out there. Mark my words. I don't put *nothing* past that little tramp. My brother, who should still be grieving—*grieving*, I tell you—for dear Katie, goes out on the prairie with that strumpet. *Alone*. Keeps saying he needs her to—I don't know, all sorts of excuses—when I have the *audaciousness* to dare *question*."

Liz vigorously macerated the cookie with strong

white teeth, seeing something Beth did not.

"Teach her the *ropes*! Indeed!" Unknowing, she plucked another cookie from the plate, giving it the same treatment. "Or they *check fences.* I ask you! Or—teaching her how to *ride proper*?" She slurped tea, nailing Beth with a sharp gaze over the cup. "Last time, he wouldn't even *answer* me."

Beth watched as her aunt snatched the sixth oatmeal cookie. She rose and pointedly fetched more, dumping them onto the plate.

"*Checking fences*!" Liz, taking on a scathing look that did her no favors, scoffed as if Luke was out burning barns or stealing horses, after Beth declined to comment.

Beth hid a smile, focusing on darning Matthew's socks, but at last took on a thoughtful look. "Does sound a *little* odd. Mayhap this *Mae* is just—a change from the usual hands. Dad gets to show off a bit." She chuckled, biting off the thread. "Better to look at than Old Tom, I'd wager. My father *is* still a man, Liz. I wouldn't concern myself—"

She was interrupted by Liz stabbing her finger on the table. "All *day*?"

Beth took on a superior look but not fooling Liz. "I trust Pa, even if you don't. 'Sides, I told you, he and I have no secrets."

"Well, I can see I am of no use here." Liz bustled about as if to leave. "My word is mocked, my fears doubted."

Matthew, closely watching the plate, wandered in to snatch the last cookie before offering, "Old Luke's just havin' a bit of—"

"—nothing!" Beth snapped. "A bit of *nothing,* Matt!"

"I reckon, if you say so, Bethy, but Luke's a growed man and can do what he likes, seems to me. Every man likes a bit a sugar in his coffee, time to time." His broad wink at his wife was killed in infancy.

"However, it isn't up to you, is it!"

"If you say so, Beth, reckon not."

"I should say not!" Liz snapped.

Later, absently tidying up, Beth replaced the sugar shaker and vinegar cruet next to the salt cellar three times. "But if you *should hear* of any—funny business, Matthew, you'd tell me." She shook her head. "No. The whole notion's a fantasy of a woman—with—with *no man* in her life."

Matthew cast a wistful glance at his wife.

Beth, smug in her place, threw Matthew a vague fond look that brightened his morning some. "Any more of them oatmeal cookies, Bethy?" he asked with forlorn hope, but his wife, scowling out the window, ignored him.

****

Luke sat on the porch, staring at the stable, his thoughts a quagmire.

He was getting royally drunk.

Correction. He was *stinking* drunk.

Liz, thankfully, was asleep after washing him with sour suspicions all evening. He wanted to tell the hands. Tell Liz. Tell the whole cotton-picking world how he felt. Alive! Happy with the world!

He took another pull from the flask of Old Overholt, coming up empty.

Reaching for the new bottle, he cracked the seal and thought rosy dreams of doing just that. Rouse the damned bunkhouse. Shout it from the rooftops. Wake

144

that sourpuss Liz. *Can't forget Bethy*, he thought woozily.

Luke took another pull and, after a hitch or two, ambled to the stable, mumbling, "Have to make my 'tentions known." As he shambled across, he didn't notice another figure enjoying the night and keeping watch.

Mae met him in her nighty, halfway past the first corral. "Luke," she whispered, "Shush! What are you doing?"

'Li'l Mae," he slurred. He lifted her, crooked her up in his arms, telling her over and over, "Have feelin's for you, little Mae, gonna tell a whole world…"

Mae gently touched Luke's face, flickering fingers over his mouth like butterfly wings, nudging his forehead with hers. Her small cool hands smoothed his jawline as she whispered, "It's all right, Mr. Luke. Go sleep."

She slid down, boneless, from his arms as he kept mumbling about '*a whole world*,' and gently took his hand, leading him back to the porch and the rocker. There she stood behind him and rubbed his head. In a moment she pumped cold water and dampened his bandana, placing it on his neck, shushing, "Shh-shhh. It's all right."

"Sorry, Mae. S'sorry," he slurred. "What must …you…?" His eyes closed, and still muttering, Luke dozed off.

Mae pressed her cheek against his forehead before scampering back to her bed.

She shinnied up the wood ladder to her refuge. Poking through the square opening, she didn't see two booted feet carelessly propped on her cot from where the figure was sprawled on her only chair. A plume of blue smoke escaped Raoul's perfect lips. "Go down or come up, *chiquita*," he drawled in his soft accented voice. "Saw the old fool was drunker than *el diablo*." Raoul sucked in deep before blasting more smoke through his nose.

Mae simmered. She scrambled on up with her fists balled. She felt threatened. This was her place, her freedom. "This is mine! Get down before Luke sees you!" Mae felt a sudden panic rise up like a gale wind from nowhere taking her breath.

Raoul smiled lazily and stretched, but there was a dangerous flick in his dark eye, like a spark off a flint. Raoul uncoiled with feline grace. In an oily glide, he gripped her waist, staring down with his dark eyes. But in place of sparks, they held the deadness of polished slate. He was looking inward, not at her, *hungry* for her admiration.

She scratched the back of his hand. She felt skin beneath her nails. With eyes like pinwheels flashing and burning, Raoul thrust his bleeding hand to his mouth and slammed her to him.

Mae twisted her head. He tried to reach her mouth but Mae stiffened her body into ungraceful, unwelcoming lines. "Mr. Farnsworth would not like you being here!" He released her like a hot poker, sneering, "Old as my *abuelo*. A toothless *viejo*. A *cabron*."

"And you are all gun and no bullets."

He grabbed her nape. "You will be sorry you say that, *chiquita*. I will show you *bullets*." He grabbed his crotch, watching her. "Many have made that mistake," he purred. "They think because I am…" Raoul made a languid gesture encompassing his whole being—his face and body. "Because I am *muy guapo,* they suppose I am weak as a *woman.*"

Stunned by Raoul's vanity, Mae had no rejoinder. His ugliness shone through his skin like sweat.

"Find someone who loves you as much as you love yourself." Mae pushed him hard.

Caught off balance, Raoul stumbled into the wall. Righting himself, he walked with stiff pride to the trapdoor. "I can get any woman I want," was his parting shot.

****

Mae cuddled the ragged-eared barn tom, king of felines for a mile around. "Oh, *Cat*," she muffled into brindled fur. "What am I to do? I dare not tell Luke. Sometimes, Luke is like he is gone from me. Sometimes, he thinks sad thoughts."

She kissed the cat's head.

"Told me once, it's 'cause he's closer to the Pearly Gates and it weighs on him some."

Yowling, Cat ducked from her head-kisses. She hugged the cat tighter. "And not to mind none when he was scratchy and short-tempered. And then, like he was funnin' me, said I was at the very bottom of the ladder to the Pearly Gates and didn't need to think on such things."

Cat commented with a snarl.

"I ken, Cat. I don't care neither." Cat scratched a paw out, catching her knuckle. "Only when he wraps those big strong arms around me, I feel safe. I never want to leave."

Cat hissed in disgust.

"Wish't he kenned. Wish't he kenned how I'm achin' like a broke arm, only it be my heart."

Cat struggled and bit Mae's chin.

Reluctant, Mae watched Cat, muttering in repugnance, hightail it off. Her tears had got his head all wet.

****

Mae heard his determined stride.

After a restive night, Luke had managed to climb the stairs and sprawl face down on his bed, with moonlight slicing his quilt to ribbons. Now, with a head like thunder booming in his skull, Luke strode with determination. His head, soul and body warred against visions of Nate and his *"chickadees." Get this over. Last night was the last night. Never again.*

However, that wasn't to happen.

Luke stepped from sunlight to the warm, redolent, dusky stable. A whirlwind hurtled toward him, a small figure that came sailing, leaping up and wrapping legs about his midriff, arms tight about his neck. Mae reared back, smiling with merry laughing eyes, and his headache vanished like frost on a windowpane.

Luke felt touched by an angel. This was Mae's way of showing he had not made a damned fool of himself last night.

Before he could speak his good intentions, Mae, near strangling him with a hug, planted a deep kiss on Luke's jaw. Luke felt his heart thud and knees weaken. Laughing from a wellspring of unbidden joy, he managed to release himself, sending straw flying and barn cats fleeing as he whirled Mae about the floor. Slowing, Luke had presence of mind to check the doors for onlookers. Finding none, he bussed Mae tenderly and lingeringly.

Mae dropped her head back, then gave a soft sigh, nuzzled her cheek against his and, sliding from his grasp, darted a smile as she raced off for her chores, calling, "Promised me another ride, Mr. Luke."

Chapter Fourteen: Waterfall

The last day of the warm Indian summer. If washed with watercolors, the days would be indigo blues, Indian turquoise, scarlets, and golds. A chinook wind ushered it in. Easterlies of cold wet breeze, presaging snow, ended it, but for now Luke and Mae, sitting saddled at the edge of a small bluff, gazed pleasurably at the splendorous scene.

Below, a waterfall spilled over the lip of a red stone bluff, cascading into a pool shaded green by overhanging peach tree willows, edged with sun-heated boulders, rushes, cattails, and purple loosestrife. An irregular black hole centered it.

"There 'tiz." Luke nodded.

Mae gave a deep sigh that lifted her small breasts. "Purely would like to go in there sometime." Dew pearled her forehead and trickled between those bosoms.

Luke looked to the distance. *Damn, I feel eighteen again.* And that, he reflected, was how long since he'd enjoyed the pond's cool green waters. Had the devil just whispered in his ear? *'Why not? No harm.'* Or was it him?

"Reckon wouldn't hurt," Luke spoke without kenning. *'Oh, no?'* his devil whispered. "Just strip to our all-togethers, 'hind those rocks over there, or…" He motioned to a fringe of ragged bushes.

Mae looked at him squarely. "I reckon that would be

mighty fine."

Wordlessly, they let their mounts mosey down the gentle rise and splash across a stream and on to the pool. Luke hobbled the horses to graze on loosestrife.

Neither noted that atop another small hillock, to the west, overlooking the pool and falls, a rider perched atop a spavined mule. His long legs dangled and an aspect of dismay and prurient interest was on his thin whiskered face, beneath a squashed straw hat. He scratched his head and hopped from the mule's back and sat cross-legged, shielded by a small hackberry tree, to await and see what he could see. Might be some profit in it.

****

The green-black water was as inviting as Luke recalled. With sweat trickling his spine, Luke couldn't wait to get into that cool glassy surface reflecting the sun in one part, yet darkest emerald under the shade of the peachleaf willow.

"You—on over to those boulders. I'll nip behind that bearberry bush and even the preacher couldn't fault us."

Liz maybe.

Mae grinned. "Nor Miss Liz, I 'spect."

Luke flashed the cleft in his jaw. Slipping into the clump of bearberry shrubs, six feet and bushy, he stripped to his cotton-underdrawers-and-vest combination, then dove in and rose, gasping from the cold, before Mae emerged in her shimmy and the long underdrawers Liz made her wear.

Luke looked up at a splash, and there was Mae, face full of delight, hair streaming behind in a black fan, doing a kind of endearing little dog paddle. He was surprised she could swim at all.

Luke recalled the shallows. Wasn't till you got to the black hole in the middle that the pond became so deep you either swam or drowned in untold feet of water. "Tried to dive to the bottom onct—never got there," Luke yelled half in warning. Then, taking long powerful strokes, with his brown muscled arms flashing in the sun and sending sprays of diamonds, he circled the pond. They didn't come near each other, but it was enough.

For a while.

Luke ducked under the crystal green surface and sprang up, tossing back silver-streaked hair, opening his eyes to see Mae, laughing in the midst of the waterfall, palms up, seeming unearthly, with crystal water splashing small arched rainbows in the sun and coursing down her body like quicksilver.

Her shimmy might as well be invisible, perfectly slamping her slim body, clearly revealing breasts with pale pink centers, the black V dividing her thighs. Mae looked like some sort of sprite, and Luke, transfixed, said it in his mind, though he wasn't quite sure what a sprite would look like. Black ribbons of hair, sluicing more water to the pond below, rippled across the rosy tips of those small firm breasts. If he ever thought of her as a girl, all thoughts vanished by the vision of this woman in miniature.

Mae, entranced by the crystalline water near drowning her, sputtered with giddy delight, lifting hands up to catch it, and didn't notice Luke's enchantment. Finally, Luke shook himself free of the spell.

"Best come out!" He cupped his hands. "You will catch lung fever or consumption."

Well, that dampened a perfect day like an old dishrag. 'Why not join her, "old man"?' his devil hissed.

Why the hell not?

Luke clambered over sun-warmed boulders with the agility of a twenty-year-old and plunged into the waterfall. Mae pressed her small body to his as if yearning to be one with him—*in* him.

Across the way, the lone figure moved away from the hackberry tree to see better. In a trice, the two figures had vanished behind the wall of water.

With the thundering splash in their ears and light moving like quicksilver across cave walls, the ripple-plunge of the falls became a wavering curtain of water separating them from the world.

Mae's embrace was as natural as the sun rising in the east. Luke groaned deep and his last inhibitions sluiced away with diamond-crystal spray throwing coronas of color in the mist.

Slamped together breast to chest, loin to loin, sealing warmth between their bodies, with the chill cascade beating down all around them, feeling her small pubic bone, wondering if Mae felt his burgeoning attention too, for once he did not care.

Luke stroked her deluge-slicked body, satiny skin sliding beneath his fingers. Water smoothed her hair back like a mythical mermaid; her whimsical face looked up to his, droplets glistening from black lashes, white throat arched, plump coral lips wet…inviting.

Luke dropped his head and savored her cool mouth, cupping the silky-smooth mounds of breast, sensing the beating throb of her heart. Mae's breath quickened; a long low moan issued from her mouth. She clutched his head, gripping his hair in a ferocious tug, tenaciously forcing his head down. Finally raising his head, Luke once again pressed his lips to hers as a starving man.

Welding her body to him, any last inhibition sluiced away with the diamond-clear water rushing down. Luke backed her into the small indentation in the rock, warm from the sun shining through behind the thundering falls…not a cave, precisely, but a hollow rounded arch like a nave, carpeted thickly with pine needles and damp leaves forming a soft springy bed, warm and dry and woods-scented.

Mae and Luke fell on their knees to the spongy fragrant earthen mattress, Mae shredding his thin union suit till it fell in tatters, he ripping her wet shimmy to explore her body with his large brawny hands, murmuring inchoate words mingled with lust; she whispering, urging, sighing, *"Luke…"* interrupted by Luke's long earth-shattering grinding kisses until gasping, staring blindly at each other in feverish longing.

Age made no difference. Luke was hard and strapping as any man half his age, and she, ready to be a woman. Luke's face—slitted eyes, silvery tangled locks—seemed wolfish; his huge body dwarfed her fragile slenderness. Mae met his strength with her own, until she dropped her head back, lips bruised and plump, small breasts swollen with desire, her thighs and belly pressed to his hard attentions. Mae fell back, opening her knees, holding her arms over her head, offering herself as if wise…or simply a Daughter of Eve.

Luke covered her without volition; hard and heated as an iron rod on an anvil, he slid hot, heavy and deep, with Mae groaning, moaning, twisting, wriggling with awakening need, arching, pressing him deeper still until, after an endless blissful thrusting, came an explosion of joy, followed quickly, both so avaricious for it, by more feverish passion long denied. They could not stop wanting each other. However, finally, each sank back, stunned into sweet exhaustion, cool moisture coating their bodies, panting and joyous and drained, murmuring loving nothings until he felt Mae stirring again and reaching, stroking gently with a light feathery touch, and he burgeoned once more…laughing joyously as he rolled her on top of his loins so he could gaze upon her lovely face as she slowly, *agonizingly slowly*, made love to him.

"Hush, little one," he murmured later as they lay side by side enjoying the throbbing of their bodies as heated blood slowed to a pulsing murmur. "We have this time. We—" he hesitated—"might again." Would there be?

Mae interrupted his musing. "But how, where?" Mae demanded, pinning his biceps with her small hands. Luke laughed, uproariously happy. She was his and he was hers, if only for this moment in time, yet already sensing an ache, a black shadow stealing over his heart, shrouding the future in darkness.

Winter was coming. They could not return to this magical place.

Still, they lingered, touching, murmuring gentle kisses until the sun slanted scarlet through the torrential cascade. Luke and Mae watched the torrent turning into fire, the cave walls flickering coral flame.

You must wed me. No other will do, Luke thought as he gazed through the moving curtain of fire.

Mae nestled against Luke's broad, battle-scarred chest, her drying curls tickling his chin and slender arms encircling him as far as she could reach, as they watched the waterfall turn more sanguine, sparkling the cave and their bodies with vermillion spangles, signaling time to leave.

She shivered. Soon a real fallout of the warm Indian summer would descend on their earthy secret. "Where can we go?" Mae whispered to his chest. Luke didn't answer. She couldn't ken what was churning through his mind. How could she? His body, heart and head warred to the death. How could something so wrong be so right? Perhaps she was an old soul and he an idiot. How could they live on the same earth and he not want more?

"Luke?" The question hovered as she stroked his chest's silky silver curls, lifting her face to be kissed. He complied. "Luke? What if…? What if—I should fall with—with a young-un?"

Luke froze.

He realized Mae was watching intently as if to read his thoughts.

"Don't be a child!" he snapped. Damn him to hell. And well she could, Luke reflected, if this kept on. *Lord!* Never entered his mind.

"It won't happen," he grated out. He thought back to Katie and what he had learned from her. He swallowed the cry in his voice, making it deep and commanding. "Of course, I would take care of you." I'd move that mountain two miles to the right so you wouldn't have to walk around it—lasso the moon and give it to you as a play ball.

Luke held her tightly, bussing the top of her head. "I didn't mean it, if I sound gruff at times. I am like an old thorn bush, full of stickers."

He kissed her fingers with sadness. "You need a young man to have babies. You will meet…" He swallowed hard, unable to finish. How could he tell her she would burnish his dreams, flavor his food, flame an old man's memories with life and joy?

Love her down to her footprints in the dust, and then collect the dust as a holy relic.

I feel winter in my bones. It comes fast. This is the last day of summer. Perhaps of my summer too. He laughed bitterly. Meeting in the barn? Making excuses to Liz? Wouldn't take long for Mae's reputation to be ground to dust, while wranglers gnawed like dogs do bones and looked at Mae as easy prey. Pestering her. Or worse.

To hell with Liz and public opinion. Luke kenned he wanted to marry Mae, make her his true and honest wife.

Mae was still quiet.

"Do you—*care* for me, Mae? Not just…" He didn't finish.

She stuck a finger where Luke assumed she meant her heart.

"My heart hurts when I don't see you. Thumps like a bird with a broke wing when you come near me. I feel like a prickly cactus just *wanting* you."

Luke feared Mae was too young to know what she wanted…but kenned her meaning, deep down.

"Then *that's* love," he said stoutly. Hoped it was true.

Mae sat on Luke's lap all the way back, her cheek on his chest, head tucked under his chin, legs hanging off one side. The horses moseyed side by side, mimicking the attitude of their two riders, as if they also wished they would never have to return. Growing dusk, yet the mounts kenned the way.

"Will…you wed me, Mae?"

Her silence killed him.

"We can't." Mae said simply to the night air. "What would good folk say?"

"Good folk! I will have it no other way. I don't care about your family. Or mine, or Liz. Will you wed me? Be my wife?"

"I—I reckon," she said slowly. "If that's what you want." After another agonizing silence. "We could have banns read right and proper?" She still seemed troubled.

He nodded, spurring his horse. "That's what folks do."

"Guess we are, what they say," she murmured shyly to his chest, "be-*trothed*?" Mae looked up at Luke for answer and away.

He roared to the setting sun.

"That we are."

Betrothed.

Him.

At his age.

He grinned wide.

Why the hell not!

And holding onto Mae, Luke startled Hell-Fire into a wild gallop.

Liz loomed large in his mind.

His jaw stiffened. Reality set in. The horse slowed. "Need the right time, my love." Do Mae no good to spring it on Liz, much as he wanted to shout it from the Baptist church steeple. "Might wait till the Harvest Dance. Announce it to the whole cussed world, at least the world of Laramie, Wyoming."

So Liz can't make a fuss.

The ranch house came to view through the gloaming. Luke felt the first unsettling pang.

From the top of a small knoll, the ranch spread out for miles, with the house a ruddy jewel, surrounded by cottonwoods, oak, sycamore, outbuildings, corral rings, and in the midst the slate roof gleaming like pewter under the moon. His ranch was so large he thought he could see the earth's curve before it gave out.

He considered. "You'll not be staying in the barn anymore. You'll be—by God!—be in the house, where it's fittin'."

"No. Mr. Luke…I mean—*Luke.*" The word was soft with tenderness. "It would never be—and you right there and all." Her words stumbled on. "I mean, I'd be a needin' you and…and *wantin'* you, and we'd be makin' eyes, and Miss Liz, she's— I'd not be mockin' her, or makin' her feel—feel…"

"Discomfited?" Luke, kenning she was correct, gazed at Mae with affection. He'd not hurt his sister, so loyal over the years and during Katherine's long illness. Liz's selflessness running the house and, truth be told, the hands too when he wasn't around, was not to be disparaged.

Not for the first time, he wisht Liz had put herself forward a tad more at hoedowns and church socials in place of sitting primly, foreboding, behind the refreshments tables, or along the wall chatting church affairs with the bespectacled, squint-eyed Baptist circuit preacher and his wife. Even *he* was wed.

He smiled, wistful. *I'll buy her the finest gowns. The best horse and buggy money can buy. Fix up the house any way she likes. Take her to Chicago on the train, show her the world, and the world her, maybe even Venice. Always hankered seeing those canals and the town where the volcano covered it all up in ancient times.* With these notions sailing around him like bright stars, Luke felt he was doing right, and all would be well.

With Liz on her own ranch, they could be neighbors

of the best sort. That day had not come. Nor would he push Liz off to Beth. Luke wasn't sure deep in his soul whether Mae was up to running a ranch from the git-go, or that Beth would accept two women ruling the roost, any more than Liz. Still, something had to be sorted.

Be damned if he'd sneak off to the barn.

Well, not much.

The notion of Mae snug in her sanctuary, wrapped in the golden glow of lantern light, and her slender white body stretched on the colorful crazy-patch quilt and arms reaching for him, caused a stirring in his nether regions and a hardening pressing like an iron rod against his jeans buttons.

I'll announce plans, by God. Marry and let the devil take the hindmost. I'll shout it from the weathervane. Meaning the frozen-in-place metal horse perpetually galloping north atop the widow's walk Liz once insisted be attached so she could watch Luke returning from cattle runs.

****

Branding time.

A hard wrench from Mae. Days filled with dust, burnt flesh, sweat, scorching sun, when the weather played her tricks, and bellowing kine. The ride on the prairie with Mae seemed a flight of fancy after a week at the Cheyenne cattle auction, then long days and nights turned frigid on the range with his wranglers. Luke wearily tossed his hat on the pegs by the door after settling his rough range mount and looking longingly up at Mae's quarters—all quiet and peaceful. He wished he could talk her into coming inside.

He wasn't even certain sure it wasn't all a blissful dream, their time together. Tomorrow would be soon enough. Still checking the stable to see if any light showed, he made his way upstairs, hallooing as he went.

At her bedroom door, he watched Liz a moment with her mouth stuck with pins industriously fitting a swath of purple muslin with yellow daisies to her canvas dress form. He began to go on to his suite of bedroom, dressing room, and sitting room at the end of the hall, when he frowned. He walked back and lounged on the door frame.

"Weren't you sewing a dress of some sort for Mae?" He gestured with doubt shading his voice. "That it?" The dressmaker's form was twice the size of Mae.

"Oh!" Liz plucked pins from her mouth to hide her flustered look. "Imagined you mighta forgot all about *that*."

Luke threw her a dangerous look. "We spoke on that subject."

Liz stopped pinning and turned to face the music on her own terms. "It's not quite—well, it *is* finished—Beth's making it, you know. I have *nothing* to do with it. Much. I don't ken how you think I can get my own chores…"

"Un-hunh. Where is it?"

Liz shrugged loftily and didn't look at him. "Imagine it's still at Beth's."

Luke seemed hesitant, but it had been a long haul these last weeks before winter set in for good. He felt grimy and worn to the bone. "Well, I'm to bed. Let me know when it's finished."

"There's buttermilk, headcheese, and a pan of cornbread if you're hungry." Liz spoke with the meekness of a contrite nun before the Pope. Luke studied her strangely but saw nothing to put his finger on.

"Right, thanks, Liz, just the ticket—any apple pie?" He found he was famished and forgot all about a dress before he tumbled bone-weary to his bed.

Chapter Fifteen: Mae's Marauders

Before daybreak, Luke strode into the kitchen, tucking in his gray flannel shirt, thoughts fixed on Mae's dear face, and maybe that had something to do with the gray shirt, even with the resolve *never* to go riding alone with her again until it was right with the Lord, and Liz. He grinned crookedly.

Till next time. Determined, he'd have the matter before the family as soon as he could get them all together in one bunch.

Wistfulness softened Luke's face as if a mountainside greened with spring flowers. By God, she was going to eat at their table and sleep where she pleased. With him, he thought with a wry expression, if that would not rain Liz's rocks of disapproval on his head.

He poured his first mug of witch's brew from the huge enamel pot, bits of eggshell still floating in it, for Liz still opined—despite his picking shell from his teeth—that egg strengthened the grounds, and maybe it did. Certainly it was black as the pre-dawn outside…

He was instantly on alert, spilling scalding coffee on his fist at the sound of pounding feet tumbling down the stairs and harsh breathing, followed by a blur of skirts and thudding boots rushing past him into the kitchen.

Lizzie! What the Sam Hill?

There was his sister, usually just in and fiddling with

her hair now askew, grim-faced and leaping to the mantel, her skirt gripped in one white-knuckled hand and the other raised high, clawing desperately for the shotgun, hollering, "*Luke! Luke!*" as she yanked it off the wall, breaking a small figurine in the effort. For Liz not to grieve over her grandmother's china shepherdess from England alarmed Luke more than anything.

She shot him a wild glance. "*There* you are!" As if she'd been calling him for a week of Sundays.

"Liz, dammit," Luke cursed and dashed the mug.

"Look there! Open your dad-blasted eyes!"

Liz jabbed the gun barrel toward the window as if to shoot through it. Luke swatted the barrel aside, drawing his Colt in an oiled movement and nudging her off, like moving a solid wall—Liz always was the stubborn one—and peered out at what she saw.

"What the Billy-blue-blazes…?"

For once Liz didn't reprimand him.

A horde at least thirty strong forged through ground mist that reached to their knees. Pitchforks, shotgun barrels, and other sharp or rusting objects jutted above the shambling mob. It seemed the throng had no feet, floating like demonic angels, but even at that distance they were no angels. Now, Luke spied the tines of more than a few pitchforks and the dull gleam of at least one axe head piercing the rolling fog.

The leader, if that was what the gaunt man in the squashed hat at the head was, seemed to be veering to the stable. Taking a bead through the cracked kitchen door, Luke's first thought was that they aimed to steal horses, or worse.

And Mae was in there.

"Liz, get back."

"Mae, stay put," he breathed.

But then the man plodded past, followed by the rest—almost at the farthest corral now. Luke cursed under his breath when Liz didn't budge, breathing easier when he spied a few rags of skirts dragging the weeds. Closer, they looked a tattered throng, all right. Outlaws, by the look of it. Even the females. Desperate range wolves preying on ranchers, or civil war renegades and camp followers, he surmised. Were any of the hands up?

He drew a bead on the leader, yet held his fire as the ragtag mob entered and exited the curling fog between the smoke house and corral like silent malevolent spirits, whole one instant, fading to gauze the next.

"Deserters?" Liz barked, poking the old shotgun beside him again.

"Ease off, Liz. Don't ken yet."

Liz seemed uncomfortably ready for a dust-up. Luke tried to squint through the mist before he made a move he might regret down at the newly elected sheriff's hoosegow, now they were a state. He walked a fence rail, here. Had womenfolk to protect, though Liz didn't seem to need it, and he hoped the mist would part like curtains so he could get a good gander. Not the first skirmish he, the boys, and Liz fought off. Where were the dang hands? Not even a curl of smoke from the bunkhouse. Felt like he cowered, which didn't sit well. Luke nudged the door a crack.

In pre-dawn chill, the *shuffle-scuff* of boots and bare feet plopping in the dust grew louder, and he detected grumbles and cursing as one tripped over something hard, probably the abandoned anvil by the trough.

Then the leader appeared from the shroud of white. Luke stepped out, legs spread, well-oiled 1873 Colt single-action army revolver held loose across his chest, Liz's shotgun barrel poking too close to his side.

"Get back, dammit, Liz!"

"Not in this lifetime, Lucian!"

He sighed deep.

The scarecrow figure carried a dirt-clotted pitchfork, no less lethal than a good carbine. Still hard to tell how many. Stragglers yet approached and the throng seemed to spread out. Thirty, even more.

Luke cocked his revolver and tightened his grip. As if in defiance, the mob emerged from the barn's shadow into the pale light of dawn. Another male, plump and pale under a grimy face, melted up beside the first man, brandishing a branch like a club. A pickax thrust through the skirling fog, closely followed by a short woman in a filthy Mother Hubbard manning a rusty hoe. As weak sun melted the fog, Luke had the oddest feeling to laugh.

Yet they were menacing, no matter how curious the weaponry.

A youth pushed the short female aside as if to rush Luke, held back by her gnarled grip. The ground fog vanished as the sun's first rays dissolved it like water on sugar.

Maybe hold them off till his wranglers woke to the fact they were invaded. He should let off a shot and rouse them, but that might begin another civil war. Nothing civil about this tribe.

Luke stepped to the edge of the porch with the Colt across his chest, wincing at the sight of the rusting axe and recalling one still stuck in the kindling stump, available to any who weren't half blind. Luke demanded, "Who's your head honcho?"

"S'pose you think it's you!" one wiseacre yelled

from the middle of the crowd.

"Liz!" Luke shoved her aside as she wedged out. "Get upstairs. Lock yourself in." Fears flew again to Mae in the barn, vulnerable, helpless save for a pitchfork or horseshoe mallet. She should have her own pistol out there.

Liz was crowding. "In a pig's eye! Staying right here. Not gonna invade *my* house…"

"Nobody said invade," he grunted from her side, hoping that was God's truth. But what the hell were they up to? The ragtag end of the ghostly mob nearing the second nearest corral shuffled jaggedly left of the porch. A boy, gaunt and starved, no older than ten by the looks of him, emerged behind an equally scrawny female. The boy resembled a feral animal but hefted a stone.

Handled worse odds, Luke told himself, but he wouldn't mind if some of the boys poked their fool heads out. Even mourning doves stopped their dreary racket. Then Luke recalled half the hands went to town yesterday to get a load of oats and the newfangled plow, and stayed over, while the other half were off to track down a valuable but amorous stud bull and probably stayed at the next ranch.

Liz silently chucked him his own rifle. He hefted it one-handed but didn't holster the Colt. Legs wide, Luke stood on the three-sided porch, trigger finger on the rifle, gun at his side. "What do you want?" he barked.

Some of the crew had more than one shotgun of their own. One, old and battered, was an ancient converted flintlock from the French and Indian wars, last used by the Confederate Army. Luke wondered, fleetingly, if it would fire without blasting the shooter to Hell and gone.

More figures in skirts waded forward. Wilted

sunbonnets. Straggly buns or hair tied in a string in back, dresses scantily pinned over lean bosoms. Children until now kept in the rear guard… Boys or girls? Couldn't tell, with their duds so characterless and hair raggedly hacked. The men were mostly bearded, hair bowl-cut if it wasn't an oily straggle. Battered hats, straw or crumpled felt, patched overalls, one coonskin cap, shirts hanging, feet in lace-less clodhoppers, those that had 'em.

"Gypsies," Liz muttered.

No, the gypsy wanderers Luke had ever had congress with, they'd had more dignity—more color— and they wouldn't handle a pitchfork on a bet. Maybe he *should* fire and get whatever boys out here. But they weren't boys. Only the cook, Old Tom, and Matt with the broke leg. Have to make do.

Luke slit his eyes into ice splinters and stared the mob down. They stumblingly halted five feet from the porch, oddly silent. That was his clue. *None yearning to be first.* "Who's your speaker, if you have one? What part do you hail from?" *'Sides a dung heap.*

"Now, now." The ragged squint-eyed man, lean like a half-starved feral dog, placated, patting the air as if to quell a riot. He also had one hand on the barrel of an old Starr Army revolver Luke spied, with a broke wood grip, stuck in his belt. "Don't git yer dander up none. Where's yer neighborly Christian spirit not to welcome friendly folk that are *almost* kin?"

His slyness was the slide of a snake's belly through grass. Brown teeth grinned an odd kind of truth. A certainty.

"Liz's my kin." Unless Pa'd held out on him. And Beth, of course. He snorted contempt. "My *neighbors.*

That why you all are totin' weapons?"

"Yes, sir! You got that right. We air yer neighbors."

The man stepped forward eagerly, halted when the nose of Luke's gun met his own, and sullenly backed away. "We don't want no trouble, mister, but yew cain't be too careful in these troubled times. Just want ta palaver some."

He shook his head mournfully and flashed another brown ingratiating grin, jabbing his finger toward Luke's chest, his manner changing like a flash storm. "But yew got somethin' of our'n, don't b'long to yew! And we didn't rightly ken how *kindly* our presence might be looked upon."

He took a half-step sideways. The rest shifted with him. Luke realized they'd soon surrounded the porch.

"You mean squatters," Luke interrupted, backing to take them all in. "In that young couple's ranch who lit out a few months ago." Luke intuited they'd never make a go of it. Maybe better the greenhorns had scarpered before they were under Wyoming dirt, yet he loathed that these specimens before him were profiting from their lost labor.

Luke dragged his mind back.

The man took another sly step, chin out. "Hit's our'n now. We lay claim to it."

"Far as I recollect, so does the Wells Fargo bank."

"Let 'em try!" He sniggered back at the mob, and spat a loop of tobacco that landed on Liz's scrubbed porch and waved his old revolver. "This is *our* law."

It was all Luke could do to nudge Liz's shotgun down.

The fleshy, loose-mouthed, jowly pale-haired man thrust past the leader again. Wobbly rolls of fat under his clothes rose in waves when he neared, along with an unwashed stench. Mean red-veined piggish eyes glinted under yellow lashes, making him even more swine-like. The gut on him told Luke he wasn't starving, and he could still smell him like old cheese from where he stood.

"Stop jumpin' around like yew got the backyard trots, Japeth, and let me take keer of grampa, here," yellow-hair half whined.

"I have nothing of yours, or would, so get on with you. I have no handouts."

The leader back-handed yellow-hair, setting his cheeks wobbling. "I'm still boss here!" He stepped to the porch, glaring coldly at Luke from under his raggedy brim. *Eyes of a ghost, colorless, dead.* "Don't wanna *hand*-out Mr. High-an'-Mighty! Ain't askin' fer none. Yew have somethin' valuable of our'n and we want it back. Either give it to us or we'll burn this ranch to the ground and drag her scrawny ass out by force."

Her. Mae?

Mutters of assent permeated the chill like rancid fat. Yellow Hair—actually not yellow, more like pale grass found under a rock, sickly and limp—glared sullen and tried to shoulder past Japeth.

"Not now, Zebulon! I'm palaverin'."

So Yellow Hair was Zebulon. Then, the mob shifted slightly. Luke spied a boy holding a firebrand and a lit lantern… *A holocaust a spark away.* And those that had them rattled pitchforks, battered hoes, ax handles and any other weapons, doubtless found on the farm, plus hefty tree limbs, moving two or three shuffles closer and more ominous, slyly surrounding the porch now.

"Now whar is she? Whar's our little Pearly Mae?"

Luke sneered at the manufactured sob, but he felt an ice-ax thrust through his chest. The stars in heaven shifted, if this be her kin.

"I harbor no one. Now git on off my ranch."

Luke gave them his back and strode to the door, detecting a shotgun cocked before a spray of buckshot peppered floorboards by his boots. Liz grunted, more of a yelp. *Don't fire, Liz.* He froze, not turning. They wouldn't shoot him in the back, would they? Again, he thought of the hands, acutely aware most were absent, except for Old Tom, maybe.

"We're not talkin' about *har*-borin'."

Sniggers from the group. Hungry feral looks from females as they surveyed Luke's robust virile frame, like they wouldn't mind "harboring" him.

Luke slowly turned.

"Hear tell, t'ween you, me and the fence post, ya'll were out on the range together. Sammy, here, he *seen* yew!" Chummily, one man to another, after throwing his arm about the shoulders of a sickly-looking slope-shouldered boy, the so-called leader announced, "Yew two, yew an' our Pearly Mae, was *real* close, out on the prairie, Sammy here sez. Iffen yew ken what we *mean*."

Luke was recipient of a brown-toothed leer and detected Liz's grunt of surprise.

"We wanna know what yer 'tentions are, now ye've done ruint our innocent young sister, niece, and datter." His complacent look was righteous as a traveling preacher.

"I'm through here. So are you. Nothin' happened. Get on out." Luke cast a disparaging glance he hoped showed confidence and turned once again for the house. Growls, as if from animals, heated the air.

Luke's neck prickled. He felt the shot between his shoulder blades.

It was a rock pelted.

He swiveled, striving not to show panic, and faced a scowling female, ageless though he guessed between twenty-five and fifty, gray hair like dirty unraveled yarn, shaking her fist and shouting with spittle spraying, "'At's right! I miss my darlin' datter. Ye've ruint her! Cain't do all the work ourselves, mister, when she's givin' it to *yew* fer free, and what *else* is she giving yew fer *free*? My boy *seen* you!"

She nodded back at the mob in virtuous affirmation. Fired by her speech, they rushed the porch, yelling garbled cries Luke only got part of. But he didn't miss the language of brandished weapons.

Luke "saw red."

One-handed, he smashed an old weatherbeaten rocker, more fixture than useful, grabbing the rocker arm with a splintered leg, wicked end still attached, and leaped off the porch, bowling into the crowd, swinging one-handed and brandishing his shotgun with his itchy finger on the worn trigger. "Hightail it outta here or some of you gets bunged up real bad. Which one a you first?" He swung the rocker leg like a scythe and jabbed the rifle barrel into a gut, a shoulder, a chest before anyone grabbed it.

The mob encircled him, though a few seemed hesitant, darting glances at their leader. The smell was overpowering. A mucky stable at high noon. The women, dragging kids, melted off, yet it wouldn't take long before a tinder lit a powder keg. Wasn't the wisest move he ever made, but Liz, bless her, sighted her shotgun at the crowd.

"That gal has a right to decide where she wants to be," she bellowed.

Luke started at that.

"'At right?" piggy man whined. "Seems to me Pearly Mae's a young'un. An' not iffen we're handfasted. Pract'ly. There be laws in this here territory. Er what I hear, this is a brand-new spankin' state! We'll dog sheriff on yew. We'll yank yew down offen that high horse. Everybody's gonna know what *yew* are. Yew and that bitch up yonder!"

Liz howled.

"Liz," Luke warned. Luke kenned useless threats. Little gals young as thirteen out here were wed, and bedded, not that he approved by a long shot. Yet this *was* a new state. Could there be laws? Either way, he already kenned Mae was too young for the likes of him, or—he shuddered—this lout.

'Mae said she was seventeen,' his devil whispered.

No, she didn't.

Zebulon snarled, looking more a swine with two teeth poking into his top lip. "We 'uz to be wedded and bedded and me on my way to bein' a pappy. Men in our fambly don't take all year to put a bun in the oven," he smirked in a way that made Luke yearn to bash those yellowed tusks back in his mouth.

"I'll take a blood price offen yew. She was ta be *mine* first!" He made a rude gesture showing what he meant.

Luke flung around to take in all of them. *Too many? Yes, dammit.* Even with Liz backing him. Now he wished she wouldn't take his orders so sincerely. *Fire, Liz, dammit. In the air.* Not that he cared if she shot off a few ears.

173

The leader's sneer took on a meaner cast. He folded arms over his concave belly. "I'm certain sure there be *law*s about who owns *who*, didn't we jest have a war over *slavery*? Better drag that little bitch on out."

"Mae's not a slave, you lying varmints!" came from behind Luke. Liz never *would* take the back seat in the buggy. She stood, rifle cocked and ready, stock wedged in her shoulder, drawing a bead. "We treat her like a daughter…" *News to me.* "And treat her better'n you lot ever did! Get on out of here you bunch of lazy diseased *pole*cats."

Oh, Liz!

Luke shifted his attention from a sudden motion. Mae in the tall loft opening. Just her pale face and hands in the dark oblong. *Stay there, Mae!*

She vanished.

Liz waved her shotgun as if deciding who to plug first. Some shrank like starving dogs, while most simply grinned evilly, shook their oddments of weapons and inched in a dedicated pincer movement. Two hopped onto the porch, flanking Liz and Luke. More thumped on boards around the unseen curve of veranda. Luke wasn't *in* the war between the states, but he kenned the maneuvers.

"Won't matter a tinker's damn who's right or wrong, iffen your head's blown clean off." Japeth set his jaw, looking about for admiration, and stuck his stubbled chin out. "Prairie's a lonely place. So's woods. Cain't *never* tell what all happens out there."

"Your last warning—Clear out!" Luke had prudently maneuvered back to the porch and shot the Colt in the air.

"What yew seem intent on is killin'," the fat man

whined. He turned to the leader. "Make 'em give 'r to me, Japeth."

Luke saw, from the corner of his eye, the boy with the lantern slither atop the smokehouse, holding the firebrand in one hand and the lantern handle in his mouth as he climbed one-handed. "That goes both ways." Luke hefted the shotgun at the boy but had no stomach for it.

"But there's a sight *more* of us. And we're fambly, not that bunch of misfits yew hire."

Maybe true enough. The leader spat another streak of wet brown spittle to splat beside Liz's boot. That did it.

Liz fired above the man's head, Luke wasn't certain sure she aimed that way, but the shot nipped off his ragged derby and struck another man in the shoulder, while at the same time a female yelped and clapped her ears.

Luke kept beaded on the boy now waving the faggot from the smokehouse roof, hoping desperately anyone cared about him, while Liz ratcheted the shotgun.

Taking on a woebegone look, Japeth ignored the bloodied man. "Wimen are the devil's play toys, sure as shootin'. That one's trouble since the day she was spat out into the world. Don't want no trouble, but we'll give yew some when yew least expect it. That there's a promise." He made a complicated gesture and spat on his hand. "Less 'n' yew all intend on makin' us kinfolk right here 'n' now."

He raised a brow, displaying brown teeth. "Seems a right thang under the state of affairs, now, seein' how Pearly Mae's damaged goods and yer the one who done it."

Luke heard murmurs of approval save from Yellow-

Hair and the wounded man. Japeth grinned, but his eyes, sludgy as axle grease, gave him away—a snake ready to strike.

"Nothing damaged about Mae."

"I done seen you out there!"

The youth with hair like brown string dipped in bacon fat thrust through, not to be denied. "You two! Doing what shunt-a be done in broad daylight, where God kin see ya. You callin' us liars?"

Had he? And what could they see? Didn't matter. Nothing could take away that glorious time. He heard another grunt from Liz. Surprise or condemnation. Was she still at his back? He didn't dare look.

Zebulon, the self-declared betrothed, balled fists pale and large as two plucked chickens, bulling toward Luke, until a man thrust a hoe handle sideways, tripping him.

"Not now Zeb-u-lon! You'll git yer turn!"

Japeth spun back to Luke with a sly grin, conciliation in his tone, whining, "Give us Pearly Mae, or make 'er honest." His squint-eyed gaze took in the large homestead, raking the bunkhouse, stable, paddocks, neat fences, outbuildings and layout. Wiping his lips, he back-handed the still-muttering Zebulon, barking, "Shet yer pie hole, Zeb," and with a crafty look, edged closer to Luke.

Darting another look at the boy on the smokehouse roof, who still cradled a torch and lit lantern, it was all Luke could do to stand his ground against the foul smell emanating from the man's clothes, body, and brown-toothed grin.

Japeth again spat and rested his shotgun. "Upon reflection, wouldn't mind bein' kin. We could all move in." He stretched his arm, encompassing all Luke's spread. "Save us all a lot of hassle. House this big. Or least somewhars close like. Lotta land here fer one person. S'pect you could spare a acre er two fer *kinfolk*."

"But Japeth!"

Japeth elbowed Zeb in the face.

"So, what is it *old* man? Let us take our young gal home to wed with Zeb, here, or do her right yer own self. Got a preacher man right here."

Zebulon darted faster than seemed possible, thrust out his yellow-furzed chin and the filthy clotted pitchfork at Luke's midriff. "I'll take keer of him. Pearly Mae's mine!"

Liz poked her shotgun at Zeb's chest in a standoff. *Bless you, Liz.* Those spikes would take him to perdition. He'd seen festering wounds such a foul thing could bring, leading to excruciating ends.

Zebulon snarled at Japeth, spitting saliva. "We got the preacher here fer a reason, Japeth! And it warn't fer him!"

"Who's leader here, Zebulon?"

Japeth turned with a shit-eating grin at Luke, and held both hands out. "Brother Bob ain't zackly *or-*dained, but he preaches up a right storm of hellfire an' damnation when he's a mind to."

With that, a woman dragged and shoved forward a small man in a greenish black suit, his black string tie hanging down on the front of a grubby homespun shirt, all topped by a flat broad-brimmed hat the worse for wear.

"He brung his Bible and all," she announced.

The "preacher" waved a tattered dog-eared black book. The crowd raised their shotguns, hoes and pitchforks—when suddenly they all swiveled as one, as Mae burst out of the barn like a scalded cat, her cameo face red with shame, fists balled into little white knots. She rounded the lot like a streak of howling fury on her race to the porch, yelling, "Not goin' nowheres with you! This be my *home! My family now*."

She took a stand on the porch before Luke as if shielding him.

"Now, Mae…" A female's wheedling voice, dripping honey, trailed disappointment like a wet gray rag as she neared the porch. "Pearly Mae? There you are, sugar. Don't ya recollect yer ma?" In one bound of long stringy legs, she stretched an equally long arm to snatch Mae fast as a striking snake, dragging her off the porch with a look of triumph at Luke and clutching Mae to her flat drooping bosom. The fat man, Zebulon, reached over the men surrounding him and tried to snatch Mae.

"Get off!" the ma hissed. "Might be worth money!"

Immediately the mob collected around the two. If Luke, watching Mae fiercely fighting that bony embrace, was angry with her for revealing herself, it would be now, but his heart ached at her doomed expression as she was swallowed in a slowly shuffling backwards knot.

Watching Mae vanish in the mob; Japeth grinned— in spite, this time. Zebulon argued something, and kept battering at the woman holding Mae. The fake preacher looked on like he wished he were anywhere but there.

Shoving the Colt into his belt, Luke swallowed his rage before he started another civil war and Mae would be gone for good. "Hey! Set and jaw a bit…" He made his voice jocular and hollered friendly-like. "Let's see what we can bargain for."

Luke showily rubbed thumb and forefinger. Maybe

settle with a bribe, even if it took cold hard cash. Moreover, it looked like that was partly why they came, and he saw no end to it.

Too late.

A female voice at the back of the pack, yelled, "Hunh, Pearly Mae! He ain't so much! Iffen yew set yer cap fer that old geezer..." The mercurial mob guffawed. "Ain't that right! Got us a *old* gander funnin' a young gal, scarce outta her cradle."

Luke felt a stone drop in his belly. He lost sight of Mae as she was still trying to struggle free before disappearing in the sea of rags, the throng shuffling back seemingly as one—even now past the third corral.

"*Luke!*" Mae screamed at the same time the boy on the smokehouse roof threw a rock, apparently from his pocket, grazing Luke's forehead, before scampering down and dashing after them. Luke staggered.

"Cain't hep ya none *now*, Pearly Mae!" Luke heard gleeful laughs wet the air.

Luke brushed at the blood drooling into one eye as if a fly had landed there. Feet stomped floorboards behind him. Luke stayed Liz with an outthrust arm. "Don't. Might hit Mae."

Liz made an oath lowering the gun. Luke clenched his jaw, still hearing that oozing-black-strap-molasses voice, *"My-my, chile. Don't know how much I missed mah little sugar plum."* Felt more than saw something whiz overhead, hearing the new glazed window sent from Cheyanne splinter and clatter to kitchen floorboards.

That did it.

Liz's shotgun, accompanied by, "Dad-blasted varmints!" discharged. A man with a battered hat writhed on the ground, holding a bloody calf, baying like a kicked dog. Side-spray peppered another's belly, and a few buckshots stitched a man's knee.

Instantly, the mob, stepping over the wounded man, turned on the little band on the porch with blood and brooding obsession in their eyes. Luke leaped off, swinging the hefty rifle stock in a blur of motion like a battering ram, stomaching one, then used it as a scythe, kneecapping four men and tripping another. One more went down with a backhand swing. Two came from behind, one grabbing the stock. After dropping a shell that rolled under a rocker, Liz wrestled with her shotgun, striving to reload.

Luke's finger tightened. His own shotgun thundered. A man fell back with grapeshot peppering his chest, blood pouring from his mouth and bleats of, "*Pappy! Pappy*," coming from nowhere. The boy ran up and threw himself on the victim.

Kenning they could have slept through the Second Coming, Luke with annoyance finally spied Old Tom and Biskits, in long-johns and singlets, stumbling from the bunkhouse with guns of their own, sleepy, disoriented—still, General Ulysses S. Grant at Shiloh couldn't have been more relieved when his fifth calvary showed up.

The agitated throng, howling defiance, not so much melted as scattered like rats fleeing a barn fire at the sight of three more guns, for Old Tom brandished two ancient Smith and Wessons, shooting so wildly he threatened to blast his own toes off, with Biskits behind him wielding his iron thirty-pound fry pan and one ancient revolver.

Luke grinned in spite of the occasion.

One of the mob got a shot off, winging it over the

porch roof, but Luke suspected most of their guns were inoperable or unreliable. Then he caught sight of a pale nightdress after one of the males stumbled, clearing a brief space as he took down another with him.

Swinging the curved rocker with one hand, bashing the rifle butt as interference with the other, Luke sprinted to get to Mae. Old Tom kept firing his pistols overhead. Helping, Biskits vigorously swung his skillet at any head available.

Meanwhile, Zebulon was somewhere leading the charge to the rear.

Luke was lost in the vanishing melee before Mae crawled out on her hands and knees. Scrambling up, she hurled rocks after her kin, some dragging off their wounded. "Stay away!" She screamed rough as a file after them with tears streaming her face. "*This* be my family now!"

"*Yew ain't heered the last of this!* Best not go ta sleep at nights," the fork-toter yelled.

Afraid they might turn on her, Luke went after her, wrapping arms about her fighting figure. There was enough blood spilt.

She was only dressed in flimsy night things, shivering either from cold or rage, he wasn't sure which, but the bones and flesh beneath the thin barrier seemed breakable. "Shhh. Hold on," he whispered. "It's all right." Was it? Two or three of the younger males seemed bent on returning. Including the one with the filthy muck-clotted pitchfork.

Liz fluttered down from the porch, still holding her shotgun, and seemed to throw cold water on their intentions.

Luke waved her off. "Liz, stand down. Never mind.

Go back."

"It isn't proper…"

"Liz, I said go back." He threw her a look. Liz threw back one brimming with hurt, muttering, "Well, I never!"

Clods pitted the ground behind them. However, the throng vanished as they arrived, melting behind the stable, barn and outhouses, though Luke was certain one of the mob had gone on before and was now wearing tattered wings and a tarnished halo.

****

Luke still wrapped strong arms about Mae's flailing figure. She, clutching a large rock continued spitting like an angry cat, battling to yank away and run after them as he held her fast, whispering urgently in her ear, "They can't take you. They will never take you."

Blinking, bewildered, Mae looked all around her after the last had vanished, as if not knowing what to expect, or whether to run or look up into his eyes. Fearful of what she might see.

In the circle of Luke's arms, her head under his chin, Mae finally raised a tear-stained face.

He spied Liz over Mae's shoulder. She looked off, with a grim set to her mouth not meeting his eyes. Not standing it any more, Liz stomped down from the porch, still holding the shotgun, barking, "Was that your *kin*?"

Mae looked at her, defiant. "Yes'm."

Liz stared meaningfully at her brother. "I warned you!"

"Liz, if you can't help, tend to your own self. You've cut your hand." Liz thrust the gun back over her shoulder and wiped her hand on her apron with a look of triumph, despite what she said next. "Now we'll have to fear the night and get murdered in our beds."

Luke wasn't certain she was far off.

"Not with you around," he placated. "You are like one of those Amazon women. Couldn't have had a better fighter beside me."

Liz snorted, tossed hair out of her face, and stomped back to the porch and banged the door. Luke pondered. For sure, he had need to set up a watch—for now. And then, he might turn the tables and go after those varmints. He shook his head, striving not to laugh. Liz was throwing pots and pans around inside to wake the dead. He ought to sic *her* on the lot.

He looked back, bemused, at Mae. She stared back with a mixed expression.

"Well!" She looked down, then back with the same defiant look. "You've met my ma and pa, and the rest of my kin, and some that ain't—aren't," Mae corrected flatly, with some bitter irony.

Luke shook his head. He had a hard time controlling his grin. "I reckon I *purely* did. Enough for three lifetimes." Then the dam broke and he roared with laughter.

Mae, after an abashed second, joined in, giggling.

"Were they always like this?" He wiped his eyes.

Mae gazed into the empty space they'd so recently vacated. "Worse. On their Sunday behavior with you," Mae vowed.

"Then you must have been found in a cabbage patch." Luke chuckled. "No trace of you in that pack." He placed his large hands on her shoulders, quirking an eyebrow. The cleft in his jaw winked. "Now, where shall we ride tomorrow? Give them something more to talk about."

Mae nodded, her eyes like stars had taken up residence.

Then and there, Luke made up his mind.

Chapter Sixteen: Revelation

The next day, a fall squall presaged Wyoming's winter fury, blustering crystal sparks of snow after Luke as he toted in a sizable armload of wood. He dumped the load into the wood box and briskly rubbed his hands, stamping before the roaring blaze in the parlor's head-high river-rock fireplace. The handwarming was more in anticipation than due to chill. Aware of Beth and Liz, both curious as cats, indulging in their favorite endeavor—gossiping, chiding over trifles, sipping whiskey-laced tea and snitching a dollop more when he wasn't looking, an old joke—he bided his time.

Beth and Liz knowingly lifted eyebrows and made *What is going on?* faces as they stiffened with interest over Luke's jovial demeanor. Matthew looked up with pleasure at seeing his father-in-law again and in such a happy mood. The occasion was a rare treat, complete with grandkids tucked snug in Liz's bed. This time, the visit from Beth and Matthew came ostensibly over a joint purchase of an expensive steam tractor and combine being offered by the Sears & Roebuck catalogue. And they'd stay the night.

Luke, his chiseled, weathered face ruddy from the outdoors, watched his family with pleasure. Reflections of the fireplace flame brightened his eyes, already lit with boyish enthusiasm, with pinpoints of fire.

No time like the present to announce his plans. Luke

did not notice the ladies exchanging alarmed looks and studying him with the inquisitiveness of Cotton Mather at the Salem Witch Trials. "Whatever's got you so het up, Lukey? Everything all right? You feeling okay?"

Liz! Lordy. He hated when Liz asked after his health. Still, no time to be irritated—a small niggle told Luke he wanted to be on their good side. Luke jabbed at the window.

"Whew! See that bank of clouds headin' south? In for a real *chinook,* we are."

Luke briskly rubbed his hands again, glancing out the window to where fat feathers of snow had already begun floating past, as if relishing the thought. "Snow weather, too."

His watchful sister eyed him as if he were addlepated. "Hummmpf! Perhaps you'd fancy feeding the chickens, breaking the ice and wading through…"

Ignoring her, Luke leaned against the mantel, contemplating the blaze with a tumbler of Old Overholt in hand, after offering one to Matthew. "Love brisk weather more each year," he declared. The women watched, wary, and Matthew, mildly intrigued, added another tipple to his unaccustomed glass. "Don't mind the first snow myself, Luke," he offered. "Real purty, 'fore it gets…"

Beth said, "Oh, shush up, Matthew."

Sticking his pipe back in his mouth, Matthew retreated.

"Air smells clean, gets the blood riling. Don't you think, Lizzie?"

"Yes, of course, Luke." Liz widened her eyes at Beth. "I enjoy frozen feet, cold cheeks and chapped lips while I'm sloppin' the hogs! I purely do."

Luke roared with laughter, again missing Liz's scorn. "You are a caution, Liz. Recall how we used to make ice cream outta snow? Remember? The first snow. Milk, sugar and a splash of Rawleigh's vanilla extract. Haven't done that in donkey's years."

"Not *especially*." Liz's voice was as cold as the snow he projected. "Guess that's why Pa bought the crank ice cream maker."

"Hey. We still have it, or how about that old sled of Pa's?"

Liz looked horrified and gripped her chair. Beth merely appeared bemused.

"I've been called many things, Lucian—but idiotic isn't—" Liz spoke tart, cut off by her brother as he still gazed happily out the window.

"I love each day. Can't wait to get up in the morning," he enthused. Luke grimaced at his reflection. He was putting it off and he kenned it.

"What's got into you, Luke?" Liz demanded, slamming down her knitting. Back in front of the fire, Luke eyed them soberly.

"Well, girls, regardless of your sour natures—not you, Matt…" Luke laughed, further vexing them. "I have a happy announcement and feel better than when I was in my twenties."

Matthew removed his pipe and grinned. "I wouldn't mind some a that."

"Matthew!" Beth warned.

"Well, out with it, Luke," Liz snapped, as if forewarned her place was in jeopardy. "I don't have till Kingdom Come."

"Yes, Pa." Beth spoke with amused indulgence. "And what brought on this miracle? Magic elixir sold by your friend, that snake oil salesman? Must get me some." She shared a rare smile with Matthew.

"I'm—well…" Luke scuffed boots on the flagstone hearth. "Thinking of getting hitched again. I know, I know, I've seen a mirror, a time or two. My jaws aren't firm as a young buck's. Got squint lines you could ride a mule through. Hair more silver than coal-tar black." Luke tipped the shot of whiskey into his mouth. "But by God, I feel eighteen again—"

He was met by leaden silence broken only by a *chuffing* as a spent log dropped in the hearth.

"Married!" Liz ended the spell.

"Yes. Liz. Beth. That. Married."

"*Who* pray tell? You haven't been off this ranch courtin' *any*body."

Luke studied the fire. "She's a tad younger'n me."

Beth looked on, entertained. Watching Liz, Beth mouthed, "*Who!*"

Matthew bounded over with a face chock full of genuine delight, vigorously shaking Luke's hand. "Why, that is grand news, Luke. Real good to hear! Congratulations. Who's the lucky lady?" He kept on, expectant, but Luke felt a dark cloud looming at an indrawn breath behind him, like the first gust before a tempest.

Beth carped, "Stay out of this, Matthew. Pa isn't finished yet. And this is family business."

Liz bawled, scandalized, "*Who,* I'd like to know? Not three years gone by since Katherine…" Horror spread across her face like dirty oil on water. "No! Never!"

She jumped up from her rocker, fists clenched at the ends of arms held stiff as two-by-fours by her side, while the rocker—the only sound in the room besides the suddenly thunderous ticking of the mantel clock—made *thump-thunk-thwacks* on the hardwood.

"That's right," Luke said with the calmness before a storm. You know her, Liz. It's Mae."

"Mae! *Mae? Never!* She will never step foot in this house. Over my dead body!" Liz swung on Beth. "I knew it! Did you hear about this? I told you! I *warned* you, Beth. There was somethin' going on and that you should be looking to your father before he did something senseless!"

She spun on Luke, hissing like a cat on attack. "What are you *thinking*, Luke!" Liz paced the room, pinwheeling her arms. "What are you *doing*? Have you gone daft?" She halted, swinging an arm out, palm up inviting her brother to explain himself.

"My brother *Luke,* and that *strumpet* in sheep's clothing! Young enough to be your daughter! Your *granddaughter*."

Her look spoke triumph.

"Liz! Liz! Stop it. I didn't think you'd carry on so. And—Mae's older than her years." Luke's black brows made ferocious furrows such that had set many a wrangler back on his heels.

Not Liz.

Luke's square jaw and fists clenched. "I was married! To *Katie!*" His face softened, perhaps recalling lush spring nights and hot summers of young love. "Katie was my life." His voice turned thick in his throat. "Always was. I miss the companionship of a woman. She made it real. I miss that. Oh, not you, Liz. You've been more than a help, more than a companion, but I need a *wife*."

"Well, gee whiz, Luke, that's just swell!"

Beth turned on Matthew like a bobcat. "I said, stay out of this! This is between me and my *father*."

"But Beth, I'm family. I have a right…"

"No Matthew Davis, you have not! You men all hang together. My Pa needs a steady shoulder and a good sounding board. Who better than me, his own daughter!"

She caught sight of Liz. "Oh, never mind, go on, Pa."

"And I needed a husband!" Liz snapped like biting wire with her teeth. "Where were you all this time, when I needed someone to cook for and share jokes with and—and—evenings after supper besides early bed with a book or the Bible?"

The sob in her voice cut Luke's heart.

"Were you out there spouting my skills to the world, or saying to me, 'Liz, put you best foot forward?' or bringing eligible men home for supper? When I wanted to invite that new seed salesman, you said no. But it was just hospitality!"

Luke looked away. *It's true, dammit! Didn't cotton to the looks of him. Never trusted redheads with cock-of-the-walk manners. 'Sides, we buy from Nate, or the feed store in Laramie.*

"Lizzie, he robbed us blind with that bad rye seed. Blighted. Killed twenty head of our good stock!" *But that wasn't it.*

"Don't care! That's not what I was getting at and you darn well know it, Lucian Farnsworth. You were too comfortable after Katie passed. I stayed here and I've cooked and I've cleaned and I've slaved for you and *I've* kept your house. No wonder you didn't have to get hitched, until you've gone gaga with old age. First Mom and Pa, then Katie. I looked after all the illness and pain. I had no time, did I, while my youth faded away like an old curtain!"

She looked off, breathing so hard Luke feared she'd faint.

He couldn't show weakness. She'd used these ploys before. Truth was, Liz was too proud to put herself out there with a smile, or a splash of lavender, or a spot of beet root on her cheeks. A suitor had to find his way to *her*. And Lord kenned that was like climbing glass mountains.

Beth still sat pensive with a faraway smile. Merely a bystander listening in. Rare as hen's teeth for his Beth.

Liz still paced. "Another thing!" Gulping cold tea, she slammed down cup and saucer and stood before them as if addressing a judge and jury.

"There was that blacksmith! Married a young girl! That trash out the edge of Red Butte. *She* ran off with a drummer scarce a year after! Never seen hide nor hair since." She nodded at Luke, triumphant. "Took *all* his savings while she was at it, and…" stabbing a finger, "that rancher over near the Sullivan's? *He* married a woman only *half* his age. Thirty-five. *She* died in childbirth. And then there was…"

"You don't need to go on! Don't need to be hit over the head with your *sacred* rolling pin, Liz!"

"I'm not finished, Lucian! Everyone knows Judd Larsen didn't pass peaceful. That young wife of his had a hand in it, sure as I'm standing. She inherited the lot and married again scarce two months later. I'm gonna get the pastor Huckabee…the good reverend…that's what I'll do! He can pound some sense into your sinful ways."

Luke looked helplessly at Beth, searched his son-in-law, who he suspected sided with him but did not want to bring thunderbolts of wrath down on his marriage bed.

His daughter finally stirred.

"Now, Auntie Liz, calm yourself. Getting all riled up over nothing. You deny Pa a few simple pleasures? You must think Pa *belongs* to you or something." Beth cast patronizing glances Liz's way. "I think it's rather sweet, Pa thinking like a young buckeroo. Doesn't bother me a whit if he has a little fling."

Matthew raised brows and threw an enigmatic gaze at his wife.

"After all…" Beth airily waved her hand. "None of our business what Pa does." She added unnecessarily, "He's a grown man. Pa's just thinking young. Probably doesn't mean it anyway."

Luke directed a sardonic gaze at her. *Thanks, my dutiful daughter, for that left-handed approval.*

"Besides," Beth continued, "Pa tells me everything. Said he was just *thinking* of getting hitched again. Isn't that right, Pa? He's funning you, Aunt Liz. Tell her, Pa."

"Beth, honey? Thought you might be a little happier for me."

"Pa! You can't mean it?" Beth laughed but had a crease between her brows.

Luke didn't bother answering. "Thought you might be more tolerant."

"Oh. I—I *am,* Pa," Beth said with all the animation of a limp dishrag. "You know I always want what's best for you, and for you to be happy. It's just that, well, that was a shock. I mean one minute this *girl*—"

Thanks for emphasizing that.

"—comes from the wrong side of the tracks, if you

think about it, not that I blame *her,* and looking like a half-drowned cat"—she chuckled— "according to Auntie Liz. Next thing I know, you're crazy drunk in *love*." Beth hooted.

It reminded Luke of banging on a tin pot.

She continued, "Of course I'm concerned. Just thought you might choose a *lady*, more *refined*, but what do I know? Just that Liz told me all about that *family* of hers." Beth studied her hands.

"Hold on, now! Don't say anything you might be sorry for. Whatever Mae came from or not, she's not of their cloth by a long shot."

"Of course, Pa. I would never question your judgment."

In a pig's eye.

Beth crossed midstream, in a way that did not fool Luke. "I remember Mama."

"We all do." *Careful. Careful.*

"I remember Ma playing with dolls. Always singing about the house, but then she'd burn the beans while she was reading out on the porch," Beth mused.

"Yeah, that was my Katie-did."

"But Pa…this is all so sudden."

"What's to understand, Beth?" Luke's words turned thick. "She wants affection. She's never had any her whole life. Mae's brave under all that cheerfulness. In that small body. I've never known anyone so brave, so caring, and I have so much to give. To make up for what she hasn't had."

"Why! Didn't know you were an *alienist*, Pa!"

"Don't use those fancy words on me." *What the hades is an alienist?*

"Beth, your mom was always young. Till the day she

died, she wasn't any older than that gal out there. In fact, Mae's older. She's had a rougher life."

Neither noticed Liz. "Older? Hah!"

"She knows her mind, Liz."

Hanging onto the newel post, Liz clutched her chest. "I'm going to my bed. I can't take any more."

"You belong in a traveling show, Liz. You purely do."

"Luke! At least I'm not a *clown* act!" Liz wailed. "Don't know what's happening to this family." Luke watched her race upstairs and turned to his daughter.

"All right! So I don't mind 'childish.' You just said your ma was more a sister. One of my Katie's many charms. She skipped instead of walked and never lost that kid-like wonder."

"Oh, I know it's my fault…"

*Fault? "*What has this to do—?"

"I was asking you all of those personal questions. And then you got to thinking. So I put the idea in your head, that you *needed* somebody *that way*, and, well, Mae is here…and not *unfavorable* looking, from what I hear, even if she does seem"—she laughed—"poor as Job's turkey."

"I don't need you to sort out my life, Beth, as much as you and Liz want to cut me up like a Christmas goose."

"Oh, Pa! Listen to reason."

"It's downright sinful…" came from behind them.

They both sighed.

Liz had crept back down, holding something that looked suspiciously like a Bible with a well-underlined passage, and it wasn't from Solomon's Love Songs.

Luke fell back in the big leather wingchair, looking

grim. "Put the Good Book away, Lizzie. Not swearing anything to you, or to God."

"Luke! Don't say she *cares* for you! She cares for *this*!" She waved the Good Book, indicating the room, the ranch, or maybe the world. "For *this*! She cares for this ranch and being carried around on a little velvet pillow. She cares for the fact that you're still handsome and healthy, with a fine spread you've slaved over, and with gold eagles in the bank. She's young. Why else would she be making eyes at an old man!"

Luke breathed hard.

He stared out into a night black as the glass between, his haunted expression staring back in the wavery panes—*an old man, gray, washed out*.

"There's nothing sinful about this, Liz, nothing sinful at all," he said dully. "I love this gal. I'd make a good home for her. I will make her happy. She needs me. She needs affection so much, Liz. And I have it to give. Mae's alone in this world." He caught the phlegmy sob in his voice. "We can give each other so much. I'll take care of her," he ended huskily.

Liz's spiteful voice intruded. "And she'll take care of *you*." But she didn't mean it in a kindly way.

Luke shook his head and dropped it back on the antimacassar head rest.

Liz collapsed in a rocker. "Where will I go? What will I do? Two women can't share a kitchen!"

"Funny, Liz. That's just what Mae said, but she's willing. She likes you, Liz. You're like the mother she would have liked."

"I wouldn't be a mother to that filthy, scheming barn cat." Scorn dripped from her voice. "No! Needn't worry. I'll pack my bags and leave, and who cares where I go?"

"You can always stay with me." Beth spoke up.

Liz shot a look of snake's venom at his daughter, disturbing Luke. "Yes," she hissed. "Suitable for stale crumbs off the table for old maid aunts. I suppose I could be granny to your *brats,* cleaning up messes and runny noses."

"Liz!" They both spoke up.

"No, I didn't mean that."

"I know, Auntie Liz. You would be welcome in our house as an honored member of the family." The gentleness in Beth's voice touched Luke. She walked over and patted Liz's arm.

Liz looked bleak as the outside weather. "I just wish… I just wish… Oh, never mind what I wish. Who cares? Who's ever cared?" She shook with heaving sobs.

Luke threw her a helpless glance. But with the two women lined up against him… Matthew had gone out to smoke on the porch after shaking his head meaningfully at his wife.

With that, Liz dragged herself back upstairs. Luke watched her. "She'll get over it." *Maybe in a million years.* "Yet frankly, Beth, I thought you might look a little more favorably on my news. You have your Matthew."

"Oh, Pa! Do you think I don't get lonely with Matthew? All he gets excited about are *seed* catalogues, as if we could plant and raise half that stuff. He ordered something called *arti-chokes* the other day from back east!"

"Beth, let's leave it at that." Luke pressed his head against the cold panes, staring out into a blanket of thick snow. He began muttering, almost to himself.

"Looks like death out there…like the dark side of

the moon. I hate the snow. I hate cold. Gets in my bones."
Sleet mixed with snow rapped the panes like bullets.
Luke's voice was lost. He waved her away. "Talk
another day. Right now, I'm tired."

"Guess I'll be going to bed too, then, Pa." She
watched him, uncertain. "Don't stay up late."

Luke shambled to the fireplace. Hunched over in the
rocker, he drew a crocheted lap robe across his knees and
stared bleakly into the dying fire, not hearing. To Beth
he suddenly looked ten years older.

"Night, Pa."

After she left, Luke drew the robe up to his chin,
shivering and muttering words too low to hear.

Chapter Seventeen: Luke Puts His Foot Down

Luke rose early with his jaw set, a look Liz, if not his daughter, kenned well. When Liz, still braiding her hair, stepped through the doorway, he was sitting at the table with a cup of tar he'd boiled himself. She glanced from him to the coffeepot. "I hope you have come to your senses now. I only meant the—"

Luke never raised his voice, but a steel blade wouldn't cut it as he announced, "This Sunday, I want the table set with the best china. What you use for Thanksgiving, or Christmas. I want a dinner with all the trimmings. We will eat as a family and not begrudging. I want us all in our best bib-and-tucker. We will be civilized folk here on the L. Devereaux ranch, by God."

If Liz looked chastened, Luke could not detect it. She nodded stiffly and raised her chin. "Yes, Luke. I'll see it's done to your wishes. You won't find *my* table lacking. But what's this *for?*"

"Never you mind. Just do it."

"I don't need to stay here and be berated!"

"We are entertaining my new wife-to-be."

Liz stared at him as if he'd said, "I slept with the preacher's wife."

"All right, Luke. If that's the way it is, it will be done!" Liz took to her heels and swept out.

"Liz!" Luke roared. "We're not through." Luke's boots struck the oak floorboards like bolts of lightning as he went after her—to be confronted by the censorious glance of his daughter just entering the kitchen to warm milk for the baby.

Good. He'd forgotten she was here.

"Liz, come back. Beth, you too." When they both stood before him, Beth jiggling the baby, Luke spoke with a deceptively calm voice.

"Where's that dress you were *slaving* over?" His face showed he meant no such thing. "The one for Mae?" He threw down the challenge like a gunslinger flinging bullets.

Liz cast a quick glance at Beth. "Why, Lucian Farnsworth, you haven't asked after that for a month of Sundays!" Liz huffed up like a banty hen. "And now here you come stompin' around *demanding*—"

"Never mind all that. I want to know what happened to it. After all this time, it should be a work of art."

"I swan!" Beth broke in. "Pa, I don't rightly recollect. Almost forgot that chore you put on us. Didn't you, Aunty Liz? 'Course, 'twasn't my particular job, what with the kids and all. More like yours, Liz. What with my children sucking up time like a twister."

"You said that," Liz bit off.

Beth stuck out her chin. "Seems to me *you* were in charge of it."

"Oh?" Liz snarled. "That why I saw *you* piecing it together? You were—"

Luke slammed the table and plates jumped. "Before you two have a donnybrook, where is it, no matter if the *devil* stitched it up."

"Well." Liz moistened her lips. "Don't rightly recall either. Must be somewhere, Beth." Beth shrugged and tested the warm milk on her inner wrist.

"Enough. What scheme have you two cooked up in your witch's cauldron?" Luke had read *MacBeth* and now took it to heart. "I gave you cash money to buy dress goods."

"Like any Christian, Lucian Farnsworth, if you must know, I chucked it into the Baptist church poor box, where it will do some good." Liz swept to her full height, almost matching her brother. "Now, if you will quit badgering us, I shall retire to my bed with a sick headache."

Luke grabbed her arm and plunked a startled Liz into a kitchen chair.

"Luke!" Liz yelped. "What's got into…?"

"What's got into me is two scheming hens pecking a young girl to death. Doesn't sit right with me! Now…"

"All right, you shall have it!"

"I have to feed the baby."

"You stay right here, Beth. The little tucker can wait." At her father's order, Beth slowly sat.

Liz disappeared upstairs, then raced back down. "Right here in my sewing basket." She thrust a large wicker basket large as a laundry hamper at Luke. "See for yourself."

Luke rummaged, muttering, "I don't see…" before he caught sight of pink cabbage roses. He withdrew a bedraggled crush of coarse fabric with the semblance of a dress if one became a mummer. Luke prodded the rough sacking like it was snake. "I don't spy anything but…"

Liz started to fluster, then stood her ground. "We made what we thought she deserved."

"Liz…?" Beth began.

"What is this abomination? A Saint Joseph's coat of

200

many colors?" Luke menacingly eyed the orange, purple, yellow, pink cabbage rose disaster with a disgust normally saved for a dead skunk under the house. He was simmering like a pot of water about to boil. *It wasn't right.* He recognized the dress Liz had whipped up was made from *feed sacks.*

He kenned many a homesteader or farmer's wife relished the patterned bags to clothe husbands and children, leave alone themselves. Last market day, one family arrived in their buckboard garbed in matching feed-sack garments. Unfortunately for the husband, the sacks his wife-mate chose were of the lurid pink rose pattern. But not for Mae.

Liz fumed, defiant, but Beth had the grace to look anywhere but at the excretion on the table. "Honest, Pa, I didn't think it would turn out like that. Besides, Liz gave me those feed bags."

Luke thrust them at her. "Somehow this seemed all right with you?"

Beth hung her head. "No, Pa. We will make her another. A nice one." She swallowed hard. "Won't we, Aunty Liz?"

Liz looked off, arms folded. "Ever since that girl got here, she's caused nothing but trouble!"

"You two..." Luke snarled and stomped out the door, letting the flimsy screen door slam off its hinges. "I'll take care of it!"

He came back chastened and watched Liz with wry irritation.

Liz didn't look exactly cowed, but resigned. "Yes, Luke. I'm sorry, it was unchristian of me," was said with a certain stiffness he did not believe for a second. "I don't know what gets into me sometimes."

"I know, Lizzie. It's hard." He meant life itself.

"Hard for both of us, but we've always had each other."

Beth looked away.

"Still do, Lizzie, but the heart can be as big as a mansion. Doesn't have to be one little cold room."

Liz blinked away tears and lifted her chin. "All will be ready, Lucian. You best be getting on this big *secret* mission then." With that she turned her thin back and made a great clatter and fuss with the dishes.

Luke saddled up Hell-Fire.

"Let's go, old friend. We can make Laramie and sleep at the Red Dog."

****

Mae looked up, hiding her surprise. There stood Old Tom and Biskits in the stable doorway, hats in hand, looking sheepish. Biskits nudged Old Tom. Old Tom blushed but looked pleased. "Heard tell you was ta be the new boss-lady here. We, Biskits and me, jest wanted ta say how—um, ah…"

"Pleased," Biskits cut in, "right pleased." He looked at his feet.

"Thank you, that's right nice of you, but…um, Miss Lizzie will still be boss-lady here." She laughed. "I'm just the same." Fizzy with happiness, Mae felt as if she had drunk a whole bottle of Luke's rye whiskey.

****

Halfway to Laramie, Luke almost halted Hell-Fire. He scratched his head under the battered Stetson, swearing. "Where the Sam Hill do you buy a dress, 'sides Sears Roebuck? That would take since Moses was a baby to get here."

Thought he saw a dress or apron or *something*

colorful hanging in the hardware store—a place that carried dry goods as well as sundries from axe heads to barrels of pickled pig's feet.

Luke stood in the doorway, fiddling his Stetson as his sight adjusted to the warmer dusk. There in a corner… Heading that way, he thought he spied a splash of pink by some mule halters. He'd get there before the proprietor could hinder him with nosy questions.

Three dresses and one pinafore hung on wire coat hangers. Luke sorted through them with despair, the clerk looking on with a whimsical expression—a gray cotton that would wrap around Mae three times over, the next, lavender with yellow polka dots; desperate, he snatched out the last, holding his hand yay far off the floor. Right size, about. Pale blue cotton with a little sheen, a low rounded neckline with white collar and lightly puffed sleeves narrowing to the wrist.

"How much?" He held it up.

The clerk scratched his head. "I'm saving this 'un for a lady till her butter-and-egg money adds up."

"Hate to disappoint the good woman, but there will be other dresses, and I'll give you top dollar."

"Yep. True enough. Getting a new stock in next month. Welp, I was a-charging her three dollars." Luke flipped a five-dollar coin at him. "That do it?"

"Well, sure. Can't bring it back," he warned.

"Wasn't meaning to."

"Want it wrapped?

"No. I'll take it as is." And Luke stomped out with the dress sailing like a flag behind him.

****

Luke announced his presence, removing his hat at the bottom of the ladder as if entering a fine house. Mae's bright face showed at the trap. "Luke!" She smiled, delighted. "Thought you were on business."

"I was. Most important business. May I come up?"

Mae grinned, holding down a white arm. "Either that or I come to you."

"Won't be necessary." Luke held up the package he had behind him. "Special delivery."

"Oh!" Like a child, she knew a wrapped brown paper package held untold delights. "Ohhhh! Is it for me? What is it?"

"I may need to demonstrate." Luke's boots hit the rungs.

As he stood at the top, he murmured, "Now, undress."

She teased, "And if I don't?"

"Then I reckon I'll have to do it for you. Though it is a bothersome chore."

She backed to her bed. "I'll have you ken I'm a respectable girl. I don't let just anyone touch my underdrawers."

"Reckon you don't want this, then." Her eyes sped to the paper parcel.

"Maybe."

Luke advanced across the small space. She, with merry eyes, circled. Luke snatched her and drew her close. "Too long, my little love. Lord, I missed you."

"Then I reckon you shouldn't stay away—or take me with you."

"Soon. For now…" He drew down one strap of her shimmy. Then the other. Her shimmy fell to her waist. He tugged it down. Mae teased with the waist of her pantaloons. In one swoop he had them off. Mae felt the delicious length of him, his belt buckle, the coarseness of his jeans, the flannel of his shirt, inhaling the tobacco-and-horse scent of him, erotic perfume. Luke relished her cool nudity.

He held her at arm's length. "No, this won't do. I want things to be proper." He grinned, ironic. "Though 'proper' right now is harder than lassoing a rampaging steer." Releasing her, he set her on the cot and handed her the package.

"Oh!" Mae ripped it. "Oh! It's so pretty."

Luke felt shamed. Just simple, rather coarse cotton, though the blue looked just about right against her pale skin. But why hadn't he braved the haberdasher or whatever they called a ladies' dress shop? If there was one.

Slowly, Luke dressed her like a doll. "Lift your arms." Mae laughed and languidly lifted them. Luke settled the sleeves gently over her hands, shoving them down her white arms. Lingering, he lovingly straightened the skirts and fastened the back row of pearly buttons, kissing her as he went. Still she wriggled with delight and wanted to turn round about, but he held her tight about the waist. "Soon I can do this every morning and unwrap you every night."

She leaned her head back against his chest. "Oh, Luke. I don't need dresses, only you."

"And I you. But you will have dresses and shoes and, and—and..."

"Stop." She swiveled around. "This is what I want most," and with the words she pulled his craggy handsome head down, offering her lips, pressing herself hard against him as if she wished to be part of him. Sheltered and cherished. He could wrap his arms twice about her slender waist as he gripped her close, echoing the sentiment in his heart and body.

"Maybe time to undress now." Luke's voice was husky with need. Slowly he tugged the gown while she stood docilely, arms up. Luke lifted her like a doll and carried her to the cot.

"No, Luke." He looked puzzled until she dragged her comforter to the open hayloft window. "Let's love each other in front of the moon."

Or God and everyone, as Liz would say, but quelled Liz's images as he tore at the brass buttons of his denims, ripped off his shirt and lay beside her, on her, she on him, rolling and laughing, tangling limbs, surrendering to each other. Luke kissed her breasts and belly, her thighs and all between while she laughed with pleasure, until neither could abide further delay. Mae reached for him and lifted her knees, murmuring, "Oh, Luke… please…" And with only the moon watching, he was already in a place where he wanted to be, and while she tightened herself around him, apparently so was she.

Chapter Eighteen: The Dinner

Luke sat at the head of a "groaning board."

Liz had outdone herself to shameless excess. The best crystal sparkled. Linen gleamed with starch. Sliced ham studded with a forest of cloves glistened with brown sugar, as well as a huge rib roast sitting, like a crown of thorns, beside pots of mustard and horseradish, cruets of brown gravy, bowls of cranberry sauce, candied sweet potatoes, green beans with bits of onion and chunks of smoked sausage, succotash, Parker House rolls, stewed tomatoes, mashed potatoes flooded with fresh butter, piccalilli, corn relish, and enough coffee to float a battleship, along with pumpkin pie and vanilla cake with plum sauce.

Mae, her hair tied back loosely with the same old red ribbon, looked a bit dazed but well turned out in the simple pale blue cotton gown. She sat by Liz at one end, with Luke at the head of the little-used formal dining table. Liz sat flanked by Beth, across from Matthew. There was Old Tom and Biskits, slicked up, plus the baby and Luke's two bachelor neighbors, Abner Smith, who brought along his excited *intended*, and Hiram, who was really too old for Liz, but how could he talk?

He would have invited Nate Solomon, but he and Hurly were in Cheyenne to purchase the next wagonful of their erstwhile wares.

Half through dinner, Beth passed a bowl of potatoes

behind Luke and bent to whisper, "Pa, she *is very* pretty, and you are an old *rogue!*" She then elbowed him on the other side, grinning as she added, "And way too nice for *you*, not what I"—she glanced at Liz—"heard."

Luke beamed with supreme pleasure as he eyed the assemblage.

Liz's face was unreadable.

At least he had *one* not to win over. He didn't want Liz vexed, of course. Nevertheless, it was his life too. He felt proud and fulsome. Mae in her blue gown chatted easily with Beth and Matthew, teased Old Tom, chuckled at something a shy, crimson-faced Biskits mumbled, and cooed at the baby. She seemed not out of place.

One hurdle leapt over with ease. Luke was giddily happy in a way that would have astounded his wranglers, who were given a few bottles of Old Overholt to aid in their bunkhouse celebration or a chance to go ride into town.

Dishes cleared, leftovers put away, a final glass of wine with Liz, and she declared she was plumb tuckered, after Luke spoke about how pleasing her dinner was, fit even for the newly elected President Benjamin Harrison.

Now Luke relaxed on the porch in a new rocker and with a last cup of joe—seventy-five percent whiskey—a rolled cigarette—eschewing Sweet Caporals—he decided to enjoy the evening stars, contemplate the day, watch the amber glow of lantern light somewhere up there, and think of Mae up in the lonely loft with the same feeling in his chest.

Wisht he could convince her to bed in the house.

For more than one reason.

He smiled and chuckled. Stubborn mite. She would be like a bowl of fresh roses perfuming the house. An icy blast coming through the stable's siding would soon convince her…and by then, they would be legally wed— as Liz would say, "in front of God and everybody."

Chapter Nineteen: Raoul

From the hayloft, Mae gazed out at the moon, her feet dangling over the edge of the opening. She loved her aerie, 'specially at night, when memories came…of Luke's lips, his arms, his manly strength enfolding her in safety and love, the smell of him, his heat, the tobacco-y aroma of leather and horses. This great, capable, strong man cared for her. Luke said she should stay in the big house till wed proper, but temptation would be too great, she reckoned. They would have been wed by now, she wasn't sure when or how, not that is mattered, in the warmth of his love, but Luke had traveled to Cheyenne on business he said couldn't be put off.

Something to do with a "trust" or a "fund for Liz," whatever that was. But something nice.

She smiled shyly at her toes.

Not that he hadn't visited *her* a few times. Yet she wouldn't dishonor Luke or Miss Lizbeth that way…and kenned Luke felt the same. Still, she yearned for his hard muscular body weighting her down, the warm, nigh overwhelming desire growing harsher, more demanding with each encounter. For now, it was enough… Still, she giggled softly, wouldn't mind if he paid another midnight visit about now.

So lost was she in the splendor of night—swallows flitting home, a few bats with wings iridescent pink and transparent against a crescent moon just sliding beyond luminous pearly clouds—there was no detecting the scented breathing as a body stealthily ascended the steep ladder to the loft, or the creak of leather chaps.

Mae felt a hand on her neck and at first supposed her longing had manifested into reality. She began to turn eagerly but then, startled, tried to jump up from her risky perch on the sill. A silky voice, warm as sorghum molasses, slid over her.

"*Chiquita.* Did I startle you, *querida*?" The voice purred like a satisfied tomcat. "I think not too much."

Mae had been aware of a cloying smell for some time now, half cinnamon or maybe cloves, mixed with the Bay Rum that some of the fellas liked to douse themselves with before Saturday night hootenannies.

Mae struggled to wiggle out from under the hard hand nailing her half in and half out the hayloft loading window.

"Waiting for me," the voice purred. "Hoping I would come. Longing for it, *querida*?" The hand pressed harder.

Mae's wriggling succeeded in her veering too far out the tall opening, and she glimpsed the ground twenty feet below. *He*—she didn't have to suppose *who* now, recognizing the musical accent—had devoured her with his eyes ever since he first showed up, making kissing motions and eyewinks when Luke was not looking. Grabbing her unexpectedly. Trying to back her into corners in the stable. His leather trousers creaked as he crouched beside her. The scents of leather, musk, sickly cologne, and his hot breath on her cheek, all made it hard to breath. Hard to react.

She tried to judge what jumble of machinery lay below them.

Sensing her intentions, Raoul gripped her by the hair, drawing her head back. Her only choice was to rise with him. He was hardly taller than she, but with his tensile strength Raoul slammed Mae against the loading frame, pinning her, twisting her about.

Her small kerosene lamp glowed a soft welcome of false safety. Why hadn't she taken Luke's offer of staying in the big house at least while he was away!

Raoul's eyes, huge, darkly liquid as they reflected the madness of the moon, bored into her angry ones. His face grew larger, blotting out the stars, until he smashed his mouth on hers before she could cry out, cutting her lip on her own teeth. She tasted blood.

Mae struggled and tried to scream past his clamped hand—*bite*—but only muffled sounds crept past his hand. Tried to wedge elbows between them and twist her face away, but the attacker had her chin in a vise. Both now teetered dangerously out into open space. Mae stared down past his hand, again judging the distance. Furious, she considered taking them both down.

Taunting, Raoul gripped her nape and thrust her farther out.

"A far drop, *gata salvaje*." Wildcat. "You fight, I might not hold you, *chiquita.* An accident might happen. So sad. I place flowers on your grave and remember you, *El Dia de la Morte*."

She'd been in pricklier situations but could not recall when. Yet using wits, and catlike as he said, spitting wrath, she had managed in the past to scratch any adversaries and send them into whimpering retreat. She could grab the dangling pulley, but then what? Keeping her face featureless, Mae tried to recall exactly what lay below—seemed to remember the hay rick with its sharp skeletal ribs.

Had they moved that since last week? Why would they, this close to winter? She kenned, with sickening certainty, the jumble of discarded farm equipment and abandoned machine parts tucked out of sight there. She might land on plowshares or rake tines, or bales of rusting barbed wire. Anyone not plum loco feared the lockjaw sickness, even if she didn't break every bone or slice herself like sausage.

Raoul, leering nastily, seemingly fearless—or in a blind lust of madness or hot blood with her hands in a death grip on his shirt, while she searched below—still grasped her waist, thrusting her out farther into nothingness.

Mae cast a brazen-faced glare back, yet quaked inside.

Not getting the reaction he desired, he drew them both back at the last teetering second. With eyes smoldering a mix of passion and rage, Raoul slid wet lips across her cheek like snails, huskily hissing, "Do not be *timido*..." He ran a cracked fingernail down her cheek, on down her neck, and gripped her small warm breast and squeezed it harshly. "I will be *gentle*." The madness shining from his eyes belied that.

With a face of revulsion, Mae winced, crying out, loathing that he touched her with his hands, where Luke's had been so pleasurably.

Chuckling nastily, Raoul ignored her. Her only options were either to jump or to somehow wriggle past him and run.

Side-eyeing the ladder, Mae shrank, striving to pivot farther into the stable loft. He shook her. "I see how *el jefe* looks at you. Wouldn't you rather have a young *caballero,* a stallion of a man, give you much pleasure?" With eyes half-closed in lust, Raoul purred the words like a satisfied cat. Red lips glistened under the tiny shaped mustache.

Mae sneered.

Suddenly at the end of his endurance, Raoul yanked her nightshift hem. The thin worn rag of a gown separated her flesh from him by a mere whisper. At least he had moved from the opening. If she could just make the ladder, she'd shinny down, never mind niceties like rungs or clothes.

Mae took a deep breath, smiled and motioned with her head.

My room. She had to get to her room, drop the bar… *Should I tell? Who? Luke?*

He'd never look at her the same. It would only reinforce the fact she came from poor, sticky-fingered trash. 'Specially after her family's visit, despite what he vowed.

Bitterness clogged her thoughts, yet she kept her face placid.

"Maybe," she murmured, looking up through her lashes.

"Ah, *chica*! Where you and *el viejo*…" Raoul's red mad gaze flicked to the half open door's welcoming glow. He dragged her across and poked his head in, eating up the inviting sanctuary.

"*Esta* might be my favorite place to have private *siestas. Me guardas este secreto.*"

He slapped her behind and shoved her roughly into the room. Mae fell to her knees.

"*Deseo ver tu cuerpo.*" I wish to see your body. "Is all of you pale as your face, *puta*?" He snatched at her shift, yanking till the flimsy scrap tore from her shoulders. Mae kicked her bare foot, catching Raoul between shin and ankle. Raoul chuckled at her effort and twisted her hair in one fist while he slapped her with his other hand.

Mae, eyes smarting tears, grabbed his fingers, digging in with sharp little nails ragged from work. He scowled, holding his hand to his mouth, and thrusting her onto her small cot, fell on top, *whooshing* breath from her lungs.

Mae pounded his back, his head. Scratched his neck. Clawed while he fumbled with his tight leather trousers. Raoul laughed. "Ah *si*! Fight, little *gata*. Scratch, claw...I will bite back." With that he sank his teeth in her shoulders. She felt his lower teeth grind on bone. Felt deep indentations piercing her flesh. Hot lips sliding across her face, her neck...his hand between her thighs.

Mae stretched both arms.

There, almost fingertipped it.

Misreading her in her attempt as she arched her body against his, Raoul sank his teeth in her ear, murmuring wetly, "Don't fight it, *puta*." Tears trickled her face. She would not get out of this whole. *There! Got it!*

Raoul's startled eyes sprang open.

He reared—a hard thunk like a rock hitting a green melon, followed by a sharp *crunch* of broken crockery. Mae's fingers had reached the handle of her little china commode with the hand-painted kittens, thick and dure as Liz's stone mortar bowl, and swung the bowl of it against his head—incidentally splashing him liberally with pee, as she had not yet emptied the little pot before bed.

"*A-ieeee!*" Raoul arched up, touched his head where

a trickle of blood leaked down his forehead, then brushed his dandied-up clothes, sniffing himself with a pugged nose. He resembled a snarling bulldog. "*Caramba! Puta!*"

He raised his hand, pulled back to strike, and saw Mae still clenched the handle of said commode connected to the jagged remnant, lethal as broken glass. The rest lay in scattered smithereens across the floor. Mae sprang away. Raoul inspected his royal blue shirt embroidered with red poppies, now soaked with blood and something else. He gazed at her with rather reptilian eyes glittering with madness, and then, enraged by the smear of blood on his new shirt and the smell of pee, Raoul dragged her back. With eyes of molten slag, he gripped her neck with both hands.

Before blacking out, with the last pinpoint sight of Raoul's crazed eyes boring into hers, Mae desperately bashed the sharp edges against the back of his knees. It was enough.

Raoul landed hard on the loft floor. Shrieking with rage and pain, he plucked out a shard piercing his tight leathers. "I will pay you for this!"

"I've heard worse. Coward!"

Mae scrambled with her weapon of cracked commode. Her hands shook—the fragment of commode dropped, shattering like the rest. Mae ran to the ladder. He lunged and cut her off. She jerked loose, kicking, with no option but to flee naked across the vast floor to the other tall loading window facing the house. She recalled the rope hanging half-down. If she could get to that…? She'd jump, even if it meant a broken bone.

Reaching out to grab the dangling pulley and its rope…

Raoul dove and grabbed her about the knees, struggling back after viewing the ground as it seemed to rush up to him. He loosened his grip. Mae was savagely pleased to see Raoul's terrified face. Kneeling, she looked desperately down. The rope dangled a full fifteen feet from the ground. She could make it.

While Mae was distracted, in a mad retaliatory act Raoul rose up and dragged her all the way up the side of the loading bay frame, exposing her unclothed body to any who might be looking.

Mae pressed back, bucking him in full view, as he attempted to thrust her out, her small breasts gleaming pearly in the light of the moon as she desperately fought. Scratching, kicking, pushing, in their silent battle—at the last minute before she fell, Mae hooked an arm about Raoul's neck.

Neither saw Lucas in the shadows of the porch.

****

Luke stood on the porch, contemplating the night. Too late to see Mae. Wouldn't be right. 'Sides, the trip had been long and arduous, and the session with the lawyer tedious, pounding out details of his trust for Liz and other sundry details pertaining to the ranch. Besides, he wasn't exactly smelling like petunias after the long ride.

Still. Good to be back and set affairs right.

Luke was content as he thought to search for the amber glow of lantern light somewhere up there, matching the glow in his chest. He looked down at his boots. Wisht he could convince her to stay in the house. His expression softened, imagining her somewhere in the house, safe and warm.

Luke jerked his head up at a muffled *scuffling* sound

across the way, past the corrals and paddocks, his body stiffening, almost as if he presaged the end of serenity. The commotion, and Mae's voice mixed with a deeper tone disgustingly familiar, came from the stable.

High up.

Luke half stood—stunned in a half crouch. His whiskey dropped, the heavy tumbler clunking nosily across the old boards. He dashed his hand-rolled to the ground.

There was Mae in the loft loading window, naked as a jaybird or near to it.

He leapt off the porch—began to run—or thought he had. But his feet felt rooted. *Something is very wrong.*

And there. *Oh, God.* Raoul, behind the slim pale body he kenned so well in both waking and dreaming.

Raoul's brown hand gripping her waist. Mae's small bosom gleaming luminescent in the moonlight. The bastard's dark head bending, kissing her shoulder, her neck, whispering to her—in Luke's mind, words of endearment. She wriggling with pleasure. Ill with revulsion, Luke saw Raoul's tongue snake out. One dark hand covered a pale breast, as he thrust her to the frame, groping, grabbing, kissing…*his hand between her legs. Her arm about his neck…*

Mae looking pale, almost blue, writhing in the moonlight, turned her face, saw Luke across the divide, and at her cry, Raoul followed her agonized gaze. Her voice, strangled, filled with meaning Luke could not translate.

Was it imagination, even from that distance, that Raoul smirked? He gave Mae a rough shove, almost toppling her from the loft. She fell to her knees. Raoul vanished. As if the floor dropped out from under him.

Luke wisht it had, straight to the blackest pit of Hell. Shaking like a dog drenched in ice water, he tumbled back in the rocker, feeling stampeded by a herd of buffalo, all the breath out of him. He clutched his arm. His chest hurt—or was it his pride?

Sucking deep, torn between rage and despair, Luke clamped the arms of the chair until the wood beneath his hands cracked.

Mae.

His Mae gazed back, white arm outstretched as if in entreaty.

Too late.

Luke rose slowly.

Blood filled his veins, but it was cold, cold and frightening.

The blood of a murderer, a killer of men, the blood of a man who might strike a woman, or beat a man to unrecognition, limbs broken and bloodied, or burn down a barn.

Luke turned his fist into knuckled rocks.

His veins throbbed and muscles stiffened before a craved lightning-release. But his head seemed filled with mud, dark churning mud that rational thought could not wade through.

Luke was halfway across the beaten hoof-marked arena between stable and porch when Raoul staggered from the wide doorways, shirt half undone, hair a ruffled mess, cursing or *something* in Spanish. Luke couldn't make out the oaths, but it didn't matter. He watched with eyes of death-dealing coldness as Raoul limped slightly, with no other sensation except a deep dark emptiness, like a crevasse in ice.

Luke's great hands flexed, unflexed, *hungry* for

hurt.

At the grate-scrape of boots on dirt, Raoul jerked his head with a peevish expression. Initially, at Luke's wrathful approach, he looked ready to hightail it, but after a second, he stood his ground and sneered, smug. Luke's long legs ate dirt. He went on the attack before half there.

"That one!" Raoul smirked, yelling as he back-peddled. "She is one *gata salvaje*…but I tired her out for *you, jefe.*" Raoul's cocky grin lit the night. A lollop of hair like slick oiled tar dropped over the cut on his forehead. He came up short against the horse trough. One hand reached behind his back. "She is mine now, *jefe.*" He stood braced, legs apart, white teeth shining, hands hanging loose at his side, holding something.

Luke stared at Raoul, then the loft.

Mae crouched in the black oblong, her long black hair hiding her shame, her face unreadable from that distance, body blanched in the light of the moon, but she seemed made of wood. He seemed made of wood himself. He couldn't, *wouldn't* make sense of what he saw. Through cotton wool he heard Raoul purr, "She enjoys my embraces, *me besas, mucho…*" Raoul wrapped his arms about himself.

Luke registered, somewhere in the lizard part of his brain, the flash of a blade.

"Ohhh, *Ra-ouul,* she beg. She enjoyed…" Raoul grabbed his crotch and thrust one arm rigid in the air. "A *young* hombre!" His other hand clutched a knife.

Stupidly—or cockily—he seemed without fear. He checked the bulk of Luke, dangerously near, with scorn. "Not a used-up old *cabrón efeminado…*" Raoul, still apparently not realizing the danger to himself, being so caught up in his mockery of the Big Man, danced about. "*Aiiiie!* What do you think we've been doing, *jefe*, while you were away, mmmm? *Dos semanas* ess a long time to leave a lusty *mujer* such as that one."

Luke caught another glimpse of Mae's pale face. She seemed a ghost.

Mae.

His heart stopped beating. Only a few times had he felt such murderous rage that turned his brain to primeval mud. Once when a cowhand was caught whipping and kicking an elderly blind hound dog, and once when a disgruntled wrangler, an arsonist with kerosene and a few lucifers, attempted to burn down his stable with terrified horses whinnying inside and the doors barred. He might have been tried for manslaughter then—not that a Wyoming jury would have convicted him—if Liz hadn't intervened with a bucket of cold well water and the hands hadn't come running.

Luke struck Raoul a short-armed blow, like a battering ram hammering a door, to the breadbasket. Raoul dropped, graceless, unable to cry out with a surprised open-mouthed look. Luke dragged him up boneless, yanking him by his shirt to an inch from his nose, snarling, "Mae? What did you say?" And threw him back against the stone trough, ready to punch him again to Kingdom Come or down below. Raoul took a wild swing with the sharp blade, missing Luke's ribs by an inch, slicing his bicep instead.

Luke didn't blink. He swatted the knife into the horse trough.

Roaul's liquid black eyes stared defiantly at Luke. "She *like* it," he spat. "She was *all over* me." He sniffed his fingers suggestively. "She cannot get enough.

Finalmente, I leave for my life. We have been"—grinning though bloody teeth, Raoul made a crude gesture—"since I got here, old man."

Raoul wasn't savvy enough or aware enough to stop. "She has eyes only for *me*, dragging me inside whenever she *see* me *alone*, you old man with no *cajones*, who cannot pleasure a—"

Raoul seemed to welcome death, or he had no brakes to his ego as he scrabbled for the knife in the trough. He did not finish. Luke walloped another anvil-hard blow on his handsome curved nose. It sprayed a fountain of blood, Luke blacked Raoul's other eye, just showing color. Raoul folded to the dust, insensate as a dead dog.

Luke strode over his body and headed to the stable. He halted. If someone looked closely, they would see a slight droop to his high broad shoulders—a shuffle to the gait, a closed look unreadable but bleak and chill as a winter stream.

He let his shoulders win the war and sag further.

The dinner. The celebration. All dust in the wind. Why bother? I saw what I saw. Imbedded as a stone in concrete. I'm what Liz said. An old fool.

He shook his head and wandered, unseeing, dripping blood, back to the house, his mouth a grim straight line, his face hacked from gray rock, lines etched deeper between his nose and mouth as if by an inexpert carver.

Can't deal with this now. "Not now," he mumbled, closing his ears to what he thought he heard—could have been the screech of wind, or squeal of the door, the mewl of a cat...*not Mae.*

Dimly, behind him, he heard the frantic thud of a runaway horse. Raoul was just disappearing on one of his mustangs. He stared hard after it. Didn't ken which one.

Not Hell-Fire.

But he didn't care about pursuing. Raoul earned it, he thought with bitterness, by showing what a damnable fool *he* was, so good riddance.

Damn Liz all to hell.

Chapter Twenty: Betrayal

As his boots struck the broad wraparound porch, the sound of bare feet raced behind him. Luke clenched his fists. *I can't deal with this now.* Rattlesnake bites alone on the prairie, saving cattle from drowning in raging river crossings, *but not this.*

"Go away, Mae. Leave me!" The bitterness in Luke's voice rivaled Liz's day-old coffee. *Don't see me like this, angry, tired. Hollowed out…*

Her voice was the wail of a spurned child.

"Stop, Mae!" Harsh, unforgiving—a voice like grinding rocks. "Go back." *Where you came from.* "I can't take it."

"Please, Luke. I *need* to speak to you. It wasn't. It isn't—"

He stepped back off the veranda, still not turning. "What could you say, Mae, that would make a pitcher of warm spit's worth of difference?"

Luke's crudity, his coldness, put ice in her bones. She pressed on, daring to tug his sleeve.

He jerked free.

"I can't! No more!" he bellowed. "What more do you want of me?"

"Cannot *what*, Luke? Please let me tell you. Give me that," she pleaded.

Luke checked the house. *All dark. Liz to bed.* In a voice like the lonely wind on the prairie, he ordered, "Sit and be done with it. And that is *all*."

He fell rather than sank onto the steps, gazing unseeing into the dark. Her slight warmth irritated as she settled beside him. She was back in her thin nightdress. Ripped. She held it together with one hand. "Sit over there!"

"I won't move, Luke. I have to see your face."

Luke turned his head aside.

"Look at me!"

"I don't like what I see."

"You see Mae. The same me. Who loves you, Lucian Devereaux."

Luke held his head in his hands, letting hair fall over his forehead, then looked, expressionless—if a mountainside could be that—and dispassionately studied her bruised mouth.

"He kissed you. Did you like it?" His voice still struck flint.

"I didn't *want* him to." Her voice was another lonely wail in the wind. Keening. "I didn't want *anything* from him. Raoul—he—"

Luke chopped his hand sideways, erasing her words, denying her. "Doesn't matter. Too old for this—*these*—" He crooked his lip and gritted through clenched jaws. "These *games*. You can't say you don't want a young buck rubbing against you. *Feeling* you."

Luke wanted her to feel his hurt. Wanted to hurt her. He'd never hit a woman. Never would. Yet he wanted to. Words would do.

Mae flinched. "Luke!" She wailed covering her face with her hands. "Don't!"

He watched her with old eyes.

"Younger men than me. Hell. Could be *anyone. Any*

young randy roustabout comes along! You will change. I've been an old fool. My own damned fault. That Mexican bastard?"

His laugh was an icy hand about her heart. "He's gone." He rubbed his knuckles. "Not that he's worth the powder to blow him up with. Weren't him, be another. *Someday*. Just when I'd start feeling again."

"*No-ooo!*"

Luke looked into the dark. "I loved you, Mae. Down to my bones. I'd fall off a cliff if you told me. I was that much caring for you. Hurts worse than any bullet to my heart. Now leave me be. Too old for this horse—"

"You, you want me to *leave*?" Mae sounded small, weak. "For—for good? Where would I go, without *you?* I will do anything for you," she wailed with despair. He watched her with a stone face.

"Leave? Hell, no. I can stand it, if you can. I ken your family. Wouldn't wish a dog on that bunch." He laughed bitterly. "And the only other work you can do is maybe down at the Red Dog."

He didn't see her flinch. "Stay, if you want. But I don't want to see you, or be near you. From now on, you are a ranch hand, like anyone else. Old Tom will give the orders."

"Luke! Please hear me!"

Luke stood. "I'm *Mr.* Farnsworth. You address me as your boss. *Mister* Farnsworth. If you must." They both half-turned.

"Luke, Lucian? Are you out there? I hear voices."

The call through the door was accusatory. The kitchen doorknob shook like a death rattle.

Luke sighed as if already seeing the long march of barren years.

Mae backed off, racing to the stable so blinded by tears she could not see. She wouldn't leave. She had no place to go, if she couldn't be where she yearned to be, but felt a rock of ice where her heart should be. She wanted to retch.

"You out there, Luke? Getting cold! You'll catch your death. Not young as you used to be," Liz scolded from the doorway. "Now come inside. I'll fix up a tot."

Luke heard her footsteps lead away.

Luke at last rose creakily off the stoop and, walking like the old man he was, trod unsteadily into the kitchen. "Coming, Liz."

He slumped in a chair. "It's over, Liz." He could dimly make out Liz holding toward him a pale wool shawl she kept on the hook.

"I told you she would break your heart, Luke, you old fool." Liz said those words softly and with pity, her voice felted by dark. The final nail. He could just make out Liz's oval of a face as she sat at the table. "Cold in here, Liz." He didn't ask what she was doing up.

"I'll heat up some coffee."

"Never mind. I'm tired."

He felt Liz wrap the shawl about his shoulders as she told him, "You gonna sit up a spell, you're gonna need this." Luke tried to swat it away, then grunted an absent thanks, huddling under it, clutching it close.

"You going to sit a while? Should I keep company?" Her voice seemed worried.

"Not dead yet, Liz."

"It's still warm." She poured a tin mug and he heard her add a tot.

Luke hunched, wrapping his hands about the mug.

"Seems to get colder every year."

He shivered. "My bones ache."

"Reckon they do."

Luke shuddered under the shawl, drawing it tighter. "Winter," he mused. Liz said nothing. "Never seems to end. And the days are long."

"A vexation to be got through." After a time, he heard her rustle. Liz kissed him on the forehead. "Well, I'm to bed. Be sure the fire's banked."

He nodded. As he had each night for decades. Seeing the long deadly stretch of years ahead, he gagged on cold burnt coffee.

Liz halted at the newel post.

"We'll go see the kids tomorrow. You'll feel better, Lucian, in time. Your pridefulness is hurt. Let preacher…"

Luke realized she had witnessed at least a part of his shame.

"I don't need a sanctimonious old preacher layin' hands on me!" he howled.

"Whatever you say, Luke."

His face dropped when she was safely upstairs. Luke's lip quivered without him kenning. He would have been shamed, if he'd thought of it, but his vision and thoughts were far away from the cold empty kitchen.

They were racing horses with sun warming their faces, moods bright as the day…and under a waterfall, Mae and he…

His mind refused to venture to that hurtful place.

Moisture trickled a clamped jaw cut out of a mountain quarry. His mouth pressed in a straight line, grim as his imaginations. Luke fiercely smeared wet with the back of one scarred, bloodied hand. He smiled grimly.

Raoul was gone.

Wasn't entirely sure of Raoul's tale of conquest.

He pounded the chair arm.

Of *course* he was telling a tale.

Luke kenned in his heart that Mae told the truth, but it didn't matter—there *would* be others. The pain was there, opportunities for such *killing* pain—*endless*. Sweet appealing Mae. The devil's temptress, Liz would say. Not far wrong. Springtime young. He, if not approaching winter was certainly in late autumn. How long *could* her affections last? How long before he went from ardent caring lover to an obsessive older husband? And any children? He would be a bent-back, creaking dad, good for nothing but sitting by the fire.

****

"I swear, Beth, I could take a whipping. I should, for all the fretting I took out on Luke over that silly gal. She had a speck of pride, she'd scarper since she's not *wanted*. Hunh! Reckon, she learned *her* place all right. Luke came in like a thunderhead. Then set in the cold kitchen without a fire and brooded. Have I told you this?"

Beth sighed but, ramming the darning egg into one of Matthew's socks, said nothing except, "Guess she was a new toy all shiny and bright."

"Well, she's good and tarnished now."

Liz complacently knifed a quarter of the chocolate cake Beth had brought over. Beth pondered when her aunt would be past marriageable material, if she kept that up, but so far, to Beth's chagrin, Liz miraculously had never lost her stick-thin figure.

****

Luke made himself scarce. There came a time when

Mae realized she had not clapped eyes on him for a solid week. Was he even on the ranch? Had he gone to some big town, not coming back? Then she heard he went to Cheyenne. Mae longed to glimpse him. Liz had come to be the one doling out chores, or if not Liz, Old Tom, who eyed her wisely, if not without pity.

"Should hightail it outta here, gal," he sidled up and said once. "Not that the place would be any purtier iffen you went, but nothing here for you but a devilish time." He sorrowfully shook his head. "A whole life out there justa waitin' fer ya?"

"My life is here," she answered simply. Old Tom shrugged and didn't bring it up again.

Mae worked like a windup tin toy. Miserably she swept the barn, mended saddles and girths, fed horses, even tended the bunkhouse sick when lung fever broke out, though Luke was ignorant of that fact.

Hiking to Laramie and hopping a train to anywhere appealed briefly, but somehow days went by and it grew more blustery after a wicked snowstorm. Liz watched her when she thought she wasn't looking.

Chapter Twenty-One: The Suicide

Luke sat brooding over a twice-read novel by Mr. H. Ryder Haggard, *Alan Quartermain*, not really seeing the words, just at the gloomy part of dusk after a day in which he'd worked himself unmercifully, with sweat pouring into his eyes and muscles burning despite the cold. He wearily glanced up, not registering the commotion initially. He frowned and rose to look out.

A wagon rattled up in a tearing hurry despite such a flimsy contraption, near losing a wheel on a sharp turn between the L Devereaux Ranch's arched wrought iron gateway and the ranch yard by the corrals.

"What now?" he grumbled.

By the time he'd stalked to the door, Luke recognized that particular rumble and squeal, would know it anywhere, and commenced to ponder what brought Nate Solomon out so late in the day. However, in the lizard part of his brain, the hectic noise presaged *danger* or *hurt*.

Something *bad* had happened.

Squinting out, Luke reached for the rifle hanging over the door. Couldn't make out quite who…but it sure sounded like Nate's rattletrap with the lidded boxes running down both sides holding fripperies, liniments, cough syrups, safety pins, and such like, the wagon the old flannel-mouth perennially vowed to replace.

An odd vehicle for racing, no lie there.

Nevertheless, to Luke's consternation, it wasn't Nate.

A strange boy jumped out, pounded to the porch and, seeing Luke, skidded to a halt. "Mr. Farnsworth!" the stranger bleated. "Hurry! He's a-wantin' you. Bad!"

Luke waited, rifle across his waist. Didn't recognize this boy, yet there was a familiarity. Something about the eyes. "Who goes there! What's the ruckus?"

The boy, scarce dressed for the weather, bounced up and down with his hands in pockets as if to hold himself back. "Mr. Farnsworth! You was always closest. Reckon that's why he's a-wantin' you. But I'm a-feared he'll try it again," the wild-eyed boy insisted.

"Who, in blazes?"

"My pappy! He—he tried his damndest to poison hisself. Took a whole bunch of his own elixir and mixed it up with God alone knows what-all. And then tried ta shoot hisself!" The boy's impatience exploded. "Ma's there, 'side herself, Mr. Farnsworth. She's fit to die, her own self, with the vapors."

"Your ma? Whose wife?" Luke demanded suddenly stubborn and confused. "And never mind Farnsworth. It's Luke."

"Nate. Nate Solomon's. My mama. Dagnab it!"

"Nathaniel? Nate's got a wife?"

"Yes, sir, he do! Nigh on thirty years. Now come on. Hit's not far. I ain't a-lyin', Mr. Luke!"

Luke studied the boy a second, then snagged his leather sheep-lined jacket and clapped on the Stetson, thought again and grabbed his denim jacket with the fleece for the boy who, whatever it was, couldn't wait for hell or high water or him. He tossed him the jacket.

"What's your name?"

"Nate Junior. So they call me, or Little Nate." He could not be mistaken for anyone else Luke now saw. The proud beak of a nose, olive skin, obsidian curly black hair, unlike his Pa's grizzled gray.

"Liz!" Luke shouted. "Gonna see a sick friend. Old Nate!" Distantly, he heard her shout, but didn't wait to hear what.

"Wait till I fetch some mustard if he's taken something." Though Lord knew Nate had enough concoctions to fell a horse if he'd a mind to, from arsenic for women's complexions to laudanum and his own elixirs that seemed pure gin.

The boy motioned, frantic. "Don't need yer gun none, nor danged mustard! He's a-askin' fer ya. Stir yer bones!"

Luke shrugged, vaulted onto the wagon, and found himself jolted back and hanging on to the low side rail as young Nate flicked the nag. He wished he rode Hell-Fire as they tore out of the yard and were a half mile down to the main road before Luke had his right leg tucked in.

The rickety wagon careened around a boulder and thudded into a crater. After the ride settled to a bone-rattling drive, Luke barked over the creaking wagon like a barge threatening to sail apart, "Now, let me in on it."

Young Nate swiped his eyes with an angry gesture. "He, he, tried—he tried ta *kill* 'imself. My daddy! He plugged 'imself. Shot a dad-burned big ol' hole in 'im."

Luke stared at the boy. "Nate? Hell's fire and spare the matches, boy. Thought you said he took some danged poison?"

"That too," the boy shouted, then with a set mouth concentrated on driving.

"Why, he's the last…" *Nate? And all his dollies?*

"How bad? Where?"

"In the bedroom," the boy snuffled.

"I mean…never mind." Maybe an accident. Luke decided to wait till he reached Nate's—wherever *that* was—chagrined he had never asked, assuming it was the far end of his rangy sales rounds. Nate. Jovial joking Nate. Always with a young girlie. What could have possessed him? Luke stole a glance at the boy. Nate never mentioned a wife. Or children. And all those girls he jabbered about?

He clapped his hat firmer on his head as the right rear wheel threatened to shake loose on a rock. "You said, Nate's *wife*. Never heard tell of a wife."

"He does! My ma…" The boy loosened up as they jounced along. "He jes' don't talk about her. She's wailing somethin' fierce. We live close by." *Close by* seemed miles over jolting, gully-washed, dried-out ridges. They'd veered off the main road onto a little-used tract some time ago. He groaned.

"Let me get this straight. Where *do* you live?" He shouted over the noise of wagon wheels crashing against rocks.

The boy snorted at Luke's ignorance. "Cemetery Road. Out near the cemetery, little bit past. This here's a shortcut closer ta home."

Luke kenned the Baptist cemetery, but they were coming at it from a different direction. Resigned, he muttered grimly, "Let's just get there, then, in one piece, and see what all this"—he started to say *horseshit* but glanced at the boy's strained face—"is about."

He finished lamely, "How bad was he?"

"Don't know, now, do I?" the boy snapped.

"Was he breathing regular?"

234

"Yes…" the boy added reluctantly, through teeth clacking from the jolting and coughing from the dust. "He was breathin' then, but…" He stopped to swipe his nose.

"But what?" Luke had lost his patience at the last jounce of the buckboard.

"Bleedin' like a stuck pig."

"Where?" Luke's first alarm.

"At the dad-blamed house!" Irritation overlaid panic.

Luke heaved a sigh. "No. I meant *where* on his body did your pa git himself shot?"

"His haid!" And the boy lashed the horse harder.

I should have ridden Hell-Fire. Luke was suddenly fearful for his old friend's life, of which he kenned little. *Flummoxed. Nate has a secret life.* Apparently, *no one* knew he had a family, or Luke would have heard from grapevine gossip. He hung on tight as the abused horse suddenly swerved the wagon on two of the four wheels onto an even smaller side trail, as if it kenned it was near home and hay, rattling up to a plain rambling wood farmhouse bereft of fields. The yard littered with barrels and wood boxes more than made up for the lack.

A swaybacked barn sat to one side, next to a shed, hog pens, and a lone cow mooing in the barn, by the sound of it. Not prosperous but not derelict either. The house was painted, but no attempt at flowerbeds or paths lined with whitewashed stones had been made. Luke could hear a woman's wailing from outside.

Chapter Twenty-Two: At Nate's

Luke, after removing his hat as if even then he entered a house of mourning, stepped inside a gloomy space smelling of must and dusty surfaces. His old friend's home was jammed with bric-a-brac and various leftover remnants from Nate's trade, apparently—boxes of cut ribbon and end bolts of cloth, a carton of broken combs, brooches with missing stones, empty elixir bottles, and evidence of random acts of trail scavenging. Luke scanned the room with overt but disgusted interest.

Piles of papers teetered on a piecrust table with one leg supported on a crate. A slick horsehair sofa held disparate pillows. He counted ten empty oil lamps. The walls were papered with pictures—etchings, a cut-out silhouette, faded prints, one watercolor of a palm tree, five portraits of stern, long-whiskered males and one of a plump female in black—plus piles of chipped crockery next to a glue pot. It did not seem a welcoming place of leisure despite the horsehair sofa.

The air was moist and thick and smelled of boiled cabbage and potatoes.

"In here!" The boy tugged a stunned, bemused Luke to apparently a bedroom, with glimpses of a rude kitchen and another room on the way. The entire homestead seemed to lack reason, with rooms tacked on willy-nilly. Luke ducked his head under the low lintel.

And there finally was Nate. His upper body, clothed

in grayed, stained BVDs, was ensconced in a swaybacked iron bedstead under a star-patterned quilt, the only nice thing in the place, his jowls studded with stubble, head wrapped round in a rusty-stained cotton rag and ripped lengths of a petticoat, woebegone and shrunken.

Luke surveyed the cramped room crowded with, presumably, Nate's sons and daughters and possibly their spouses, all keeping morbid watch, with undercurrents of sullen anger tightening their expressions.

Nate, seemingly mortified, took in Luke through half-slitted eyes. "Didn' ask you ta come," he fretted and turned his face obstinately to the wall, studying a stain in the shape of a rooster.

Luke put fists on his gun belt, trying to summon up what to say, besides what he thought. "What the hell, Nate?" His question was drowned by cries and protests. He forged through the death watch. The males, with the unmistakable stamp of Nate, showed degrees of sorrow, boredom, anger, sullenness, but little pity. From somewhere came the wailing. Luke found the source held onto by two older sons with long sideburns and beards.

When she spied Luke, the plain, plump little woman with frizzy gray hair and a nose like a small potato swiped a sodden handkerchief across her eyes, stumbling away from her boys to clutch Luke's arm as though he were a lifeboat, while continuing incoherent weeping.

Luke had patience for one more minute, gazing with consternation, and no little pity, at Nate. As he thrust her away, Luke addressed the squalling woman. "What's all the ruckus, Miz Solomon? He's not on his last legs." He cast a look at Nate. "Yet," he said heavily.

"Oh! Mr. Farnsworth! You gotta help him! He tried to *k-kill* himself," she wailed afresh. "He took the gun out and writ me a note. Oh, I heard the shot!" She clutched fleshy fists to her chest while her sons clung, scowling at the man in the bed.

"Old son of a bitch. Doin' this to our ma!" The redhead, the one on the left, burst out.

"I don't know what to do-*oooo*!" Tears wet the bosom of her dress.

Suddenly Luke felt suffocated. *Have to get out of here.* The very air spoke of broken visions, hopes and promises—of life.

"Without my boys here, I…" The woman sucked in all the air in the fetid room. Plus, she was raking in the whole pot for drama, when Nate should be the hub in the wheel, the old cuss. Hell, he hadn't even kenned Nate *had* kids. Or a wife. What else had the codger kept close to his vest?

Luke sucked a tooth and scrutinized the pitiful creature on the ticking pillow.

"He see a doc?"

"Jest a scrape!" One of his sons bawled sullenly. "We done took care of it."

"I see you did." Luke didn't try to keep skepticism from his tone. Looked like a wild goose chase, at any rate. Other than seeming as wretched as a drowned cat with a stained neckerchief about its head, Nate seemed all right, at least physically. Looked like he shot himself in the ear. Nate wasn't near kicking the bucket…unless, *he* gave him a boot.

Luke pushed through the mob to the end of the iron frame. He nodded to one of the sons, in a *Get her out of here* way, but the boys didn't budge. Luke sighed, bent down and grunted. "What's all this about, then, Nate?" he asked, as kindly as he could.

"It's all *over*." Nate blubbered dolefully, rolling his eyes toward Luke. Luke noted his grizzled head where the bandana had slipped—half his left ear was not only bloody, caked with gore, but the rest was gone, just the fleshy part of the lobe left. He meant it. Probably. Who kenned?

"*What's* all over?" Luke spoke menacingly quiet. "Why did you do such a hare-brained stunt? This— *whatever* it is…"

"It's *over,* Lucian!" Nate suddenly grabbed Luke's cowhide vest. "I got something important ta tell ya." His voice was a raw whisper.

"Spit it out!" Luke snatched his vest away and moved back, angered, sad—and Nate's breath stank like an old mule.

Clutching bedcovers, Nate wouldn't look Luke in the eye. "I don't want to go on."

"You said that, Nate. Anything else before they shovel dirt in your face?"

"It's all over for me, but…"

"You keep jawing that. What is? Are you sick, Nate? Did a doc say—?" He felt for his old friend, whatever ailed him, recalling the other deaths he had reported on. Luke smacked the railings, making them clang a discordant tune. "Nate!"

Nate weakly shook his head and rolled to his side. He lay silent a moment, then rolled back and struggled to a sitting position. Luke was aware of his audience, pressing. "Can't you give the man some peace?" If anything, they huddled closer.

Nate ignored his family and nailed Luke with dead eyes. "I haven't been with a woman for years, Luke. Haven't had *affection* for all those years. Our marriage was arranged like in the old country. We *never* cared for each other." His voice was leaden as a coffin liner, until the wife began histrionic incoherent cries again. "She hates me and I can't stand her. Never have."

Fresh wails and a sudden rush from the corner, as Nate's wife stormed the bed, beating at the covers.

Luke turned to the mass of onlookers. "Take your ma!" He nodded forcefully and herded them, protesting, out. A lone girl Luke hadn't seen behind her ma glared before she left. Alone with the supposedly dying man now, Luke folded arms, leaning one hip against a wall flaking whitewash. "What the Billy-blue-blazes, Nate?"

Moaning, Nate wagged his head side to side. "I don't know why I told ya all that hogwash about me bein' with *this* dolly, and *that* chickadee. Even the gals at Red Dog laugh at me. Don't even hide it none."

Luke had the idea the nice girls at the Red Dog saloon didn't laugh so much because of the performance of Nate's John Henry as much as at his laughable appearance, with his squashed hat and dumpy figure. Even then they would take it all in stride. Bad for bizness otherwise.

Luke fiddled with his hat. "Nate, takes more than a bit of fun with a gal to be a man. You have years…"

"Hogwash!" Nate continued, groaning. "I ain't been with a woman, I tell ya, or been *good* for one, for years…ten at least, but that's what it's all about. Being *close* to someone, even if it's jest ta palaver some. I haven't had an ounce of affection. Or a kindly touch. My kids're just waiting for me to kick over. It *ain't* too late…don't wait, Luke, till it's too late to be a man…to know the sweetness of a woman. Have someone *care* for you…"

Nate cast a bitter glance at the woman who had crept back in. "I haven't had a *kind* word from *anyone* in this house, or a warm bed. I go around half-dead inside and make jokes and a damnable fool of myself, pretending all the ladies find me—sought after—a man!"

At last Luke felt a burr in his saddle for his old friend. "Nate? You're not too…"

He was interrupted by Nate's angry wave of words. "My life's been empty, *a waste of a life,* Farnsworth. It's what I said." Nate lurched up straighter, desperate for Luke to understand.

"Don't be like me, Luke. Don't wait!"

"So." Luke shook his head with a half-smile. "You told tall tales. Hell's bells. Never did really believe 'em, Nate. Don't mean you don't have friends, or those who—respect you." He slapped him on the shoulder. "Pull yourself together…for your sake, if nothing else. And no more foolishness. Stop by, see me," he ended, clumsy-like. "Not just to sell me anything. Have a drink, sit and talk a while. We're *compadres.* And Nate"—he looked sternly at the wife—"if your kids aren't helpin' you, they are old enough to make their *own* way."

The woman began sobbing anew.

Nate grabbed Luke's hand. "This won't go no further?"

"What won't go no further? I'm just here jawing with an old friend." He winked a smile. "Be seeing ya, Nathaniel. Get better. And don't be long coming over."

"Sure, Luke." Nate sank back and seemed to fall into a swoon. Luke's smile faded as he watched his old friend's grizzled and half-shaved, sunken-jowled face in repose. But he seemed more at ease. Maybe it helped just to spew all that poison out.

The boys, men really, still crowded around their ma in the messy parlor, and rounded on Luke when he emerged from the bedroom. "Don't you listen to nuthin' that old coot says. Look what that old fool did to our ma! He oughta be horsewhipped," the redheaded one yelped.

"Well, I won't be the one doing it," Luke said as he clapped his Stetson on. "And he put decent food in all your bellies." He looked at one pudgy man with a full beard with hints of gray, looked him up and down and then straight in the eye. "Just how old are you anyway? Still sucking on the teat, are ya? Never see you working with yer pa."

The man flushed and started forward, but thought better of it.

Luke, turning on the others, continued, "And the rest of you. What are you grown men still doing at home? Oughtta be ashamed!" Luke took another long enigmatic look back at his friend and strode out.

By the time he hit the porch, something flashed in Luke's head like a shooting comet lighting up the sky, or the blinding flare of gunpowder—*clear, bright. Explosive.*

All he could see in the distance was *not mountains or sky* but that dismal room, sick with accusations, lost hopes, bitterness, and morbid stink. Luke shook his head as if coming up from a deep dive into sunlight. His heart expanded till he thought his chest would burst.

"I'm gonna *live*. By thunder! I'm gonna *live till I die*."

Luke clenched his fist until his bones cracked. "Damn my hide if I won't!"

Chapter Twenty-Three: The Dressmaker

Grim, determined like a man in the front line on a battlefield, stunned by sentries of mannequins with saucy, smirking, cupid-bow lips blindly eyeing him while lording it over fripperies, clouds of petticoats, bustles, flimsy white lacy tops with tiny straps that could never keep out the cold, Luke entered the new Fine Apparel Emporium with a vision in mind.

Luke stood, back plastered to the door, as a youthful female with spit curls in the middle of her forehead and an older man with a goatee, probably the owner, descended through aisles of furbelows and pastel clouds like the prow of Old Ironsides.

Luke fervently gave thanks. A *man*. An island of safety. Until the man rubbed his hands as if spying a juicy steak and in fluting tones not much heard in Wyoming, trilled, "Good afternoon, good sir. And how may we accommodate you?" The gentleman's eyes not so much flashed as winked.

"I have a *niece*"—Luke turned to the lady—"about yay size and 'bout yay tall." He held his hand big as a small skillet a little over five feet from the floor. "And I want, ah, a *dress*, a—real pretty one. With—you know?" Know? But he didn't, suddenly overwhelmed by choice as he gazed desperately about.

He scrutinized the assistant again with the studious manner of purchasing a horse. About Mae's height, and though pale blonde and insipid-eyed where Mae was dark-haired and wicked-eyed, the assistant was just as slim. A bit lacking in the uppermost part… "Umm, 'bout your size, but—" He pressed hands to his chest, dropping them instantly.

"Oh!" The man fluttered, whispering in discretionary tones, "You mean the young lady is, er, more *robust* up here but otherwise…the same?"

"Umm, yes." Luke sweated, nearly knocking over a pair of lacy drawers hanging on two pins, so thin they were shameful, and those too would *never* keep out the cold.

"Then I know precisely, good sir."

Whew! Luke mentally exhaled, running his finger behind his neck bandana. Rather be riding a horsefly-bitten Brahma bull.

"Do you have a *color*—hue—a shade in mind, sir?"

He weakly asked, "Color?"

"Why, yes. What shade does your niece prefer? Young ladies," he sniffed, "are *very* particular." The haberdasher raised one plucked brow. At Luke's frustrated silence, he sighed to his patent toes. "What *color* are her *eyes*?"

Luke took himself in hand. *Have to stop acting like a schoolboy in a cat house.* "Sort of greeny-blue, like, like clear water…" And abruptly Mae's big-eyed elfin face, with the little pointed chin and hair grown into curling soft ebony silk flowing down past her shoulders, swam into view.

"What is the occasion, sir?" His young assistant fanned long lashes at Luke.

"A—like a party," he half-snarled in his impatience.

The proprietor raised one brow. "Miss Gordon,

please bring out that sateen turquoise number." He added in a whisper, "*The one that didn't fit Miss Oglethorpe.*"

"Yes, Mr. Bottoms. I ken the one."

Professionally, she swept out, returning with a frothy thing over her arm that looked like foam on water, bedecked with lace and roses and what all, holding it up to herself.

Luke wondered if the gown would be wearing Mae, 'stead of t'other way round. Besides, where could one wear it? Even the Harvest Dance was too countrified for such a thing. Cheyenne, at least, if not Chicago or San Francisco, to wear such a get-up. Instinctively too, Luke intuited Liz would have a conniption if he brought such a confection into the house meant for Mae.

"Not on your life."

Mr. Bottoms looked nonplussed.

"What *is* the occasion?"

"A country dance, or a good Sunday-go-meeting dress."

"Ah, then this one is not appropriate," Mr. Bottoms uttered wistfully, glowering at his assistant as if it had been her fault to bring forth such an abomination. Luke got the impression he mourned the chance to offload this pricy fluff unsuitable for anything but a coronation, in Luke's estimate of women's attire.

Mr. Bottoms' hand flicked for his assistant to whisk it off, as if the gown were fit for the rubbish bin, but just then Luke's eye caught another wisp of color.

He strode through a gauntlet of sheer underdrawers and frilly tops and laced-up corsets, to an alcove where hung a simple pale dress of indeterminate color, not pale green, or blue, but with a faint hint of silver. The exact shade of Mae's eyes.

Plain taffeta, with a sweeping skirt whispering secrets when it swirled, a fitted V waist and a neckline called a "sweetheart," though Luke was ignorant of the term, edged with the faintest tad of black lace, an unusual combination, but one he kenned would suit Mae to the bone, enhancing eyes, hair and pale skin. The sleeves were long and fitted, with pointed wrist openings.

Luke grinned. Somehow, he recognized that tiny-waisted dress was the right one.

"Oh, *that* one!" The proprietor sniffed. "Made exclusive for one of the—" he whispered, "*doxies* at the Red Dog. She felt the neckline was *choking* her." His eyes flashed insult.

"That will suit Mae fine."

"Well, if you *insist*." And made a gesture for his assistant to wrap it up. His slight blonde assistant simpered demurely at Luke and promised many things with her eyes, but not before he also purchased a dainty pair of pink leather slippers.

He had one more stop to make.

****

"There!" Luke plunked the fat, beige paper package, tied foursquare with red twine, onto the scrubbed kitchen table as if he would entertain no arguments. He stared at Liz, telling her he would suffer no spouting off, either. But Liz was not to be quelled so easily. She stared at the red string, intuiting immediately, from some feminine sixth sense unknown to Luke, where it was from and what it contained.

"Yes, Luke. Why not buy her a *pony* while you are at it?"

"By God, I just might do that. I want you to do the Christian thing and help her red-up. She's not from your

247

background, to have your *womanly ways* with dresses and such, having never been exposed to them, but it is high time."

Liz rolled her eyes at that and sniffed, partially mollified. Luke kenned his sister's bluster hid underlying shyness. When hoedowns sprang up, she tended the punch bowl and pottered around the trays of vittles, or saw to the washing up, never standing even on the fringe to be plucked up like a summer—he amended, an *autumn*—rose. "Too many thorns," he muttered and reached over to pluck a curl to let drop over her forehead.

"Oh, you!" She swatted him away but left the curl. "But what's it all for?" Liz demanded.

"The harvest shindig, dammit!" It was two days away—near full winter, but folks finally got to lay down most their labors. "I bet half the territory would like to come sparking you, if you let your hair down."

Liz flushed. "Oh, go on with your foolishness. I don't have time for folderol!"

Luke strode off, allowing the screen door to slam a tad harder than necessary. Fulminating, he spoke through the screen. "See she's dressed proper, hair and all."

Still, she had finally pried out of unusually tightlipped Lucian Farnsworth, a brother from whom she had no secrets, part of what it was all for. Well, except for that pack of store-bought Sweet Caporal cigarettes and *The Pasha and the Harem Girl* novel that Sadie Ledbetter had slipped into her reticule after the Ladies Aid meeting. Sadie had whispered, "Let no one see this, and give it back when you're finished, Lizzie." That was three weeks ago. Liz read the indelicate novel quickly at first, eyes as rapid as her breathing, then, more lingeringly. She smiled bitterly at the thought that she had never had such delicious forbidden or illegal experiences.

And here was Lucian, her older brother, acting like a wet-behind-the-ears schoolboy.

Liz stared at the beige paper package as if it were a copperhead ready to strike. Then, after eyeing Luke as he galloped off on Hell-Fire, she tentatively touched it—pressing, prodding, poking, finally ripping a tiny corner—and stuck her finger in to rub the smooth cool taffeta. Though curiosity seared her soul, if not her finger, she would allow herself to go no further until she had to. Suddenly Liz did not want to set eyes on...*whatever* it was—a *dress* of some sort.

Chapter Twenty-Four: The Harvest Dance

"You look mighty fine, Lizbeth." Luke didn't want to say that in her tan velvet she resembled a potato. Liz had no notion of what she looked good in, he concluded, no matter how finely it was stitched and embroidered or gussied with lace. Her ears sported her ma's garnet eardrops, and she looked fetching despite the potato dress. So did his daughter, in her blue silk with the little sprigs of flowers he kenned well. She took after him, though. Tall, rawboned, and square-jawed.

Luke was in his best striped whipcords, dress shirt and a silk bow tie in place of his usual Indian turquoise bolo, his hair slicked with water but already springing up into its lion's mane. He touched his pocket. Still there. It felt warm to his touch. Beneath it he felt his heart thumping.

Taller than most, Luke looked over the heads of nearly everyone in the vast barn of flying chaff, past swirling dancers, and blurs of whirligig hues like a jigging rainbow, as knees lifted, teeth flashed, arms sawed, with the thunder of stamping feet, breathless laughter and the caller's exhortations making it difficult to communicate.

He nodded to the tall string bean of a fellow dimly made out in stiff new overalls, a string tie fastening the clean shirt's collar. Liz glanced over sourly, puzzled. The farmer he indicated looked undecided on whether to go home or undergo the chagrin of being turned down.

"Look. There's Jim Bensen. Nice fella. Owns quite a large farm close by Red Butte, I hear. Not too far away," he said heavily.

Liz watched the farmer with her gimlet eye, sniffing.

Luke felt an irritant like a speck in his eye. "Could do worse than a nice buck like Jim, Liz. Not hard to look at, either."

True, Luke decided. Black hair, dark blue eyes, a firm jaw. Engaged to be wed when his sweetheart passed of scarlet fever last year. He watched a female, recently widowed, eye Jim with more than motherly interest, while his finicky sister gazed at the tall thin farmer with a scorn she ought to reserve for pickpockets and stagecoach robbers.

"I *could*, if I wanted a long drink of water, but I'm not *that* thirsty."

"Then you might go for a long *dry* spell," Luke uncharacteristically shot back.

Liz lifted her chin and looked off with a hint of moisture in her eye. "I have to see to the punch bowl…make sure there are not too many *additions*."

"Yeah, wouldn't want that. Can't have folks having *too* much fun." Luke chuckled, sighed and moved away. He'd done his duty. He'd dance with her once, as always.

Chafing. He was chafing. He'd had to lag behind and haggle through a roustabout's payday challenge, for each hand had a different and more optimistic sum in mind than had Luke, and they were more intractable than usual. By the end of haggling, Luke was willing to give them the ranch, just to be gone. Also, he slipped a flask of whiskey to Matt, still too bunged up to withstand a wagon's bouncing. He'd barely had time to slick up. But now he had important business. He hoped it was not too late.

He swiveled desperately, searching for Mae in the throng.

Luke felt his heart thump and stop…then thud a steady beat so loud he wondered if others could hear it.

Luke sucked in a deep sigh of pleasure.

An elk horn chandelier, one of three with a forest fire of candles, blazed above Mae, resplendent in the pale taffeta matching her undefinable eyes, long, slightly curling black hair cascading almost to her slender waist, pale bosoms sweetly rounded above the neckline. His throat felt full when he noted the bedraggled red ribbon she had tied over her crown. She stood forlorn, looking about, bewildered, through the maze of intertwined dancers, as if placed on display. Liz had told her nothing.

Without a word, not that Luke could speak, he strode through the whirligig throng.

Mae looked up.

As if a magnet drew them, they not so much fell as collided into each other's arms. Mae clasped Luke about the neck, clinging as she would to a rock in a raging sea. Luke, his large hands spanning her waist and welding her to him, buried his face in her hair scented with vanilla and cloves.

Mae tucked her neck under his chin. "Luke, *Luke*," she sighed, oozing contentment.

"Mae, Mae, I love you, my darling little Mae."

Mae looked up at him with eyes sparkling from more than the candles.

The country waltz caught them, netted them, with its agreeable strains of fiddle and harmonica. They began to sway, oblivious of others, lost in their dream.

"Obvious as white on wool there's something goin' on."

"What is that old goat doin' looking all lovey-eyed at that innocent child?"

"Not so innocent, some would say." One onlooker smirked, darting meaningful glances and pursing her lips.

"After all, he has a nice place there, worth some coin, and that ain't confederate, by gum."

"Rumor has it, some say..." and several names were mentioned, including the Sauerbecks.

Luke grinned. *Already the subject of heated speculation, it seems.* Liz's eyes blazed through narrowed lids. There would be cold biscuits, if any. More than that would change. Had to.

Mae's eyes darted to the speculators and out through open barn doors to the cricket-filled unseasonably warm night where couples lingered deep in the shadows of hay ricks and carriages.

"This is not exactly how I pictured it," Luke began. "I was thinking of a trip to Cheyenne, or..." Luke didn't get to finish. Mae grasped his large brawny hand in her small one and pulled him to the night.

Barely away from the gawkers, Mae grasped his leather vest and raised her face to his, gazing up with eyes luminous with love as she tugged Luke down. She stood on tiptoe, almost reaching his lips. "Kiss me, Luke. Kiss me like you mean it." Her face was a perfect cameo under the harvest moon. Eyes closed. Soft lips half-open.

He sighed deep within *and told his angel to go to the devil*. Raising her up, he brushed her lips with his, then kissed her thoroughly and long.

"Little Mae, are you sure? I'm older..."

"Oh, Luke," Mae breathed. "Look at me! I am a woman grown."

"I am a man, *more* than grown. I'd be stealing your youth." Why was he saying this? How many chances did he have?

Mae had the angry kitten look again. "I don't care. I don't *want* a boy! I'm lovin' you, Luke. I ken we can't never be *proper*-like wed, but I don't care. I want to be with a man, a *real* man, the first…"

He brushed the back of his hand on her soft cheek, afraid he would cut her with his rough calloused palms. "Who says we can't?"

Luke's arms almost wrapped twice around her tiny waist. He lifted her up—looked at her with such longing, and kissed her tenderly—and she put her arms around his neck, hugging him tight as if he would vanish should she release him. "I'm yours, Luke, any way you want me…and forever long."

Luke's last misgivings, if he owned any, fell away like a thunderclap.

He dug in his pocket like any first-time blushing swain, then held out a polished gold ring with a small ruby cabochon like a winking eye in the center.

"Will you wed me, Mae?"

Mae gravely held out her hand. Luke gently slid the ring on her finger. Mae studied her slender hand and the ring with wonder.

"We'll take a train to Chicago, hire a whole car just for ourselves. We'll honeymoon there. I want to show you to the whole world. Maybe even Europe. We could do the grand tour!" He laughed giddily. Mae just watched him, dazed. He wondered if she kenned yet how much her life would change. Luke gazed down at the scrap of a woman with flyaway hair and huge eyes, soft mouth and pert little chin who held the power to turn him into a willing slave, a ferocious protector.

His little hellraiser, his hoyden, his beautiful treasure.

With that, Luke scooped Mae into his arms and strode long steps back to the dance still aswirl with jolly madness, wending to the middle of the floor where he twirled Mae in the midst as if clearing a space.

Bending his head, he whispered, "I wish I were carrying you to our marriage bed."

Mae's response was a soft giggle in his neck and tightening her arms as they danced and swayed and twirled under the gimlet gaze of most attending. Luke fended off, with a look that would turn butter to stone, any interloper who dared to try cutting in. The mob, clapping in time to fiddles and banjos, parted with good humor at the sight of the two of them so enthralled—the tall iron-haired rancher and the thistledown of a girl in his arms smiling gravely up at him.

Luke halted finally. "Listen up, listen up, friends!"

Then, Lucian Devereaux Farnsworth, slowly turning, addressed them all—the fiddler stopped and the crowd quieted with eager speculation at this new turn of entertainment, save for Liz eyeing the pair from the refreshment table with shock and dismay coloring her pale face.

Her shoulders drooped.

The cake knife dropped from boneless fingers. She started toward the couple with singular attention, then halted, turned, and made her way outside so no one would see her.

She would not make a spectacle of herself as her

brother was apparently dead set on doing.

Luke's craggy face, flushed with exuberance, glowed with pride. "As many of you with eyes in your head might have guessed…" He paused for the general good-natured laughter. "I love this little gal that fell from heaven, apparently, square in my lap." His announcement was greeted with more friendly hoots and a few elbow digs. "Love her down to my boots…" This was interrupted by a man calling from the back, "And everyplace in between!" The man was shushed by a landowner's wife, albeit with a twinkle in her eye and a smile on her lips.

"That may be true too," Luke said amiably. He sobered and pressed Mae to his side. "Mae has consented to be my dear wife for however many years we own."

The mob surged to the two, slapping Luke on the back so hard he kenned he would feel it on the morrow, and the fiddlers started up a merry jig.

Liz in the meantime, watching from the wide barn door, gazed with speculation across the dancers and well-wishers at the lanky black-haired farmer.

She fancied men taller than her, as she was taller than most females. A hard task, but maybe she *was* thirsty. And besides, he *was* taller if she removed her shoes.

And maybe the rest of her garments.

The lanky farmer glanced up with hopeless admiring interest as Liz made a beeline toward him.

A word about the author…

I pen novels and scripts in Myrtle Beach, South Carolina, on ships at sea, in the car, or any place there's a phone, laptop or paper napkin.

My first feature script, *Sary's Gold*, captured ScriptPimp's Grand Prize and was shortlisted as Best Western in the Chanticleer Book Review Awards.

Sary's Gold, based on true events, concerns a fictional widow in a brutal Deadwood-esque outpost: Big Bear, California, and is now published as a novel by The Wild Rose Press.

Sary's Diamonds is Book 2 in Sary's adventures, set in 1910 Africa.

Book 3, *Sary and the Maharajah's Emeralds*, has a torrid Northern India locale.

Danforth The Dragon is a children's book written and illustrated by the author.

The Girl from Convict Lake: Psycho/Suspense in the icy wilderness of Michigan's Upper Peninsula.

The Wylder Ghost and Blossom Cherry is a Paranormal/Romance set in 1890s Wyoming.

The Dishwater Duchess of Wylder, Wyoming: A sequel.

My other novels are:

Beast in the Moon, an erotic dystopian Sci-Fi.

The Crawl Space, an adult, coming-of-age horror story.

Thank you for purchasing
this publication of The Wild Rose Press, Inc.

For questions or more information
contact us at
info@thewildrosepress.com.

The Wild Rose Press, Inc.
www.thewildrosepress.com